The Perfect
Lady by Mistake

李 白

The Perfect
Lady by Mistake

AND OTHER STORIES BY
FENG MENGLONG (1574–1646)

————————

translated with an Introduction by
William Dolby

PAUL ELEK   LONDON

To Ann Grace

Published in Great Britain 1976
by Elek Books Limited
54–58 Caledonian Road
London N1 9RN

ISBN 0 236 40002 9

Printed in Great Britain by
Unwin Brothers Limited
The Gresham Press, Old Woking, Surrey

Contents

A Note on the Illustrations

The frontispiece shows a woodcut portrait of Li Bai (Li Po) of unknown date, reproduced in *Li Bai quanji* (an edition of the complete works of Li Bai), published by Guangzhi Shuju, Hong Kong, 1959. The illustrations in the text are woodcuts from an early Qing edition of stories ascribed to Feng Menglong, and are reproduced from an original edition in the library of the School of Oriental and African Studies, University of London.

Introduction

In the long history of Chinese literature the vernacular short story was rather a late-comer. Long before their writing came into being, the Chinese were no doubt telling stories orally, and they continued to do so throughout the centuries. The earliest recorded Chinese myths and legends, such as the laconic accounts in the *Shan-hai jing*, 'Book of monsters', often seem to be summaries of full and elaborate oral story cycles or sagas, although it is difficult to prove that they are such. Embedded in many works of the Zhou (1027–256 BC) and Qin dynasties (221–07 BC) are also numerous lengthier and more sophisticated anecdotes, fables of Aesopian scope and style and well-structured parables and historical tales. During the Han dynasty (206 BC–AD 220), philosophical, historical and quasi-historical writings were often very close in character to fictional novellas. For example, some of the biographical sections of the *Shi-ji* ('Historical Records') written around 100 BC by the Grand Historian Sima Qian (147–90 BC) are almost certainly a mixture of fact and of what, if not downright fiction, is an extensive and imaginative elaboration of probabilities and possibilities. In construction and style these biographies are models of gripping, coherent narration, and they were as much an inspiration for later fictional literature as for historiography.

During the period of the Six Dynasties (222–589) it became a very popular literary pastime to write collections of anecdotes. These included collections of jokes, such as the *Xiao-lin*, 'Grove of laughter', attributed to the Imperial Counsellor and Doctor Emeritus Handan Chun of the third century, collections of accounts of famous men, and collections of ghost stories and

I

tales of the supernatural. The latter in particular were often fairly long and intricate, for example some of those in the *Sou-shen ji*, 'Assembly of spirits', attributed to Gan Bao (late third–early fourth century), and many of the tales in the *Yu-ming lu*, 'Records of the darkness and the light', by Lin Yiqing (403–44). The authors were frequently otherwise celebrated or eminent figures, among them an emperor and various ministers, and possibly that is one reason why these tales often tend to come within the realm of *belles lettres*, being pithily instructive rather than complexly narrative. The prevalence of this genre no doubt paved the way for the writing of more complex, more lengthy, and often more overtly fictional short stories which became a widespread practice during the Tang dynasty (618–907). These Tang stories, known as *chuanqi*, 'marvel tales', are in many cases ones that we readily recognise as novellas, written with a clear concern for plot, for dramatic tension and a high level of structural cohesion and stylistic beauty. Their elegant, concentrated language indicates authors of considerable orthodox literary education, and the writers of *chuanqi* were often literary men and officials of high standing such as Niu Sengru (779–847), a prime minister at one time, Pei Xing (fl. c. 860), an Imperial Commissioner and Censorial Minister, and Yuan Zhen (779–831), a famous poet and holder of many high-ranking posts including that of Imperial Commissioner. These authors firmly established the novella written in classical, literary Chinese as a major item in the Chinese tradition of letters, and such stories continued to be written in later centuries in fundamentally the same elegant manner and literary language.

Although it is safe to assume that the Chinese told stories orally as far back as prehistoric times, there is much debate as to when the first professional oral story-tellers appeared. They existed at least as early as the eighth and ninth centuries AD, and probably much earlier, but as a widespread social institution they seem first to have established themselves during the Sòng dynasty (960–1279), when vernacular story-telling became a common form of public entertainment. All the same, the roots of Sòng vernacular story-telling clearly extend deep into earlier ages, and not only thematically. Surviving texts, known as *bianwen*, 'incident texts' (?), 'transformation texts' (?), from the Tang and Five Dynasties (907–60) periods include partly vernacular narratives which must have been delivered orally or based on something delivered orally, some for the purposes of Buddhist preaching, others more probably for only nominally religious or for secular oral delivery, such, for instance, as the *Wu Zixu bianwen*. Direct speech is a prominent feature of them, and the performers of *bianwen* and indeed the written texts themselves no doubt prepared some of the ground for the Sòng professional raconteurs. But there must have been a great variety of other reasons why professional oral story-telling flourished during the Sòng. The great concentrations of population in its huge capital cities, Bianliang and Hangchow, the rapidly expanding commercial prosperity (creating the requisite surplus material wealth), and favourable intellectual, social and administrative attitudes must all have played their part in fostering the fashion for such entertainments and in establishing the necessary physical conditions for them. The increasing predominance of the secular philosophy known as Neo-Confucianism may conceivably have been more conducive to secular than to religious story-telling in general, although it is doubtful whether any clear-cut distinction between secularity and religion prevailed among the populace. It seems, at least, that there was some administrative restraint on the story-telling activities of Buddhist priests. The considerable interest shown by the Sòng intelligentsia in other, literary kinds of fiction may well have been another, stimulating influence on oral story-telling. The Sòng literary-man's tales, as found in such collections as the *Qing-suo gao-yi*, 'Lofty deliberations of the green window-lattice', by Liu Fu (fl. c. 1100), were racier and written with freer zest and humbler level of subject-matter than the Tang *chuanqi*, and were no doubt influenced by as well as possibly influencing the oral story-tellers.

In the enormous amusement parks, known as *wazi*, 'tiles', *washe*, 'tile-booths', or *washi*, 'tile-markets', that existed in Bianliang during the eleventh century and in the yet larger ones of Hangchow during the twelfth and thirteenth centuries there arose regular audiences for the arts of oral entertainment. Such audiences enabled the performer to maintain a regular livelihood, or at least a livelihood that was not limited to fairs and feast days, although festivals remained the more intense

3

periods of entertainment. In the *wazi* a great variety of performances co-existed in close proximity and constant emulation and cross-influence. Besides the story-tellers there were balladeers, acrobats, puppeteers, singing-girls, clowns, comedians, proto-dramatic play-actors and many other kinds of entertainer, their arts often sharing common features and constituting together something more in the nature of a fluid continuum than a range of separate categories of skill. The story-tellers were sufficient in number, ability and appeal to be able to specialise in different kinds of story: historical tales (even specialising in a particular period), tales akin to detective stories, Buddhist and supernatural tales. Some seem to have ranged more freely, with tales of love, everyday personal drama, and fictions that were perhaps not even nominally linked to recognisable historical facts or to venerable texts. Precisely what form all these oral tales took and in what manner they were delivered we cannot say, and very little can be gleaned on the subject. We can be fairly sure that prose and verse were often intermingled, and that a story was often carried on day after day, the daily episodes presumably ending on a note of dramatic suspense or anticipation. Who were the story-tellers? Some were literate, but most were probably men of little if any formal literary education.

Questions that spring readily to mind are whether the story-tellers used oral or literary sources for their material, and whether they used the classical literary language referred to as *wenyan*, 'Classical Chinese', or the everyday vernacular language referred to as *baihua*, 'plain speech'. Here again, the direct evidence is sparse and frail, and we are to a large extent left to rely on inferences from other ages and possible parallels to be drawn from the story-telling of other countries. In neither case is comparison necessarily reliable. In other ages there may have been radically different conditions for oral story-telling. The advent of mature drama and of the novel during the thirteenth and fourteenth centuries, for instance, may have greatly altered the nature of other forms of entertainment. Likewise, the unique importance of writing in Chinese society poses problems in deducing from non-Chinese traditions. Fairly pure oral and vernacular traditions have existed in China, as, for instance, the nineteenth-century cycle of tales of

4

Nian rebels, assembled under the title *Quan-quan zhan*, 'Round-and-round warfare', but both the *bianwen* that preceded the Sòng and the major written 'vernacular' traditions of Chinese narration after the Sòng made ample use both of ancient literary sources and of Classical Chinese. Sòng oral story-telling flourished in Bianliang and Hangchow, and in such concentrated centres of Chinese civilisation its themes must almost inevitably have been heavily influenced by the great weight of ancient Chinese literature, as evidence indeed suggests it was, as well as no doubt utilising purely oral legends and tales and the resources of imagination.

How the story-tellers reached the ancient literature and how they would render it to their audiences are problems more difficult to answer. Literate story-tellers could cull it straight from the written sources, and the greater diffusion of printing during the Sòng must have facilitated access to ancient works for a much greater number of people than during earlier dynasties. There seems to have been little social stratification in many of the Sòng entertainments. For instance, entertainers were often 'commuters' between imperial banquets and the markets and seamy *wazi*. There were seemingly no rigid barriers between literate and illiterate in the realm of entertainment, and even illiterate story-tellers cannot have found access to literature very difficult, either through direct aid from the literate or second-hand from other oral entertainers. We need not assume that the Classical Chinese of the sources would be any great obstacle even to illiterates. Although Classical Chinese was in many ways very different from the basic colloquial tongue, the relationship between the two was decidedly dissimilar to that between Latin and the European vernacular tongues in certain respects. Through the ages, even ordinary everyday speech in China has contained a great deal of Classical Chinese, and Classical Chinese has never really been a 'dead' language. Many proverbs, much popular song, and all kinds of official pronouncement and ritual formulae and so forth have been couched in Classical Chinese. It is quite feasible that the Sòng oral story-tellers translated their Classical Chinese sources into more purely colloquial language. Almost certainly they often did, especially when the source was over-erudite, over-laconic or otherwise abstruse. But it is also

5

perfectly possible that, as in many printed 'vernacular' tales of other periods, they quoted whole passages of Classical Chinese unaltered, sometimes with a colloquial exegesis and sometimes without, and that their audiences took it as a matter of course.

Another key question is whether the story-tellers ever wrote down, or had written for them, versions or outlines of their tales. It seems quite likely that some of them did. We know that during the thirteenth century there existed *shuhui*, 'writing societies' which supplied written texts for entertainers, and it is in theory quite probable that such societies also supplied some story-tellers with written material earlier in the Sòng. If the story-tellers had prompt-books, however, they may well have been no more than generalised handbooks listing various set patters, formulae, rules and tricks of the trade. A large number of titles of Sòng and Yuan (1279–1368) stories survive that are regarded as referring to oral story-telling, but there is no proof that they had corresponding written story-tellers' versions of the tales in Sòng times. All the same, the Sòng oral story-tellers must have had a considerable effect on Chinese literature. How they affected contemporary literature is difficult to gauge, but one feels that they must have been a vital influence on the first mature Chinese drama, the Yuan *zaju*, 'miscellany play', that flourished during the thirteenth century. This drama was able to avail itself of a considerable public familiarity with various old stories and story-cycles, a familiarity that must surely have been fostered by proto-dramatic and other entertainments, including the story-tellers. Some actresses and playwrights of Yuan *zaju* were performers or authors of narrative ballads, and the relationship between the various entertainments was undoubtedly very close.

Whether or not the story-tellers themselves had written versions of their stories, it would have been a fairly natural thing for publishers and authors to produce books that borrowed their material or imitated their style at least partly. During the thirteenth and early fourteenth centuries a section of the publishing world availed itself of popular oral entertainments. The thirty Yuan editions of Yuan *zaju* which survive were a product of this trade. Some of these *zaju* were printed with only their arias; some have their arias and a few stage directions; and others have arias, stage directions, and dialogue or speech in amounts ranging from some for the main roles only to a fair quantity for various roles. None of these *zaju* editions seems to give nearly as much speech as there must have been in actual performance, and their varied composition bespeaks a somewhat haphazard treatment or heterogeneous derivation of the material. Before their printed titles they have the words 'newly printed' or 'newly published' or 'newly written'. These words, presumably intended as an extra attraction to buyers, are also found at the head of the titles of the stories published during the thirteenth and early fourteenth centuries.

Five of the six surviving stories of this period were published during the period 1321–23. They are known as *pinghua*, 'plain stories', all being historical tales or sagas of the length of a short or average English novel, short by later Chinese standards for the novel. But whereas the Yuan *zaju* editions, to some extent or other, undoubtedly reflect plays actually performed, the relationship of the *pinghua* to oral story-telling is difficult to prove with any certainty. The convenient episodic divisions, the frequent use of direct speech, the dramatic mood, the use of devices that in later ages were regarded as story-tellers' devices, and various other features seem to suggest some connection, but only vaguely so. The language of the stories is sometimes colloquial, but not on the whole so, and frequently includes extensive passages from ancient works, for instance Sima Qian's *Shi-ji*, and poems which are classically complex and concise in their wording. This does not disprove any connection, but certainly does not prove one either. Unlike the *zaju* editions, the *pinghua*, although often rather roughly, woodenly, and snatchily compiled, are fairly similar to each other in general arrangement, are full, if often terse, narratives, and are moderately well-produced editions, with copious illustrations. We cannot, in short, assume parallels with the *zaju* editions. The purposes for which the *zaju* were published are anyway far from clear. It is quite possible that the *pinghua* were published as a literary or historiographic endeavour quite separate from oral story-telling.

Whatever the nature of the *pinghua*, they undoubtedly played a part in the later developments of Chinese written fiction,

7

being one source of inspiration and material for the novel. The Chinese novel is traditionally said to have arisen in the late Yuan or early Ming dynasties, and Luo Ben (identified with Luo Guanzhong, c. 1330–1400) is acclaimed as the father of the genre and the author of what as far as we know is the earliest novel, the *San-guo zhi yan-yi*, 'Romance of the Three Kingdoms', and, less reliably, of a number of other novels. The earliest extant edition of the *San-guo zhi yan-yi* bears a preface dated 1494, and the earliest known biography of Luo Guanzhong, written by a friend in 1422, mentions him only as a *zaju* playwright and composer of riddles. Late fifteenth-century and early sixteenth-century works also associate Shi Naian, identified with the playwright Shi Hui (late thirteenth century–early fourteenth century), with the origins of the novel. It is clear that by the late fifteenth and early sixteenth centuries the genre was well established, but much doubt surrounds what went before. If Luo Guanzhong or Shi Hui wrote tales, it is quite possible that they were of another nature, for instance chantefables, narrative ballads, or indeed something akin to *pinghua* (although almost certainly of a more polished literary form than the surviving *pinghua*). The *San-guo zhi yan-yi* derives much of its material from the formal literary and historical sources. According to one Qing scholar, it is 'three tenths fiction mixed with seven tenths of fact',* a statement perhaps best taken as referring to the novel's large-scale reliance on the orthodox historical sources rather than to its absolute factuality! This, and more markedly, some of the later novels show distinct signs of inspiration from the *pinghua*, although the manner of narration is altogether smoother, more sophisticated and more minute.

During the Ming dynasty (1368–1644), starting, it would seem, in the late fifteenth century, there began a period, reaching its climax in the late sixteenth and early seventeenth centuries, of widespread, intense re-examination and editing of old works from the Sòng and Yuan, and of early Ming works purportedly of Sòng or Yuan provenance. This was paralleled by more wholly creative activities that were in many respects

*See Lu Hsun, *A Brief History of Chinese Fiction*, translated by Yang Hsien-yi and Gladys Yang (from his *Zhongguo xiaoshuo shilue*, 1923–30), Peking, Foreign Languages Press, 1959, pp. 167–8.

8

intimately involved with the reappraisal and revival of old works. Emperors showed considerable interest in stories. Emperor Wuzong (r. 1506–21) paid the great price of fifty taels for a copy of one particular book, and Emperor Shenzong *WATER /MARGIN?* (r. 1573–1620) was an avid reader of the novel *Shui-hu*, 'Fen-lands'. It was during this period that the earliest novels came into circulation, that other great novels were written such as *Xi-yu ji*, 'Journey to the West' or 'Monkey' (c. 1580), and *Jin Ping Mei*, 'Golden Vase Plum-blossom' (written during 1580–90), and that many, heavily edited versions of Yuan *zaju* plays appeared. In the case of these *zaju*, it is clear that the Ming editors very often provided all or most of the dialogue and that they very often substantially altered the arias and stage directions. On the other hand, it seems reasonable to assume that they did base their versions on some kind of genuine Yuan text or upon a text which derived from a Yuan text. In the same period there were also published a number of 'vernacular' short stories, known as *huaben*, 'story-bases' (?), some purportedly Sòng works or founded on Sòng editions, others, in similar style, more frankly admitted to be Ming creations. Whether the 'Sòng' *huaben* were of Sòng or even Yuan origin, or in fact entirely Ming creations simply borrowing the label or aura of the Sòng to acquire an air of venerability, is one of the vital questions in the history of Chinese fiction. *[RUBBISH]*

The earliest *huaben* that survives was, as far as is known, first published in 1498, appended to a play. The earliest collection, the *Qing-ping shan-tang hua-ben*, edited by a certain Hong Pien, was published around 1550. The lateness of both dates must surely arouse our suspicions. The stories in the collection are a veritable motley in length and style of composition, ranging from terse touching-ups of *chuanqi* tales and colloquialisations of Sima Qian's *Shi-ji* to the fresh and charming verbosity of *Kuai-zui Li Cui-lian ji*, 'Li Kingfisher Lotus, the naggy shrew', which is mainly in verse and is very similar in mood and manner to various kinds of narrative ballad. There is, as far as I know, no proof that any of the stories of the collection existed as such before 1550. There are strong indications that many of them were based on the stories of *zaju* plays, or, in some cases, upon plays of the *nanxi*, 'southern play',

9

drama which coexisted with Yuan *zaju* drama in central and southern parts of China during the late Sòng and Yuan dynasties. Although we cannot rule out the possibility of earlier *huaben* or skeletal or rudimentary tales upon which the *huaben* may have been based, as far as we can tell the *huaben* may not have arisen till the early or mid Ming.

Other collections of *huaben* appeared. Feng Menglong (1574–1646 or later) published three collections during the years 1620–27: the *Quan-xiang gu-jin xiao-shuo*, 'Fully illustrated stories ancient and modern' of 1620, also known as *Yu-shi ming-yan*, 'Evident stories to enlighten the world'; the *Jing-shi tong-yan*, 'Universal stories to warn the world' of 1624; and the *Xing-shi heng-yan*, 'Constant stories to awaken the world' of 1627. Each collection contained forty stories, and they are jointly known as the *San-yan*, 'Three stories'. Some of the stories they contained followed earlier, known, extant *huaben*, often with little alteration, but a number concerned the Ming, being thus clearly not based on any Sòng or Yuan *huaben*, while many others seem to have culled their material from a variety of non-*huaben* sources such·as the Tang *chuanqi* and official histories. There may have been earlier versions of the latter tales, but most likely they were written by Feng himself, possibly in some cooperation with friends or associates.

There was clearly a strong fashion among literary men in the late Ming for re-editing old texts and claiming antiquity for new ones. Anthologies of 'Yuan' *sanqu* songs abounded, in which a large number of the songs were probably later than the Yuan. And, as mentioned, fragmentary or sparse drama texts were being supplemented and offered to the public as the genuine Yuan article. In 1615 and 1616, just a few years before the *San-yan*, Zang Maoxun (d. 1621) published his *Yuan-qu xuan*, 'Selection of Yuan songs', which for centuries afterwards was to prove the standard collection of 'Yuan' *zaju* plays. In a large proportion of the hundred plays in this collection much of the dialogue and stage directions were provided by Zang himself, or conceivably also by some team of editors working for him. Even the arias, the very core of the plays, were altered. Such late Ming editors rarely proclaimed very loudly either the fact of their editing or the supposed antiquity of their works. By and large, they did little more than attach the label of antiquity to the works. Indeed, as in the case of Zang Maoxun, they would sometimes quietly, but, even with a certain amount of pride, confess to their editing activities, or would leave enough clues for such activities to be obvious to anyone bent on ferreting them out. Feng Menglong himself published a greatly expanded version of an earlier novel originally attributed to Luo Guanzhong, entitled *Ping-yao zhuan*, 'Extirpation of the warlocks', doubling the number of chapters contained in the previously current version. Such an expansion can hardly have been a serious attempt to fool anyone as to the antiquity of the work, and no doubt Feng's object was better literature. Claims of venerability are a common stock-in-trade of raconteurs and entertainers, and need neither be taken too seriously nor in any way condemned. A true understanding of the way in which these Ming publications came into being might indeed enable us all the better to appreciate the true creative splendours of that age.

It was Feng Menglong who firmly established the *huaben*, the 'vernacular' short story, in the Chinese literary world. He and the general literary, publishing and social climates combined to inspire others to write in a similar direction, principally Ling Mengchu (1580–1644), whose sparkling stories were often yet more obviously his own creation, and who in some ways surpassed Feng as a story-teller. The genre continued to flourish during the last years of the Ming and the early Qing dynasty (1644–1911), till around the end of the seventeenth century, but its full flowering was surprisingly short, since the novel, also within the 'vernacular' tradition, went on to conquer new peaks during the eighteenth century, and remained a vigorous part of literature into the twentieth century, when it enjoyed a considerable vogue as late as the twenties and thirties with the works of Zhang Henshui. Towards the end of the Ming, forty tales from Feng Menglong's and Ling Mengchu's collections were assembled, slightly edited, under the title *Jin-gu qi-guan*, 'Marvellous vistas ancient and modern', by a certain Bao-weng-lao-ren (a pen-name meaning 'Old Man Embracing a Cask'). This survived as the only generally current collection of *huaben*, and a sequel to it appeared in the late nineteenth century. By and large, the main achievements in the realm of the short-story during the Qing took place in the *chuanqi*-style or literary Classical Chinese tale, rather than in the 'vernacular' *huaben*. Such eminent story-writers as Pu Songling (1640–1715) and Yuan Mei (1716–98), for instance, both preferred the more purely Classical Chinese style, although Pu's tales in particular have a liveliness and freedom of a kind that might well have been stimulated by his well-known acquaintance with other forms of 'vernacular' literature.

It is customary to distinguish the 'Classical Chinese' from the 'vernacular' traditions in Chinese literature. In fact, works classified as the former are far from always wholly or purely Classical Chinese in their language, although in some particular genres pure Classical Chinese is *de rigueur*, while works included in the 'vernacular' tradition, which embraces such forms as the *pinghua*, the novel, the *huaben* and the drama, although sometimes largely colloquial and vernacular and usually to some extent so, are also in some cases largely in Classical Chinese. The real and useful distinctions indicated by the two categories are those of general attitude rather than of specific language. The most obvious distinction would seem to be that the 'vernacular' tradition *as a whole* countenances the wholesale mingling of all kinds of languages, from the most abstruse and ancient Classical Chinese to the most racy colloquial and dialect. This attitude alone seems to justify the distinction made between the two traditions, although not the terms used to describe them. But better terms are difficult to find.

Little is known of Feng Menglong's life. He came from Wu county in Suzhou (Soochow) in Kiangsu province. In his younger days he experienced romantic life in the singing-girl quarters. Some time after 1628 he became a Senior Licentiate and embarked upon a career in government service. In the last years of the Ming, after Qing forces entered China, he engaged in the composition and dissemination of patriotic or loyalist propaganda, and followed the Ming government when it sought refuge in Fukien province. During the years 1634–38 he was magistrate of Shouning in Fukien province. It is likely that he died for the Ming cause. Numerous works are attributed to his authorship and editorship, among them a number of works of lofty Classical Chinese scholarship, and, besides the *huaben*, numerous works in the 'vernacular' tradition, including plays, novels, jokebooks, and collections of folk-songs. Not all the attributions are reliable, but there is no doubt of the considerable extent and variety of his contributions to Chinese literature.

Of the six stories in this volume, most, if not all, have at some time been translated into a European language, but some of the translations are long out of print. My versions have been prepared independently. 'Yang Jiao' comes from the *Yu-shi ming-yan*, 'Li Bai' from the *Jing-shi tong-yan*, and all the rest from the *Xing-shi heng-yan*. Four of them are found in the *Jin-gu qi-guan*, and for my translations of these I have used the Peking, Renmin Wenxue, 1957 edition. 'A joke over fifteen strings of cash' I have translated from the *Xu Jin-gu qi-guan*, Hong Kong, Wen Yan Book House, 1964 edition. I wish to thank Dr H. C. Chang, who helped me and fellow-students through this story in years gone by. Any shortcomings in the translation are my own fault. 'On Big Tree Slope' I have translated from *Xing-shi heng-yan*, Hong Kong, Zhong Hua Shuju, 1958.

Various common features will readily be noticed in the stories, such as set narrative devices and the oral story-teller's mood, and the frequent use of verse to introduce and demarcate scenes, to describe scenery and persons, to summarise a moral, to anticipate trouble, and so forth. Each main story is introduced by another, shorter story of the kind generally termed *ruhua*, 'entering story', which serves to reinforce the message of the main story and to be its curtain-raiser, creating anticipatory dramatic tension. Morals are stated most explicitly, a practice which tends to disturb a modern Westerner, but which is often an excellent foil for good theatre. The Chinese of the stories varies from the most involved Classical Chinese, often quoting ancient works unaltered, to a rough and sometimes vulgar colloquial. Regional dialect is sometimes used.

All the stories here translated were based in part or wholly on earlier tales or accounts. 'On Big Tree Slope' and 'Two magistrates' both seem basically to derive from much terser Sòng literary-style anecdotes, and 'The perfect lady' seems also to have been inspired by such material. We note that Shen

Zijin, a contemporary of Feng's and a celebrated playwright and musician, wrote a play called *Wang-hu ting*, 'Lake Prospect Pavilion', on the theme of 'The perfect lady'. The topic of 'Yang Jiao' can be traced back as far as the *Hou Han shu*, 'Official history of the Latter Han', and the anthology of literature known as *Wen-xuan*, 'Selection of writings', both compiled during the Six Dynasties (222–589). The story is found in an incomplete version in the surviving portions of the *Qing-ping shan-tang hua-ben* collection, with much of its wording identical to that of Feng's story. Undoubtedly he took the story from there, supplementing it and polishing it and adding a more extensive *ruhua*, but the precise extent of his alterations we cannot know. 'A joke over fifteen string of cash' is likewise found, in almost identical form, in another collection of *huaben* entitled *Jing-ben tong-su xiao-shuo*, 'Capital editions of vernacular tales'. This collection has often been regarded as an assembly of genuine, pristine Sòng vernacular tales, but scholarly opinion now strongly suspects it to date from the Ming, and it is not unlikely that the collection took it from Feng, rather than vice-versa. The theme of the story served as the subject of a Kunqu play called *Shi-wu guan*, 'Fifteen strings of cash' in twenty-six acts by Zhu Hao (fl. c. 1644). In revised form this play enjoyed considerable nationwide celebrity in China in 1956 and subsequent years, both as a stage play and in its colour film version. The tale has indeed inspired much other literature, including a Qinqiang play in sixteen acts, a Peking Opera in nine parts, a *guci*, 'drum lyric', narrative ballad occupying some two hundred pages of modern print, a *tanci*, 'strum lyric', ballad of some ninety pages of modern print, and various other ballads.

'Li Bai' is a synthesis and elaboration of a body of history, legend and literature concerning China's most famous poet, Li Bai (701–62), who through Arthur Waley's translations has become widely known in the West under the romanisation Li Po. Most of the basic features of Feng's account can be traced to earlier material, including some of Li Bai's own poems and the biography of Li in the official history *Xin Tang-shu*, 'New History of the Tang', by Song Qi (998–1057), but Feng far from exhausts the wealth of earlier fact and legend about the poet, and his story, both by its selection and its elaborations, creates a unified over-all mood all its own.

Recent translations of Feng are found in a number of works: Harold Acton and Lee Yi-hsieh, *Glue and Lacquer*, London, Golden Cockerel Press, 1941, reprinted as *Four Cautionary Tales*, New York, A. A. Wyn, 1947; Wang Chi-chen, *Traditional Chinese Tales*, New York, Columbia University Press, 1944, reprint New York, Greenwood Press, 1968; J. L. Bishop, *The Colloquial Short Story in China, a Study of the San-yen Collections*, Cambridge, Mass., Harvard University Press, 1956; Yang Hsien-yi and Gladys Yang, *The Courtesan's Jewel Box*, Peking, Foreign Languages Press, 1957; Cyril Birch, *Stories from a Ming Collection*, Bloomington and London, Indiana University Press, 1958; Liane Bettin and Marianne Liebermann, *Die Jädegöttin*, Berlin, Rütten and Loening, 1968; André Lévy, *Etudes sur le conte et le roman chinois*, Paris, École Française d'Extrême Orient, 1971; André Lévy, with René Goldman, *L'Antre aux fantômes des collines de l'Ouest*, Paris, Gallimard, 1972. Spirited translations of Ling Mengchu are given in André Lévy, *L'Amour de la renarde*, Paris, Gallimard, 1970, and John Scott, *The Lecherous Academician*, London, André Deutsch/Rapp and Whiting, 1973.

Among the steadily growing number of incisive works in Western languages on the *huaben* and Chinese fiction, in addition to studies contained in many of the above works, there are the following books and articles: Cyril Birch, 'Feng Menglong and the *Ku-chin hsiao-shuo*', *Bulletin of the School of Oriental and African Studies* (London) vol. 18, 1956, pp. 64–83; Jaroslav Průšek, *The Origins and the Authors of the Hua-pen*, Prague, Academia, 1967; Glen Dudbridge, *The Hsi-yu chi*, Cambridge, Cambridge University Press, 1970; W. L. Idema, 'Story-telling and the short-story in China', *T'oung Pao* (Leiden) vol. 59, 1973, pp. 1–67; Patrick Hanan, *The Chinese Short Story, Studies in Dating, Authorship, and Composition*, Cambridge, Mass., Harvard University Press, 1973.

Edinburgh, July 1975   *William Dolby*

The Perfect Lady by Mistake

Wine-pleasured in our fishing skiff
day by day we stray,
And mid the deepest bulrush thickets
the breathy flute we play.
The wind withdraws from the face of the lake,
cloud-images disperse their haze,
And heaven mirrors in the waters
its tranquil azure glaze.

This poem was written by Yang Bei of the Sòng dynasty as he toured the Great Lake by boat. The Great Lake is some thirty miles to the south-west of Suzhou. What sort of size do you imagine it to be? It is two hundred miles east-west, one hundred and twenty miles north-south, and five hundred miles in circumference. It embraces seventy-two mountain peaks and is surrounded by three sub-prefectures. Which three? No lesser regions than Suzhou, Hangchow and Changzhou! And all the rivers of the south-east make their way into the Lake. Another name for it is Thunder Lake, and it is also known as Spread of All-Providence, Bamboo Rain-Hat Lake, and Five Lakes. Now why should it be called Five Lakes? In the east it joins with the River Sòng up to Changzhou, in the south with the Torrent Crash Stream from Wucheng, in the west with the Bramble Stream from Yixing, in the north with Lake He as far as Jinling, and in the east again with Leek Stream from Jiaxing, these five stretches of water accounting for the name Five Lakes. At the same time, since the waters of these 'five lakes' are still branches of Thunder Lake, the whole

玉堂春

has thus come to be referred to as the Great Lake. In the Great Lake proper there are also the famous Five Scenic Lakes: Water Chestnut Lake, Drifting Lake, Watercress Lake, Tribute Lake, and Xu Lake. Besides the Five Lakes, there are the Three Small Lakes: the one to the east of Mount Fujiao, called Lake Plum Blossom Bridge; the one west of Duqi and east of Yucha, called Lake Gold Tripod; and the one east of Linwu, called Lake East Paddy Hamlet. In Wu people apply to all these lakes the collective name of Great Lake.

Of the seventy-two mountain peaks in the Great Lake, the biggest are the two Mount Dongtings. The Eastern Dongting, known simply as Eastern Mountain, and the Western Dongting, known as Western Mountain, surge some way apart from each other in the middle of the Lake. Various other mountains far and near loom hazily through the misty blur of waves and billows. A poem by the Yuan poet Xu Qian captures the scene:

> Fed by myriad swirling waters,
> girdled by provinces far and near,
> Floating west to horizon mountains,
> and southwards where land may ne'er reappear.
> Hence the Three Rivers home to the sea,
> straight their course 'twixt mightier streams,
> Yet mid hasty white waves in the autumn wind
> the fisherman's boat still leisurely dreams.

The two mountains, Eastern Mountain and Western Mountain, lie well out in the middle of the Great Lake, and being surrounded by water on all sides cannot be reached by horse and carriage. If anyone wants to take a trip to them, he has to rely on water transport, which not infrequently entails some dangers. A long while ago the Sòng dynasty Prime Minister Fan Chengda encountered a storm on the Lake and embodied his experiences in a poem:

> White mist floods the sky, white waves trough
> deep,
> my boat like some leaf of bamboo tossed by the
> water at the whim of the wind;

> I shall not now dare to rise late from my sleep,
>   no more such casual habits keep,
> since these mountains and these waters have been
>   printed on my mind.

Now the people living round these two mountains are masters of the arts of fortune-building and roam the whole country far and wide engaging in trade, which is why in the merchant world there is the dictum 'Heaven-scouring Dongting'. We are solely concerned with the Western Dongting, where there lived a wealthy man by the name of Gao Zan, who in his youth had made a practice of plying the provinces of Hupeh, Hunan, Kwangtung and Kwangsi as a trader in grain. Later, as his wealth grew more substantial, he had opened two pawn emporiums, the management of which he had entrusted to four assistants while he himself remained at home to enjoy the benefits. His wife, née Jin, had borne him two children, a son called Biao and a daughter called Autumn Fragrance, the girl being two years older than her brother. Gao Zan employed an elderly tutor, who lived in and had his meals with the household and gave private instruction to the children. Autumn Fragrance was very alert and intelligent. Beginning her studies at the age of six, by the age of eleven she was thoroughly versed in the classics, and her literary compositions were invariably excellent. She did not proceed into any academy when she reached the age of twelve, but instead remained at home to cultivate the feminine arts of needlework and all the refinements of embroidery. As she stood on the verge of fifteen, she had blossomed into an unusually attractive young woman. A lyric to the tune 'West River Moon' provides an apt description of her:

> Her face is like the flower of the peach
>   with dew all lightly laden,
> Her body is as whitest snow
>   cupped to the form of this shapely maiden.
> Across her eyes there lie
>   the ripple spills
> of shimmering autumn rills,
> Beneath two eyebrows black as sloes

two superb pure-swerving bows,
And her fingers are slender,
fine as the new
tender shoots of spring bamboo.
No longer cite Xi Shi as the zenith
of willowy charms and seductions!
And this lady yields nought to Miss Oriole,
in gay allure and soft attractions.
Slim, golden-lotus feet
petal-light,
All her moves one heaven
of grace and delight.

Conscious of his daughter's attractiveness and intelligence, Gao Zan was disinclined to marry her off to any Tom, Dick or Harry; he was determined on the contrary to find some young scholar gentleman, as handsome as he was talented, to be her partner. Whether such a partner could manage to provide lavish betrothal gifts or not was of no object to him. Providing the suitor was to his liking, he was perfectly willing to give his daughter a more than usually generous dowry when she married. Offers of marriage from numerous powerful and wealthy families arrived daily, but upon discovering that their young scions were of no special abilities and of only average looks, Gao Zan in every case withheld his consent.

Although Dongting lay in the middle of a vast stretch of water, it was situated upon a key communications route between the three sub-prefectures. Gao was moreover a man of considerable means. For these reasons the news was spread far and wide by match-makers, who lauded the gifts and beauty of Miss Gao and disclosed that her father was ready to contribute generously to the marriage if a sufficiently presentable husband could be found. Every young man with the slightest scrap of talent and the vaguest hint of good looks sought to do himself a splendid good turn by slipping into the breach, and would beg some go-between to try and arrange it for him. The go-betweens would duly make out the young men to be as handsome as Pan An and as brilliant as Cao Zijian, those two paragons of old, but under the stronger light of closer investigation it was more often than not revealed that they were very run-of-the-mill in both respects. Fed up with having the wool pulled over his eyes by this gang of go-betweens, Gao Zan had a firm word with them.

'From now on,' he said, 'you can cut out all the chitter-chatter. If you really come across someone special, just turn up here with him, and if he's what I'm looking for, we'll settle matters on the spot without any rigmarole! Nice and straight and simple!'

After this advice, the go-betweens no longer ventured to approach him with frivolous propositions. Now it was a case of:

> It is only true when your eyes have seen it,
> you cannot rely on what you hear,
> Now the touchstone is here to assay with
> the silver-debaser turns blue with fear.

Now we shall let our story take a different tack for a while. In a place known as Pingwang in Wujiang county in Suzhou prefecture there lived a young scholar by the name of Qian Qing, courtesy name* Wanxuan. He had read and absorbed a prodigious amount of classical literature, was as profoundly knowledgeable in modern matters as in those of antiquity, and to cap all these qualities was the very picture of brilliance in appearance. Here is another lyric to 'West River Moon' to describe him:

> Life has brought him
> full red lips, teeth of resplendent white,
> And eyebrows clear-cut, fine-carved
> for eyes that shine with noble light.
> Panache and gallantry reside in *him*
> not in some coat fresh cut to fashion's whim,
> Foremost in handsome looks and deeds,
> all other men in this he leads.
> His writing brush but touches paper,
> a thousand words he dashes off,

---

*Further name taken at the age of nineteen, or sometimes earlier in youth.

　　　　sublimely phrased,
He wields his pen in composition,
　　all lookers-on admire and are amazed.
Epitome of sterling attainments
　　of fame well deserved, far and near,
Inspiring in others at very first sight
　　the urge to acclaim and revere.

For many generations past the Qian family had produced scholars, but the household was very poorly-off. It was a grave misfortune for Qian Qing that his parents had both died early, for this had rendered his situation all the more bleak and stinted. Thus when he came of age he lacked the wherewithal to take himself a wife, and simply lived together with an old serving man, Qian Xing, the two of them existing in mutual reliance. Every day Qian Xing would engage in a little small-scale trading in order to provide for his master, but not infrequently his means would not stretch to a meal and every now and then they would have to go hungry. By good luck, when Qing graduated there was a cousin of his living outside the northern gate of the town. This cousin was very rich, and invited him to come and pursue his studies in his household.

The cousin was called Yan Jun, courtesy name Boya. He and Qian Qing had been born in the same year, both now being seventeen, but as he was slightly older than Qian Qing, a mere three months though it was, Qing would address him as 'Elder Brother'. His father had passed away, leaving only his elderly mother, for like Qian Qing he was neither married nor even engaged.

Come now, story-teller, Qian Qing was not married because he was poor—but Yan Jun was rich! Why on earth would Yan Jun not have acquired a wife by the age of seventeen? Well, there were reasons. Yan Jun was afflicted by overweening ambitions and had sworn that he would not contract any marital obligations until he was able to choose himself a girl of really outstanding beauty, and this accounts for his slowness in attaining a match. To add to his problem, he was remarkably ugly to look at. How do you mean? Here's a further lyric to the tune 'West River Moon' to convey some notion of what I mean:

Murky-mugged like the bottom of a saucepan,
Great ball eyes like big bronze bells,
Cannonball head dense-nailed with pock-scars,
Mouse-hair sideboards, drooping rat-tails.
Teeth covered over with a plate of goodly gold,
Body knocked together from iron bent, and tough
Fingers splayed like drum-sticks ready-made:
Call him Handsome Yan and raise a handsome
    laugh!

In spite, of his ghastly looks, his greatest delight was to tog himself up in gaudy finery, put on a low, seductive voice and force a cavalier laugh, in the strange conviction that all this somehow made him into a really dapper dandy. A further disadvantage under which he laboured was that he bore not a drop of the ink of culture in his whole being and could scarcely commit a line of literary worth to paper, while at the same time he was for ever pontificating upon everything ancient and modern in an attempt to show off how learned he was. Qian Qing was perfectly aware that they were not at all attuned to one another, but since the use of Yan's premises was of considerable benefit to his studies he would unfailingly lend his support to Yan in all he did. Yan Jun for his part was very happy with such a situation and would seek Qian's advice in all his enterprises. So the two of them got on very well together.

Let's not be long-winded. On with the story. One day, early in November, Yan Jun received a visit from a distant relative, a man called You Chen. He was a small trader, quite an enterprising fellow, and had borrowed a little capital from Yan Jun, which had enabled him to open up a fruit shop at his home which earned him his livelihood. On the day in question he was on his way back from Mount Dongting after having bought a few loads of oranges, and called in to present the Yans with a bowlful of the fruit, by way of a novel present, the oranges being the first of the season. Over on the Mountain he had heard how Gao Zan was in quest of a son-in-law, and now, in the course of conversation, he chanced to relate the matter to Yan Jun, quite casually, without any particular motive in doing so. Strange to say, however, Yan Jun was very taken with the idea.

'I've always been on the look-out for a fine partner in matrimony,' he thought, 'but none of the possibles have been to my liking. And now this chance drops upon me out of the blue! With my looks and my ability, and my wealth into the bargain, all I need do is ask a go-between to pop across and say a few sweet words to them. How can I fail!'

That night, try as he would, Yan Jun could not get to sleep. He rose at daybreak, washed himself and combed his hair at breakneck speed and went round to You Chen's house.

You Chen had just opened his door and was coming out when he saw Yan Jun. 'What's pulled you from your bed so early this morning, dear sir?' he asked.

'A rather important matter I'd like to bother you with,' said Yan Jun, 'I was afraid you might be going out, so I made a special effort to be early.'

'What could it be that you wish me to do for you, I wonder, sir,' said You Chen. 'Please come indoors and sit down and tell me exactly how I may be of assistance.'

Yan Jun entered and after bowing and performing various courtesies sat down.

'Well, sir,' said You Chen, 'just you instruct me as to whatever it is you require of me, and I shall do it to the very best of my endeavour. My only fear is that such a useless fellow as myself can scarcely be of any use to you.'

'One thing and one thing only,' said Yan Jun. 'I would like to ask you to act as intermediary in a matter of marital union.'

'I am most grateful that you think of giving me the chance to earn a nuptial gratuity,' replied You Chen. 'Might I ask whom you have in mind?'

'The people you mentioned yesterday,' said Yan Jun, 'the Gaos of Western Dongting Mountain. Might I trouble you to arrange things on my behalf?'

You Chen gave a stifled guffaw. 'Don't hold it against me if I speak rather bluntly,' he said. 'If it was anyone else you wanted, I should be only too glad to do the arranging. But if it's the Gaos you're after, I would suggest you look for someone else to negotiate it, sir.'

'Why are you backing out?' asked Yan Jun. 'It was you who mentioned the matter in the first place. Why tell me to find someone else for the job?'

'Well, no then, I'm not trying to back out,' said You Chen. 'It's just that old Gao is a queer old nut. Not easy to talk to. So I was a bit hesitant.'

'Anything else might pose difficulties,' said Yan Jun. 'In other matters there is usually room for some beating about the bush or waffling or playing hard-to-get which might make it difficult to get down to terms. But not when a match-maker comes to try and draw a couple together in blessed wedlock. Unless of course the father has no mind to marry off his daughter, in which case there is nothing to be done about it. He has to deal through a go-between, no two ways about it, and I don't give a damn how queer and crotchety he may be, he must know that it will do him no good to get on his high horse with a go-between. So why on earth are you so scared of him? No, I think it's you who's deliberately being awkward and refusing to help me achieve the marriage I have set my heart on. Never mind—I'll ask someone else to go and arrange things. And when it's all fixed, you needn't expect a drink from the wedding cup!' With these words, Yan Jun leapt up to go.

Having borrowed his capital from Yan Jun, You Chen always made a habit of keeping on the right side of him. Now, perceiving the young man's displeasure and hostility, he rapidly changed tack. 'Come on now, sir. Don't go off in a huff. Just be seated for a bit and we'll talk it all over. We'll leave no stone unturned.'

'If you agree, then go!' said Yan Jun. 'If you refuse, then that's that. What is there to discuss!' But in spite of this forceful utterance, he turned round and sat down once more.

'No,' said You Chen, 'I wasn't just being awkward, the old fellow really is a funny customer. I know other people make a fuss about inspecting a prospective daughter-in-law, but he insists on inspecting his son-in-law of all things! He's only prepared to give his daughter away if he sees the man face to face and likes the look of him. So you see, with every sign of trouble in that direction I was worried that all my efforts might turn out to be a sheer waste of time, and worse still that I'd just be landing myself in hot water with you.'

'If what you say is the case,' said Yan Jun, 'I really don't see where the problem lies. Quite simply, if he wants to see me

24

in person, we can let him have a good eyeful of me. I'm not deformed. What is there to worry about!'

In spite of himself You Chen let out a huge guffaw. 'My dear good sir,' he said, 'I'm not trying to insult you, but let's put it this way. Even though you may not be bad-looking, there are men a good deal more handsome he's still turned down as impossible. If you try without meeting him face to face, you won't stand a chance in a hundred, but maybe you'll stand a chance in a thousand. If you meet him in person, you haven't a chance in a million of marrying his daughter.'

'They often say "A marriage is never brought high and dry without some teeny-weeny lie",' said Yan Jun. 'You go and tell a tall story for me. Say I'm a thoroughly splendid chap. Maybe my luck will be in and he'll agree on the spot without wanting to interview me first. You never know.'

'And what if he does want to interview you?' asked You Chen.

'We'll sort out that problem when it arises,' said Yan Jun. 'All I'm asking you now is to hurry over and have a word with him.'

'Well, since it's you that's asking me,' said You Chen, 'I'll be off, come what may.'

As he was on the point of leaving, Yan Jun repeatedly urged him to do his level best. 'If you manage to pull it off,' he said, 'there'll be twenty taels of silver to express my gratitude to you, and as a first step I'll hand you back that loan-deed. On top of that there'll be the wedding gratuities.'

'I'll do all I can,' replied the other.

Shortly after taking his leave of him, Yan Jun had five taels of silver popped into a packet and delivered to You Chen to cover the cost of hiring a boat the following day.

That night was another sleepless one for Yan Jun. 'If he goes there without putting his heart into it,' he thought, 'and just reports back here with any old story trumped up on the spur of the moment, it will all have been a sheer waste of time and effort. I'll send someone else along with him, a smart lad, to take a mental note of what he hears him say. Yes, yes, that's a first-class plan.'

25

When dawn broke, Yan Jun called a young servitor named Xiaoyi and instructed him to accompany You Chen to the Mountain for the marriage negotiations.

Xiaoyi set off, and Yan Jun felt all on edge. After a quick wash and smarten-up, he marched round to a nearby Temple of Sacred Lord Guan to seek a divination, so that he could predict his destiny and tell whether he was to be blessed with success in the marriage. Without ado he burned incense and made repeated obeisances, then gave the canister of divination-lots a few rattles with his hand. Out jumped a divination-lot, and he picked it up to read it. He saw that it was lot number seventy-three, and upon it was written the following four-line oracle:

> Yearning for orchid chamber and love's
>   shared delight
> sudden news comes casting disappointment's
>   blight,
> Infatuated hopes of twined columbine and rose
> but concord is not the flower that in
>   this garden grows.

For all his lack of education, the meaning of these lines was pretty plain to Yan Jun; he could scarcely avoid grasping their message. This spot of fortune-telling put him in a furious temper. 'Rubbish! Rubbish,' he repeated again and again, and with an angry flourish of his sleeves marched out of the temple gate.

Reaching home, he sat down for a while. 'Of course he'll agree to the marriage,' he thought. 'No one can tell me he would really be put off me simply because he thought me too ugly. A man, if he's worth his salt, is not judged in the same light as a woman. As long as he manages to raise himself above the crowd in life, that's all that matters. Does Gao really have to choose some fabulous beauty-boy like Chen Ping or Pan An?'

As these thoughts coursed through his mind, he picked up a mirror to take a look at himself. He twisted his head this way and that, but it was no good, he could not deceive himself.

Even he could not bear the sight. He flung the mirror down onto the table, heaved a disconsolate sigh, and sat there in dumb and helpless gloom. All day long he felt miserable and fed-up. We'll leave him to it.

Meanwhile, that same day You Chen and Xiaoyi boarded a fast three-paddled boat and were cradled across the calm, windless waves to the sound of the boatman's shanty-calls, until they moored directly before the gate of the Gao residence. By then it was early afternoon. Xiaoyi sent in a name-card by way of introduction and Gao Zan issued forth to welcome them. Gao inquired the reason for their visit and was informed that they wished to discuss the possibility of a marital union with his dear daughter. He asked the identity of the suitor.

'He is a relative of mine,' answered You Chen, 'domiciled in my own poor county. He comes from a family of not insubstantial means, and both socially and economically would be a very fitting match for you, my lord. And he is just seventeen and a very erudite young gentleman, too.'

'What about his disposition and appearance?' asked Gao Zan. 'I've already let it be known that I must see any suitor face to face before I can even think of entertaining his offer.'

Seeing Xiaoyi hanging close behind him, right by the back of his chair, You Chen had no option but to do what was expected of him and tell some whopping lies. 'No need for the slightest worry on that account,' he said. 'A massive, imposing figure of a man, with divinely perfect looks. And a veritable treasury of literary talents he is, too. Took the junior exams when he was thirteen and came slap-bang top of the county, way ahead of the rest. His father's sad decease a few years ago has prevented him from enrolling in any academy, which is why he has so far been unable to obtain a degree, but a number of elder scholars who have looked at his writings have judged that he's fit to take the imperial examinations in the capital. I must apologise. I'm not accustomed to this match-making business and I cannot really do justice to the young gentleman. It was just that I come across to this mountain year in year out to buy fruit and I chanced to hear that your dear daughter was as fair as she was gifted and that you, venerable sir, were most anxious to find a suitable son-in-law. So one thing led to

another and it occurred to me that this young relative of min
was the very man for you and I have made so bold as to pay
you this unsolicited visit.'

Gao Zan was highly delighted to hear all this. 'If you
relative is such a handsome and able young man, then o
course I can scarcely refuse,' he said, 'but I still cannot fee
entirely easy about the matter until I have set eyes on him
myself. If you would be so kind as to bring him to my humble
abode for a brief while, we could there and then conclude the
affair without further ado.'

'You can take my word,' said You Chen. 'I have not praised
him loosely or lightly, as you yourself will be able to confirm
in due course. The trouble is that he's one of those young
gentlemen who are always buried in their books, a real young
literatus, and he may not be willing to make the trip over here
Even should I succeed in encouraging him to do so, all will be
fine as long as the marriage comes off, but if by some chance it
doesn't, what a fool he will have made himself look, returning
home empty-handed! And in that case I'm bound to bear the
brunt of his resentment.'

'Since he's such a thoroughly presentable, all-round young
man,' said Gao Zan, 'there's no question but that we'll reach
an agreement. But it's my nature to weigh up everything with
minute care, so I must have a look at him first. If he doesn't
feel like coming over here, let me go over to his place and you
can bring him out, casually as if by accident, for me to observe
him. No possible harm in that, eh?'

Alarmed at the very thought of old Gao's paying a personal
visit to Wujiang and discovering what an ugly sight Yan Jun
really was, You Chen hastily changed his tune. 'If you really
feel you must meet him, respected sir,' he said, 'I shall bring
the young man here to pay his regards in person. I couldn't
for a moment think of troubling you to travel all that way.'

With these words he tried to take his leave. Gao Zan,
however, adamantly refused to let him go and instead straight-
away called for wine and sweetmeats to be set forth for a feast
to entertain him. They dined well into the night and Gao Zan
wanted him to lodge there overnight.

'I already have a bed laid out for me on board,' said You
Chen, 'and I must be off early in the morning. When my young

relative presents himself before you, I hope then to burden you with my company once more.'

Gao Zan brought out a packet of money and gave it to him by way of payment for his voyage. Expressing his thanks, You Chen went down to the boat. The following morning a favourable wind filled the sails to the full and in less than half a day they were back in Wujiang.

Yan Jun was standing dumbly lost in thought at the gate, waiting for the news. As he saw You Chen returning, he came out to meet him. 'Sorry to have put you to all this trouble,' he said. 'How did things go?'

You Chen narrated all the ins and outs of his conversation in elaborate detail. 'He insists on seeing you, sir. What's to be done?'

Yan Jun pondered silently and uttered not a word.

'See you in a while then,' said You Chen, and went off home.

Yan Jun walked back indoors and shouted for Xiaoyi, whom he subjected to a thorough-going interrogation, in case You Chen hadn't been telling the truth. But Xiaoyi's version of what had happened completely tallied with You's. After he had brooded on the matter for a long time, a scheme occurred to Yan Jun. He went round for another conference with You. What stratagem did he have in mind? Ah, yes,

> Yearning for a lovely bride, Passion burns
>   so bright,
> lacerating his soul with longing, sleepless
>   night on night.
> Yet Providence, it always was, decided every
>   wedding,
> Hymen does not come, wedlock is not
>   won at Passion's bidding.

'About what you said just now,' said Yan Jun, 'well, I have a plan. There's nothing to worry about.'

'What plan can possibly do any good?' asked You Chen.

'I have my cousin Qian Qing studying with me in my house,' said Yan Jun. 'He's much better educated and better-looking than me. I'll beg him to accompany you over to their place tomorrow. You can pass him off as me and cheat Gao until all the betrothal formalities have been gone through—I don't think we need worry about Gao's trying to back out then.'

'Yes, if he sets eyes on Master Qian,' said You Chen, 'he's dead certain to give his consent to the marriage. The only thing I'm pretty doubtful about is whether Master Qian will cooperate.'

'Qian's a very close relative of mine and we get on together like a house on fire. All I'm asking of him is to stand in for me for a few moments. That's not asking much. I'm absolutely sure he won't refuse.'

Yan Jun said goodbye and went home. That night he went to the study-apartment to join Qian Qing for supper. He had arranged an extra slap-up meal of wine and savouries for him that night.

'Here am I imposing on you all this time,' said Qian Qing in astonishment. 'Why on earth have you gone to all this trouble to give me such a lavish spread tonight?'

'Let's just have a few drinks together,' said Yan Jun. 'There's a little job I would like you to do for me, if I might bother you with it. You won't refuse, will you?'

'Anything whatsoever I can do for you, you only have to issue the order,' said Qian Qing. 'What sort of job?'

'Well, I won't beat about the bush,' replied Yan Jun. 'You Chen who keeps the fruit shop opposite has been acting as go-between for me, trying to fix me up with the daughter of a certain Gao over at Western Dongting Mountain. On the spur of the moment he got carried away and praised me up no end, claiming I was the pinnacle of good looks and learning. He quite lost himself in his own eloquence. Old Gao, though, insists on inviting me there to meet him face to face before agreeing to any engagement. We were talking it over yesterday, and concluded that if I went myself I might not match up to my description. You Chen has lost enthusiasm and the marriage will be a hard one to pull off anyway. So I would like you to pretend to be me, go along with You Chen, roll up under my name and trick old Gao so that we can wangle the wedding. If you'll do that, I'll be enormously grateful to you, and I'll certainly repay you in no small way afterwards, you can rest assured of that.'

Qian Qing mused on the matter for a moment. 'Anything else I wouldn't mind,' he said, 'but I don't think things would work out right in this case. Even if we managed to deceive him for a while, when he got to know of it later there's no telling what sort of a mess you and I might find ourselves landed in.'

'But that's all I want,' said Yan Jun, 'just to deceive him for a while. Once the engagement formalities are over, it won't bother me even if he does realise what's happened. Anyway, he won't know who you really are, so even if he feels aggrieved he can only vent his wrath on the go-between. Why should that bother you! What's more, he lives at Western Dongting Mountain, a hundred miles away, so it may take him a good while to discover. Just you stop worrying. No call to be timid and scared.'

Qian Qing pondered in silence. If he gave in, he would be letting himself in for something decidedly unethical. If he stood firm, he would incur a grudge and would be unable to carry on studying on his cousin's premises. He was on the horns of a dilemma.

Perceiving his brooding indecision, Yan Jun spoke up again. 'Look here, dear fellow,' he said, 'there's a common saying, "If the sky collapses, there'll always be someone taller than you to prop it up." I'll look after everything, so don't you fret.'

'Yes, yes, that's all very well,' said Qian Qing, 'but all my clothes are so ragged and scruffy. I just wouldn't match up to your image.'

'I already have that matter in hand,' said Yan Jun.

The following day Yan Jun rose early and went straight to the study-apartment, where he had a boy valet fetch out a leather trunk full of clothes. They were mainly of rich satin and silk, turquoise-dyed in the most fashionable patterns and piquantly perfumed with ambergris and other scents. These he handed to Qian Qing for him to change into when he set off, together with immaculate socks and silk shoes to wear underneath. Only the caps did not fit, so he at once had a new one specially made for him. He further made up a packet of two taels of silver and handed it to Qian Qing. 'Just a meagre contribution towards your stationery and other studying expenses,' he said. 'I'll have more offerings of gratitude for you in the future. This suit of clothes is a present for you to wear, dear younger brother. I would only beg you that in time to come when it's all over and done with you'll not disclose any of these goings-on to anyone else. I'll go today and make arrangements with You Chen, and you can set off early tomorrow.'

'Just as you say,' said Qian Qing, 'but I shall only borrow these clothes for the while, and return them to you when I get back. As for the silver, I wouldn't think of taking it.'

'In ancient times, when people shared their chariots, horses and fine fur coats with their friends, there was none of this awkwardness between them,' said Yan Jun. 'There's nothing remarkable about my offering you these few poor clothes. A meagre gift. Just a token of my feelings. If you refuse them, it will upset me very much.'

'Since you are so very kind to me,' said Qian Qing, 'I'll take them against my better judgement. But I certainly cannot accept the silver.'

'If you insist on refusing it,' said Yan Jun, 'I shall feel that you are trying to back out of our enterprise.'

Only then would Qian Qing accept it.

That same day Yan Jun arranged a meeting with You Chen. You Chen was most reluctant to undertake the affair, but simply in order to avoid offending Yan Jun he forced himself to assent. Yan Jun arranged for a boat, and had put on board supplies of such things as bedding and food. Besides Xiaoyi, who had gone on the previous occasion, he assigned another two page-boys to serve on board, making three in all, and in their silk shirts and felt caps they looked most dapper and impressive. By nightfall everything was fully prepared. Yan Jun also instructed Xiaoyi and the other page-boys that when they arrived they were always to address Qian Qing as if he were their own real master, Yan Jun, and that they must never let slip the name Qian. The night passed and the following morning he got up very early so as to hurry Qian Qing along with his toilette. As he changed into the most fashionable and sumptuous under and outer garments, his every movement wafting perfume, Qian Qing seemed more handsome than ever.

Clearly milord Xun Yu
    whose scent lingered on
    unfading after he had gone.
Surely handsome young Pan An
    whom girls in pursuit
    tossed gifts of fruit.

Yan Jun had invited You Chen across to his house and they and Qian Qing had breakfast together. Then You Chen and Qian Qing embarked with Xiaoyi and the two other page-boys, and once more blessed by a favourable wind they sailed without let or lull straight to Western Dongting Mountain. It was growing late when they arrived, so they spent the night on board.

The following day, waiting a decent interval until he estimated that Gao Zan would have risen, Qian Qing made out a visiting card, filling it in with Yan Jun's name and modestly appending a self-depreciatory remark. Xiaoyi took the card to the Gaos' gate to deliver it and announced that Squire You had brought the young master of the Yan household for the purpose of rendering a visit. Servants of the Gao establishment recognised Xiaoyi and rushed to inform their master. Gao Zan sent word for the guests to come as soon as possible. With the fake Yan Jun leading the way and You Chen following on behind, they strode into the main reception hall. One glance at the young man with his lofty, noble air and splendid apparel was enough to fill Gao Zan with utter delight. Upon completion of the formal introductions Gao urged him to sit in the place of honour, but Qian Qing self-depreciatorily pointed out his host's seniority and persisted in declining the honour, so that they were obliged to sit in the more proper order of precedence. Gao Zan was inwardly rejoicing. Here indeed was a modest and unassuming young gentleman.

When all were properly seated, You Chen was the first to speak, apologising for having disturbed their host by his visit on the previous occasion. Gao Zan made a long-winded reply.

'So this is your relative young Squire Yan?' he then continued. 'I failed the other day to ask his courtesy name.'

'I am too young to merit a courtesy name,' said Qian Qing self-effacingly.

'My relative's courtesy name is Boya,' said You Chen, speaking up on his behalf, 'the *Bo* meaning "senior" and the *ya* meaning "refined".'

'Most fitting elements for his name,' declared Gao Zan.

'Oh, I could scarcely venture to claim that,' said Qian Qing.

Then Gao Zan questioned him about his family background. Supplying a full answer to each question, Qian Qing flowed with eloquence and genteel culture.

'Well, he acquits himself very well in the external manifestations of culture,' thought Gao, 'but this gives me no certain idea of how well-educated he is. I'll ask our tutor and my son to come out and meet him and give him a thorough going-over to see just how erudite he really is.' After a couple of rounds of tea had been served to the guests, Gao instructed his servants to enter the study-apartments and invite the tutor and the young master out to join the gathering.

Presently a Confucian scholar aged over fifty appeared, followed by his pupil, a young boy. All of one accord rose to their feet and bowed. Then Gao Zan introduced everybody in turn by their names. 'This is my son's teacher, Mr Chen, who is at present a prefectural Master, and this is my son, Gao Biao.'

Casting a glance at the boy, Qian Qing perceived that he had sublimely carved, lively facial features and was altogether a superbly handsome lad. 'If that's how the boy looks,' he thought, 'you can just imagine what the sister is like! What a lucky devil Yan Jun is going to be.'

Another round of tea was served. Gao Zan turned to the tutor. 'This gentleman is my guest from Wujiang, Yan Senior Refinement, of venerable attainments for all his tender years.'

Mr Chen took his employer's hint. 'Ah yes,' he said, 'Wujiang is a hive of geniuses. I guarantee his knowledge and learning are unusual in their extent and profundity. Yes, there is the Shrine of the Three Lofty Hermits in your region, good sir— whom is it dedicated to, now?'

'To Fan Li, Zhang Han, and Lu Guimeng,' replied Qian Qing.

'How is it they came to be accorded such high esteem?' the other inquired.

Qian Qing proceeded to expound upon each of the famous

men in great detail. Then the two of them went on to probe each other's knowledge for a while. Detecting that the tutor's level of erudition was a fairly average one, Qian Qing purposely steered the conversation towards abstruse topics of universal implications, ranging freely over antiquity and modern phenomena, in a manner that rendered the teacher so speechless with astonished admiration that he was only able to utter 'Brilliant, brilliant!' again and again. This pleased Gao Zan so much that he was soon jigging and jumping around with delight. Quickly he summoned his servants and with tactful unobtrusiveness instructed them to produce a more hospitable spread for the guests. Acting upon his command, they dragged forth tables and piled them with every kind of sweetmeat and dainty. Gao Zan took up chopsticks and wine cups to allot places for the feast. Qian Qing made a formal courteous reply to the invitation, going through the motions of polite refusal, and then insisted as before on his host's taking the seat of honour. Soon the tables were fully laid with various varieties of soup, main dishes and side-snacks, all whisked into view with breath-taking alacrity.

How was it that everything was so marvellously to hand, you might wonder? Well, you see, Gao Zan's wife, Madam Jin, was very fond of her daughter, and when she heard that the go-between had brought young Squire Yan across, she had hidden behind a screen to observe him unseen. Seeing such a highly presentable and well-spoken young gentleman, she had at once been favourably struck by him, and taking it for granted that old Gao would be of the same mind had set about preparing the feast well in advance, long before it was ordered. That was how, as soon as the command was given, everything flowed so smoothly.

The little group of five, hosts and guests, alternated between the wine and food, feasting on until the red sun pecked the mountain top. Then Qian Qing and You Chen rose to take their leave. Most loth to see them go, Gao Zan eagerly pressed them to stay on for a few days. Qian Qing was quite adamant. Gao Zan made a few more attempts to retain their company but was then obliged to resign himself to their departure. First taking his leave of Tutor Chen, Qian Qing then thanked Mr Gao, apologising that he would have to set off very early the

35

following morning and would thus be unable to come and say goodbye again. Gao Zan for his part most politely expressed the hope that his guests had not been offended by their make-shift and quite inadequate reception. Young Gao Biao also bowed a courteous adieu. Madam Jin had ready a present of various titbits for the journey, tasty dishes with wine, rice, fish and meat, and as a further gift there was a packet of 'money for the boat'.

Gao Zan drew You Chen aside. 'Young Squire Yan's looks and education leave no room for further debate,' he told him. 'If you would be so good as to mediate for us and bring the match to fruition, I shall be endlessly grateful to you.'

'I will do as you ask,' said You Chen.

Gao Zan saw them right on board before parting from them, then he and his wife spent the whole of that night discussing young Squire Yan. Yes indeed:

> No need for Pei Hang's pestle of jade,
> no engagement gifts of rich gold need be made,
> Their feet are linked by a silk cord of red
> and the Moon Man has fated them to be wed.

To continue with the story, the following day Qian Qing and You Chen set sail, but wind and currents failed to run right for them and it was late at night before they reached home. Yan Jun was still sitting up by a nightlight, waiting intently to hear the good news. The two men knocked on his door, entered, and related all that had happened the previous day. Convinced the marriage was already in the bag, Yan Jun felt beside himself with joy. He hastily selected a propitious day that same month for the betrothal formalities, duly handed back the loan-deed for twenty taels of silver as a grateful present to You Chen, and chose the third day of the twelfth month as his wedding day. Gao Zan, very contented with his prospective son-in-law and having, moreover, already had the wedding trousseau put by for some while, for his part made no objections whatsoever.

The days passed and the months went by until suddenly it was nearing the end of the eleventh month and the happy day was approaching. Now when the people south of the Yangtse

36

get married, they do not follow the ancient ceremony whereby the groom personally goes to the bride's home to collect her. Instead the bride's female relatives and brothers escort her to the bridegroom's home. The female relatives are known as 'bridesmaids' and the brothers as 'best men'. But having managed to pick himself such a magnificent son-in-law, Gao Zan was boasting of him all over the place and had determined that on this occasion the son-in-law should come and collect the bride in person. He made preparations for a grand banquet and invited all his friends, relatives and neighbours from far and near to come and drink a nuptial cup. He sent someone first to inform You Chen of these arrangements. You Chen gave a jerk of horror and rushed round to tell Yan Jun.

'Well, this time I'll have to go myself,' said Yan Jun.

'When we called on him,' said You Chen, stamping his foot in frustration and exasperation, 'the whole household had a thoroughly good eyeful of the prospective son-in-law. They could paint his portrait from memory. And now at this stage he's suddenly changed his face and build! How is the go-between going to explain that one away? The wedding will be a disaster before it's even started and I shall be marked down for humiliating treatment.'

Hearing this Yan Jun switched his resentment to the go-between. 'That's what I said in the first place,' he grumbled. 'It was in my destiny to marry her and it would have come about of its own accord anyway. If I had gone to her house myself the first time, this impossible dilemma would never have cropped up! It's all your fault for muddling me. You deliberately told me old Gao was an awkward customer, refused to let me go and sent my cousin Qian instead. Yet it turns out that old Gao is a thoroughly well-meaning old fellow, and agrees to the proposal as soon as it's made without kicking up the slightest fuss or bother. I tell you, I was fated to marry that girl. Providence has fixed it that I should be Gao's son-in-law. You don't imagine that the only reason he agreed was because he saw my cousin Qian! Anyway, he has already accepted my engagement gifts, so his daughter is mine. You can't tell me he'd dare say no at this stage. If I do go in person this time, what do you think he'll be able to do to me? You're not going to say he'll try and back out of the marriage contract!'

'I can tell you it won't come off!' said You Chen, shaking his head. 'The man will be in his own house and home, when all's said and done! Where will all your fierce talk get you there? If they refuse to put the girl into her sedan-chair, there'll be nothing you can do about it.'

'I'll take a few extra men along with me,' said Yan Jun. 'If he's amenable, all well and good. If he turns out awkward, we'll fight our way in and bring her back here by force. Even if he takes it to court, I've got the nuptial certificates here as proof. He'll be in the wrong for breaking the agreement. I won't have done anything illegal.'

'Good squire,' said You Chen, 'don't talk big! There is a common saying, "An angry dragon doesn't tackle a serpent on its home ground." However many followers you may take with you, how could you match him there on his own territory, with his manpower likely to increase as each minute goes by? And if, by some chance in a million, you pulled it off, and it got into court and the old man said the bridegroom was a different man from the suitor, the judge would be bound to call me in for interrogation, as go-between. And under torture, I'd have no option but to tell the whole truth and nothing but the truth. And it would be no laughing matter for Master Qian's career prospects either!'

'If that's the case,' said Yan Jun after a pause for thought, 'I won't go, after all. I'll trouble you to go and give him an answer tomorrow. Tell him that since we've already met on a previous occasion, and since in our county we don't follow the custom of collecting the bride ourselves, it would be better if he stuck to our traditions and brought the bride to us.'

'Even more hopeless,' said You Chen. 'Having taken a great fancy to his super son-in-law to-be, old Gao has been praising up his looks and culture to all and sundry, and all his relatives, friends and neighbours are banking on the collection of the bride as an opportunity to get to know him in the flesh. There's nothing for it. We have to go there.'

'What on earth can we do then?' asked Yan Jun.

'In my opinion, for what it's worth,' said You Chen, 'our only workable policy is to beg your cousin Master Qian to go once more and cheat them to the bitter end. When we've tricked the bride over the threshold, you can rely on the size and power of your family and rest assured that the Gaos will not try to snatch her back again. Once the wedding is over, let them object as much as they like, there'll be no need for you to be afraid of them.'

'There's sense in your suggestion,' said Yan Jun, 'but all the same it is my wedding after all, and that would be handing over all the glory of it to someone else. And there'll be a lot of awkwardness trying to persuade him to do it, too.'

'At this stage and as things stand,' said You Chen, 'you have no choice. And what is a moment's glory compared with the whole lifetime's pleasure you are going to enjoy!'

With very mixed feelings, Yan Jun left You Chen, went home and made his way to the study-apartment. 'My noble younger brother,' he said to Qian Qing, 'can I possibly trouble you to do something else for me?'

'What further problem can be facing you, I wonder?' asked Qian Qing.

'The third of next month is the date for my wedding,' said Yan Jun, 'and on the second I have to go and collect the bride from her house. If everything is to work out right, I shall have to trouble you, if I may, to make the trip there once more.'

'The last time I went in your stead, it was a trivial affair,' said Qian Qing, 'but collecting the bride is a ceremony of great moment. I couldn't possibly stand in for you this time! Absolutely not. On no account.'

'Of course you're perfectly right,' said Yan Jun, 'but you see because it was you they met that time, they only know you, and if I suddenly turn up instead they are bound to be mighty suspicious! And I'm afraid that if things go wrong, not only will the wedding be a dead duck, but it may well lead to a court case. If it comes to that, then you will be involved, too. It would be spoiling the ship for a ha'p'orth of tar, wouldn't it, and by your refusal you would yourself have caused the ruination of everyone's happiness including your own, wouldn't you? On the other hand, if you went and collected the bride, you'd hear nothing more about the whole affair once the wedding was in the bag. We're in a desperate pickle and we have to resort to desperate methods. You know as well as I do that there's no point in upsetting the boat when it's nearly home and dry. You can't refuse.'

In the face of this earnest and pointed exposition of the state of affairs, Qian Qing had indeed no choice but to consent.

As his next step, Yan Jun summoned all the wedding musicians and others who were involved in the expedition to collect the bride, warned them on no account to divulge the secret, and assured them that on their successful return there would be generous rewards for them all. Of course, none of them would have ventured to go against his orders.

On the second of the following month, You Chen went across to the Yans' house first thing in the morning to lend a hand with arranging all the 'bride-collecting' presents and the various customary gratuities and tips and packing them all up with appropriate care. All the clothes, the Confucian scholar's hat, the round collar, the silken sash and the black felt boots for Qian Qing's use were brought out, and catering arrangements were made for the various boats. There were two big boats, one for the bride and one for the go-between and the bridegroom, four medium boats bearing the main body of attendants and four small boats, two as protection escorts and the other two for various other tasks. Thus ten or so boats set sail across the Lake together, amid the sound of gongs and much clapping. It was a most exciting voyage, with fireworks and firecrackers going off ceaselessly all the way. Yes, truly there was:

> Much great rejoicing far and wide
> as a splendid groom comes to claim his bride.

It was past noon by the time the boats reached the Western Mountain, where they moored about half a mile away from the Gao residence. You Chen went on ahead to announce their arrival to the Gaos. Meanwhile the 'bride-collecting' presents, the flower-bedecked, gaily coloured sedan for the bride to ride in, and several hundred lanterns and torches, were all made ready. Qian Qing, clad in splendid attire, had his own plush sedan lined with green silk, and four bearers on the ends and four at the sides. Borne in this and heralded by the sound of pipes and other music, he headed straight for the Gaos' mansion. The local populace from far and near, informed of the brilliance and sublime appearance of the Gaos' prospective son-in-law, gathered to try and get a look at him, jostling shoulder to shoulder along the route, as noisy and festive as if they were viewing some rumbustious Buddhist marvel play. Qian Qing, upright and dignified in his sedan, dazzling as a jewel in a crown, inspired universal shouts of admiration. A woman who had once met Autumn Fragrance passed a glowing judgement upon him: 'That will be a real marriage of beauty and genius. The Gaos have run their eyes over no end of suitors and now at last they've picked a real winner.'

In Gao Zan's house preparations for an enormous feast were well under way. The place was crammed with relatives and friends and even before dusk fell all the main hall was bathed in the crimson light of the decorative coloured candles. Then, to the deafening sound of music, the people at the gate announced that the bridegroom had reached the gate. The Master of Ceremonies, clad in the prescribed red attire and flowers, hurried out to perform his ceremonial bow before the sedan, recited the customary verses, and invited the groom to alight from his vehicle. With plentiful expressions of delicate and reverent courtesy all made way for the visitor and he was ushered into the middle hall, where he ceremonially handed to his father-in-law the ritual gift of the 'goose', symbol of marital fidelity. These ceremonies over, he was introduced to all the relatives and friends, all of whom were overwhelmed with admiration for his superb looks. Tea was served and everyone partook of sweetmeat snacks, then the places were laid for the banquet. This time, in contrast to the previous occasion, the bridegroom sat in the specially reserved privileged position facing southwards, while the relatives and friends sat round him, all drinking wine, the music of loud pipes and drums in the background. Provisions for the entertainment of the groom's entourage were being made in the side rooms.

Meanwhile Qian Qing sat there, hearing everyone constantly praising his brilliance and good looks and congratulating old Gao on his excellent choice of son-in-law. 'They look as if they've seen some spirit!' he chuckled inwardly, 'and I feel as if I were in a dream. When the dream is over and I wake up, it will all seem just a meaningless lot of nonsense. And I wonder what will become of all these ghost-struck people?' Then another thought occurred to him. 'Here am I now, standing in for someone else, accepting a façade of glory that doesn't really belong to me. I wonder when, if ever, I shall enjoy such things in my own right? I don't suppose I'll ever attain such heights of splendour.' This train of thought left him beginning to feel rather dispirited and he felt too listless even to drink his wine.

Gao Zan and his son took it in turns to serve him with wine, waiting upon him with eager attentiveness. Not wishing to delay the consummation of his cousin's wedding, Qian Qing made attempts to get away as soon as possible. But Gao Zan was most insistent that he stay longer, so he sat there a while more and soup and rice dishes were served. At about three o'clock, when his retinue had more or less finished their wine-party, Xiaoyi came up to Qian Qing and urged him to depart. Qian Qing instructed him to distribute the gratuities and rose to say goodbye. By about five o'clock in the morning, Gao Zan had all the trousseau and dowry sorted out and placed on board the boats and all that remained was for the bride to mount her sedan. At this juncture men from the boat came running up.

'There's a gale blowing out there,' they announced. 'How can we set sail now? Better to hang on till the wind has slackened.'

In fact a great storm had arisen at midnight. And what a ferocious storm! What a sight:

> Trees uprooted mid winnowing dust-clouds there
>   in the hills,
> Billows surging and waves rearing there out on
>   the Lake.

The great noise of music and entertainment in the hall had left the company unaware of the storm till then. As Gao Zan called the musicians to a halt, the all-pervading howl of the wind fell upon their ears, a weird, eery note. Everyone was dumb-founded, and You Chen began hopping from foot to foot in terrible impatience. Most disconcerted, Gao Zan could only invite the company back to their places at the banquet, at the same time assigning some of his men to keep a watch on the weather outside.

As dawn approached, the storm grew even more frenzied, packing the sky with dense pinkish clouds and filling the air with wildly whirling, dancing snowflakes. All the company stood up and went to observe the weather, discussing it among themselves.

'Doesn't look as if this storm is going to let up,' said one.

'Storms that start in the middle of the night don't die down till the middle of the following night,' said another.

'In a snowstorm like this they couldn't travel even if the wind did drop,' declared another.

'Hm, I reckon the snow is going to get even heavier,' predicted another.

'With such a gale,' predicted yet another, 'when the wind does stop, the lake will freeze up.'

'Oh, you don't need to worry about the Great Lake ever freezing up,' came the quick rejoinder. 'It's the snowstorm that worries me.'

All this prattle in no way improved the situation. Gao Zan and You Chen both sank to the depths of gloom. They hung on a bit, then breakfast was taken. Afterwards the wind was blowing even more wildly and the snow was falling yet more heavily. It seemed there would be no chance of crossing the Lake that day. And once having missed the specially chosen propitious date for the wedding, there might not be another suitable day that month. Moreover, the groom had arrived with such joyful pomp, heralded by music and in a perfect atmosphere, that it seemed impossible to send him away empty-handed! Gripped as they were in a seemingly insoluble crisis, one of the company, an old man called Zhou Quan, intervened. He was an old neighbour of Gao Zan's and a dab-hand at settling local problems. He noticed that Gao Zan was brooding and at a loss what to do.

'In my opinion,' he said, 'we are not faced with any real dilemma at all.'

'What scheme do you have in mind?' asked Gao Zan.

'Since today is the appointed date for the wedding,' said Zhou Quan, 'there is no question of our not keeping to it. You have your son-in-law-to-be here in your house, so why not have

43

the wedding here on the spot? Throw a feast and follow it up
with the wedding night. And when the storm has died down,
they can return home at their leisure. Perfect, eh?'

'That's the best thing to do,' everybody agreed in unison.

Gao Zan had in fact been thinking along precisely the same
lines, but he was delighted that Zhou Quan had spoken up to
put his own ideas into words. There and then he instructed
his servants to make ready the wedding chamber.

Qian Qing, although present in body, had not really felt
involved in the proceedings, and the state of the wind had at
first seemed of no great moment to him. When Zhou Quan put
forward his suggestion, however, he experienced an inward
start of sudden alarm, but still thought there was every chance
of Gao Zan's not following it up. Gao Zan, however, joyfully
concurred. In great consternation Qian Qing cried out within
himself against the injustice of it all. He was going to ask You
Chen to speak up on his behalf, but, what do you know—You
Chen, always fond of drinking, had been further spurred by the
coldness of the weather and his own mood of displeasure to
quaff down great gobletfuls, on and on until, blind drunk, he
had retired for a doze in an empty chair to one side of the
gathering. So Qian Qing had to speak up for himself.

'We must not be hasty and makeshift about such a momen-
tous affair that occurs but once in a lifetime,' he said. 'We can
quite easily choose another day, and I can come and collect
the bride again.'

Gao Zan would not hear of it. 'We are now one united
family,' he said. 'What odds does it make if it takes place here
or there! Your good father, moreover, is no longer in the land
of the living, so you can take the decision with your own two
hands.'

With that, Gao Zan marched off to the back of the house.
Qian Qing made repeated attempts to convince the relatives
and friends that the wedding should not take place there, but
everyone took sides with old Mr Gao and none would agree
with Qing's point of view.

Feeling by now helpless to extricate himself, Qian Qing left
the room on the pretext of going to the toilet. Once outside he
called Xiaoyi for a consultation. Xiaoyi also felt that he should
not go through with it and advised him to refuse, but other-

44

wise could produce no trump card from his sleeve.

'I've already refused again and again,' said Qian Qing, 'but old Gao will take no notice. If I refuse too adamantly, he'll start to get suspicious. My sole motive in all this has been to bring about your master's marriage. I would never for a moment think of deceiving him. If anything compromising happens, I shall not know where to hide myself for shame.'

As the two of them conferred, the others gradually gathered round them in a crowd. 'What a splendid moment this is,' they said, 'and your father-in-law to be has already made up his mind. There is no need for you to hesitate or entertain any doubts, good sir.'

Qian Qing, glumly pensive, uttered not a word in reply. When the midday meal was concluded, arrangements were made for another banquet. Then the Master of Ceremonies cloaked in red declaimed the ceremonials and the young couple clad in their robes ascended the hall, performed the required customary rites and 'mid red wedding candles' were married. Ah, yes:

> Wed this night till life shall last
> a blissful conjugal scene!
> How sad in this bliss there is something amiss
> for one is willing and one not so keen.

Late that night, when everyone else had drifted off, Gao Zan and his wife personally ushered the bridegroom into the wedding chamber. The bridesmaid removed the elaborate jewellery from the bride's hair and tried again and again to persuade the bridegroom to make himself at home, but he would not comply. Mystified by his conduct, all she could do was help the bride into bed without him, after which she herself left the room. The girl-servants left behind closed the door and again urged the young man to get into bed. His heart beating as wildly as the flailing hooves of a fawn in flight, he was obliged to fob them off with what sounded like a promise that he would. 'You go off to sleep first,' he told them. The maids had had a wild night of it and sprawled and tumbled off to snatch some sleep.

45

It was Qian Qing's original intention to sit up by candlelight till the morning, but in the confusion of it all he had neglected his chance to ask for more than the few candles left at his disposal. When these were used up, he did not think, in the circumstances, that he could very well shout for more, so suppressing his feelings of utter misery he forced himself to lie down, on the outer edge of his side of the bed, fully clothed, completely ignoring which end the girl had her head and which her feet. Next morning, at the first light of dawn, he rose and left the room and went into his brother-in-law's study-apartment to wash himself and comb his hair. Gao Zan and his wife simply assumed that he was young and bashful, so took no offence at his behaviour.

That day, although the snow stopped, the wind still did not die down. Gao Zan held a celebration party. Qian Qing drank himself thoroughly fuddled and sat around till the late hours of the night before entering the nuptial chamber. Once more the young lady had gone to sleep before him. Lacking the stamina to keep himself awake for long, he went to sleep fully clothed as before, not so much as venturing to come in contact with her bed-quilt.

One more night over, he rose early, and seeing that the storm had somewhat abated was eager to depart, but Gao Zan insisted that he stay one more day before he would let him go. Qian Qing, try as he would, could not override him, and had to resign himself to another day of drinking. In secret he conferred with You Chen and mentioned how he had spent the nights fully clothed. You Chen dutifully expressed belief, but secretly was far from convinced. Since things had reached such a pass, there was nothing he could do about it anyway.

Now the young lady, Autumn Fragrance, had been stealing furtive looks at her bridegroom since their marriage, saw that his looks corresponded with the general claim, and was secretly overjoyed. What she could not fathom was why for two nights in succession he had failed even to undo his belt. Could he be annoyed because she went to sleep first without waiting for him? On this the third night she instructed her maids that when the master came into the room the first thing they were to do was to help him to bed. Acting upon these orders, as soon as the newly wed husband came into the room

46

the maids undid his robe and removed his hat. Sensing that something was going awry, as soon as they took off his head-gear, Qian Qing rapidly bounded onto the bed, and sticking as close to the inner edge of the bed as possible went off to sleep still by himself and still not undressed. Decidedly put out by this, Autumn Fragrance herself went to sleep fully clothed. Yet she felt it would be too embarrassing to tell her parents.

On the fourth day the weather had cleared up and was quite mild. Gao Zan had already seen to the provisions for the boats to escort the bride to her new home, and he and his wife now set off to accompany her across the Lake. The bride and her maids travelled in one boat, while Gao Zan, Qian Qing and You Chen travelled in another. The ships were bedecked with multicoloured streamers, the sound of music rocked the heavens, and it was a lively, merry voyage. Xiaoyi, however, having been entrusted with his special task by his master, felt wretched and very much on edge, and so took a tiny, fast boat and sped back ahead of all the others.

To shift the scene back now to Yan Jun . . . Ever since he had sent them all off on their 'bride-collecting' voyage, he had been waiting in anxious suspense. At midnight on the night of the second, when he heard the great gale and snow-storm blow up, he took it quite calmly. He simply assumed that the boats would be delayed in the snowstorm and might be late. It never occurred to him that they would be unable to cross the Lake at all. With everything ready for his wedding banquet, all laid out down to the last detail of perfection, he waited a whole night. There was no sign of anything happening, and he became deeply depressed.

'In such a storm, better if they don't board the boats,' was his first thought. 'What a worry if they were travelling across the Lake in that.' Then another thought struck him. 'If they haven't embarked, once my father-in-law realises we have overshot the appointed date, you can bet your life he won't bring her across just any old day. Oh no! He'll have to go through the business of selecting another properly auspicious day. And when that will be is anybody's guess. Ugh, it makes you sick to death!—But if You Chen manages to use some gumption and initiative and get round old Gao to bring her over regardless, I personally won't give a damn whether it's a propitious date or not. The sooner I can enjoy my pleasures the better.'

With these thoughts rioting through his head, Yan Jun could not remain seated, but was for ever restlessly walking out to the gate to see if anything was coming. When on the fourth day the wind dropped, he felt certain there would be some news. And sure enough, soon after midday Xiaoyi came into view, returning ahead of the others with his report.

'The bride is being brought here. She's only ten miles away,' he announced.

'We went past the chosen date,' said Yan Jun. 'Surely they would not agree to let the bride embark?'

'Yes,' said Xiaoyi, 'the Gaos were desperately anxious not to miss the fixed date, and insisted on the wedding taking place. Squire Qian stood in for you for three days, as bridegroom, sir.'

'If they've been married for three days,' said Yan Jun, 'has Squire Qian been sleeping in the bride's room then?'

'They slept on the same bed, but neither of them so much as touched the other,' Xiaoyi assured him. 'Squire Qian resisted temptation and did no more than keep her company in bed.'

'Stuff and nonsense!' snarled Yan Jun. 'Don't try and give me that. What did I ask you to do for me? Why didn't you make him refuse? Why did you let him do such a vile, immoral thing?'

'I did have a word with him,' said Xiaoyi, 'but Squire Qian said, "My only wish is to accomplish your master's marriage. May the gods of Heaven bear witness that I have not the slightest intention of ever playing him false!"'

At these words Yan Jun's:

> Wrath boiled up from his heart
> and vicious spite sprang in his gall.

With one clout he knocked Xiaoyi aside, then in blind fury stormed out through the gate to wait for Qian Qing, entirely bent on having a mighty row with him.

At that moment the boats drew into the bank. Qian Qing had been very circumspect, and had asked You Chen to stay with old Gao and keep him company while he himself jumped ashore ahead of them all. Since he felt no cause to be ashamed of himself, secure in the confidence that he had behaved with moral impeccability, he strode with leisured pace and lofty dignity towards the gate of the Yans' residence, and seeing Yan Jun some way off, began to approach him all smiles and affability, to bow a greeting and unburden to him all that was on his mind. Yan Jun, however, presuming to judge this noble man's emotions and conduct on the basis of his own mean-minded, narrow-souled self, now viewed him as his bitter enemy. He glared at him with enormous, bulging eyes, and allowing him no time to open the conversation waded straight into him.

'Heaven smite you dead!' he ranted viciously between clenched teeth. 'You must be mighty cock-a-hoop with your-self now!' He lunged out with clawing fingers, clutched Qian Qing's hat and hair in one fistful and rained wild kicks and a flurry of punches on him. 'Heaven strike you dead, you swindling rat!' he hissed. 'Someone else forks out his money and you get all the fun!'

Qian Qing made attempts to defend himself verbally, but Yan Jun was busy hailing blows and curses upon him and would not listen to a single syllable he uttered. Nor did the servants dare approach and try to persuade Yan Jun to calm down. Panicking at the beating to which he was being sub-jected, Qian Qing kept on shouting, 'Help, murder!'

As the noise of the rumpus reached their ears, the people on board the boats came ashore to see what was happening. When they arrived on the scene, they saw an ugly-looking fellow thrashing the bridegroom! Completely mystified as to what it was all about, they rushed up to try and persuade him to stop, but all their efforts failed to halt his attacks.

Gao Zan questioned Yan Jun's retainers, and, realising they could no longer keep up the pretence, they felt compelled to disclose the truth. That really set the cat among the pigeons! As soon as he heard their explanations, he blazed up, swearing furiously and cursing You Chen for a vile rogue, a lying, swindling go-between, and a seducer of people's daughters!

He followed this up by snatching hold of You Chen and beginning to thump him, one blow after another. His indignation was shared by those of his household who had come with him to escort the bride, and united in one accord they plunged into action, determined to trounce the ugly fellow. Rallying to the defence of their master, Yan Jun's retainers also flung themselves into the battle. First it was Yan Jun fighting Qian Qing, next Gao Zan walloping You Chen, and in the end all the members of both households were milling together, locked in combat. A crowd of spectators gathered, and the crowd swelled until the whole street was blocked and no one could pass along it. As when

They marshalled themselves in battle array
and warred by Nine Mile Mountain,
They fought each other do-or-die
before the walls of Kunyang City.

Strange coincidences do occur. It chanced that the governor of that county was at that very moment riding back after seeing off a superior. On reaching the northern gate of the town he heard the thunderous uproar of rowdy brawling and saw people tangled in combat in the street. Halting his sedan, he shouted to his men to arrest the offenders. Once they realised that the governor was out to make arrests, the crowd all melted away, leaving only Yan Jun still clutching hold of Qian Qing, and Gao Zan still gripping You Chen. Utter confusion ensued as they all simultaneously tried to expound their grievances, and the governor could not make head or tail of the situation. He ordered them all to accompany him to his court so that he could interrogate them one by one, and forbade them to continue their altercations.

In view of Gao Zan's seniority in age, he was the first to be called to the upper end of the court-hall for questioning. 'I am a commoner from Western Dongting Mountain,' he explained, 'and my name is Gao Zan. In choosing a husband for my daughter I made a special point of inspecting suitors as to their looks and education, before eventually agreeing to marry her to one of them. On the second of this month the man I had chosen to be my son-in-law came to my house for the collection of the bride. A snowstorm prevented them from returning and I kept the young man back at my house for the completion of the wedding ceremonies there. Now today when I arrive here on my way to escort my daughter to her husband's home, I am astonished to come across this fellow giving my son-in-law a cruel thrashing. I inquire what it's all about, and learn that the ugly fellow there has bribed the go-between to obtain my daughter by fraud, and sent that young man Qian to my house under the ugly fellow's name. All you have to do is ask the go-between, my lord, and you will find out all their treachery.'

'Who is the go-between?' asked the governor. 'Is he here?'

'You Chen,' replied Gao Zan. 'There he is, down at the foot of the steps.'

Barking the order for Gao Zan to withdraw, the governor summoned You Chen forward. 'By your distortion of the truth and your foul deceits you have been the author of all this trickery,' he fulminated. 'Confess the whole truth and nothing but the truth if you wish to avoid very severe punishment.'

At first You Chen prevaricated, trying to fob off the governor with devious denials. Infuriated, the governor called for the ankle-press to be fetched forth in readiness. Although from the rough tradesmen's quarters, You Chen had never experienced judicial torture and felt obliged to confess the truth. Now he related everything in minute detail, how first of all Yan Jun had asked him to go and negotiate the marriage, how Gao Zan had proved awkward in wanting to select a son-in-law of the right looks and ability, how subsequently scholar Qian had been imposed upon to go and visit him under Yan Jun's name, and finally how the wedding had proceeded from beginning to end.

'Now we have the truth,' said the governor with a nod of his head. 'This fellow Yan Jun, for all his efforts, was pipped at the post by someone else. One can scarcely wonder that he got into such a state! But he erred in his original intention to deceive.'

He next summoned Yan Jun in order to consider his statement. Having heard that You Chen had already confessed the truth and perceiving that His Worship's tone of voice was fairly affable, Yan Jun felt he had no choice but to give a faithful account of what had happened, and the two men's statements tallied completely.

Finally the governor summoned Qian Qing. The sight of Qian Qing's youthful good looks, and also of the injuries which he had suffered in the fighting, evoked a certain sympathy in the governor for the young man. 'Here you are,' he said, 'a graduate scholar who has studied the scriptures of Confucius and Mencius and is fully acquainted with the ethical precepts of the Duke of Zhou. How could you bring yourself to impersonate someone else and go in his stead to be interviewed and to collect his bride? How could you collaborate in such fraud and behave in such a perverse manner?'

'From the beginning I had no wish to do it,' replied Qian Qing. 'I only did so because Yan Jun was my cousin and my senior and because I myself, being destitute, was pursuing my studies in his home, where I was provided with my board and lodging. My cousin implored me incessantly until I could no longer refuse and had to agree in spite of myself. My only idea was to step in and help things along for a while so that he could achieve the marriage he desired so much.'

'Come now!' said the governor. 'If you went there out of cousinly affection, then you should surely never have married the girl.'

'Originally,' replied Qian Qing, 'I was only going to collect the bride for him, but there was a great storm for three days running and it proved impossible to take the boats across the Great Lake. In view of this fact, Gao Zan, who was most anxious lest the appointed date go past without any wedding, required me to get married there on the spot.'

'But,' said the governor, 'aware, as you were, that you were merely standing in for someone else, you should have refused.'

'That's it, my lord, you're quite right!' kowtowed Yan Jun from the side. 'From the very fact that he went through with the wedding, you can tell he was carrying out a premeditated swindle.'

'That's quite enough from you,' bellowed the governor. 'Constables, drag the fellow off out of our way!'

Then he turned once more to Qian Qing. 'Are you trying to tell me,' he said, 'that in going through with the wedding, you had no selfish designs?'

'You have only to question Gao Zan,' said Qian Qing. 'I refused again and again, but he wouldn't give in. I was afraid after that to refuse any more, in case I aroused his suspicions and ruined my cousin's chances of concluding the marriage. That was the reason why, as a temporary measure to meet a crisis, I went through the nuptial ceremonies. But although I shared the same bed with the bride for three nights, I went to sleep fully clothed and never violated her in any way.'

The governor burst into loud guffaws. 'Since time began,' he laughed, 'the only man who has ever been able to resist a woman's charms when she was placed in his lap was Liu Xiahui. Even the Man of Lu, for all his virtue, felt he had to bar his door to a female neighbour seeking refuge from a snow-storm which had destroyed her house. Oh, no, no, you're a young blood, still not of an age to have achieved emotional equilibrium and steady control over giddy passion. Are you trying to tell me that you shared her bed for three nights without doing anything to her? Whose leg do you think you can pull?'

'You may not believe my statement of what happened, Your Excellency,' said Qian Qing, 'but if you were to tell Gao Zan to go and ask his daughter himself, you would see whether or not I have spoken the truth.'

'Hm,' thought the governor, 'If they *did* make love, the girl will surely not be willing to admit to it now?' Then suddenly an idea occurred to him and he ordered his constables to procure a certain trustworthy midwife. She was told to go to the boat and test whether Miss Gao was still a virgin and to report back as soon as possible. In no time the midwife was reporting back to the governor that Miss Gao was indeed still a virgin, pure and undeflowered.

From the foot of the courtroom steps, hearing the news that she was still undefiled, Yan Jun yelled out, 'If my wife is still undamaged, I'll be only too glad to fulfil the marriage!'

'Keep your mouth shut!' the governor warned him again.

Then he called Gao Zan. 'Which one in your heart would you have preferred your daughter to marry?' he asked.

'Well, I took to Qian Qing from the start,' said Gao Zan. 'And then my daughter did go through the wedding with him. Even though he took no advantage of sharing a dark room with

53

her and even though there has been no conjugal love between them, they have been through the marriage ceremonies. If it were a question of having her marry Yan Jun instead, well, not only I myself but my daughter too would be most reluctant to agree to it.'

'Precisely the train of my own thoughts on the matter,' said the governor.

Qian Qing inwardly rebelled against the trend of the conversation. 'My activities,' he said, 'were for the benefit of another, not for selfish motives. If the girl is assigned to me, it will completely nullify the whole value and purpose of my having slept with her for three nights without even unfastening my belt. I would prefer her to marry someone else. I could not think of risking the suspicions of others and of incurring unfavourable gossip.'

'If this girl is married off to someone else,' said the governor, 'you will be deemed to have blotted your copybook in twice crossing the Lake and practising deceit, albeit on another's behalf. Such a situation would constitute a great stumbling block to your career prospects. If I today settle the marriage in your favour, it will be possible for your errors to be overlooked. Moreover, it is patently obvious to me that you are well inclined towards the girl, and since there is every willingness on her and her family's side, there will be no question of others being able to hold anything against you. Do not be over-adamant in your refusal. I shall now deliver my verdict, which will set matters aright.'

Raising his writing brush, the governor proceeded to pass his formal judgement:

It was quite in the normal course of events for Gao Zan to interview would-be sons-in-law, but Yan Jun's use of a more presentable stand-in for himself was certainly a rare and remarkable device. The father of the girl, once having selected a splendid husband for her, could scarcely have been expected to know that 'the ox would be changed for a sheep', to use a Mencian term. On the other hand, even if the other party finds the methods of selection objectionable, that does not entitle him to 'foist off a deer as a horse', to recall the Qin dynasty anecdote. The young gentleman, Qian Qing, in twice crossing the Lake on his embarrassing

54

mission performed a service no less arduous than that of Liu Yi, who, we are told, once delivered a letter to the Dragon King's palace deep under the waves. Furthermore, in maintaining his distance from the young lady for three nights, while yet sharing her bed, he would not disgrace comparison with Lord Guan Yu, that general and divinity who once, you will remember, when allowed but one room for himself and the two wives of his sworn elder brother, whom calamity had placed in his charge, stood outside with a candle all night long, rather than risk any suspicion of impropriety. In our present case, the God of Wind took the role of go-between and the Lord of Heaven drew the young couple together in marriage, a splendid couple most fitted for one another. That Yan Jun ended up by being deprived of the wife he had sought was but a proper, self-instigated reward for his own iniquities. I hereby declare that Miss Gao shall be assigned to Qian Qing, dispensing with the need for any further wedding ceremony. Yan Jun did wrong to fabricate the fraudulent plot in the first instance and later transgressed by being the prime mover in the outbreak of a brawl. Since his wedding schemes have now come to nought, we shall provisionally spare him further punishment, but the money expended upon the nuptials shall, it seems only fair, be considered as apportioned to Qian Qing in compensation for the physical assault upon his person. You Chen by his falsehood-brewing missions to and fro was the real instigator of the feuding and shall be severely punished as a warning to others who might think to follow in his path.

His judgement delivered, the governor shouted to his constables to administer thirty heavy blows of the rod to You Chen, after which punishment, however, he excused him from the obligation to sign a confession and finally had him driven from his presence, the reason for this latter dispensation being that he desired to allow the minimum possible enduring publicity to Qian Qing's impersonation. Gao Zan and Qian Qing bowed their thanks to him, and all those involved in the case departed through the gate of the county court. Yan Jun, his face the very picture of profound humiliation, and not daring to utter a word for all his fury, skulked off with his

head buried in his hands. It was a good few months before h
dared show himself in public. You Chen returned home t
nurse his wounds. But enough of them.

Meanwhile Gao Zan invited Qian Qing aboard his boat and
although one might perhaps have expected other reaction
expressed most fervent gratitude to him. 'But for your nobl
character and conduct, which inspired the governor's admira
tion, dear son-in-law,' he said, 'my daughter might easil
have been married to that villainous bandit. A most unsuitabl
match! Now, would you do me the honour of accompanyin
my daughter to my house and staying with us a little while
Might I ask, dear, noble son-in-law, if you have any peopl
at home?'

Qian Qing answered that both his parents were dead and h
had no other relatives at home.

'In that case,' said Gao Zan, 'there is all the more reason
for you to come and live with us. I shall make all provision
for your studies. How would you feel about that, dear son-in-
law?'

'I should feel it an enormous favour to receive your kind
support, dear father-in-law,' replied Qian Qing.

That night they sailed away from Wujiang, sleeping through
the voyage. When they reached Western Mountain the
following morning, all the local people, once appraised of
what had taken place, spread it far and wide as an item of
spicy news. Acquainted with Qian Qing's moral integrity and
sincerity of heart, they all without exception accorded him
their profound respect. Later, at his very first attempt, he
passed the imperial examinations with flying colours and
secured himself fame and fortune, and he and his wife grew
old together in joyful concord. Here is a poem to sum it all up:

> Shall ugliness by swindle
> deserve a beautiful wife,
> And his cousin devoted to his cause
> come off worst in life?
> The tender moon above Wujiang
> has pity for their sake,
> And serenely lights the lovebirds
> as they wing across the Lake.

Li Bai*, God in Exile, Drunken Drafts his 'Letter to Daunt the Barbarians'

Most worthy object of our admiration,
Li Bai, God in Exile, poet supreme,
Who long ago, on a gallon of wine,
would flood forth poems in torrent stream.
The brocade splendours of his soul
put the paragons of his age to shame,
The prodigal power that poured from his pen
surpassed the ancient bards of fame.
With a rough-drafted letter he cowed
frontier lands and barbarian hordes,
With his songs of nation-o'er-bowling charms
he seduced music fashion's latest chords.
A prodigy of dashing panache,
of gay genius the ultimate height!
And above Li Bai's tomb at Coloured Rock
the moon shines ever bright.

In the reign of the Tang emperor Xuanzong (712–56) there lived a literary genius called Li Bai, whose courtesy name was Taibai, meaning 'the planet Venus', and who was a ninth generation descendant of the Emperor Li Hao, Promoter of Sagedom and Military Splendour, of the Western Liang dynasty. Li Bai came from Jinzhou in Szechwan. He was born after his mother had dreamt that the Long Grain Star

*Better known in the West as Li Po.

had entered her body and made her pregnant. The Long Grain Star is also known as the Great White Star (Taibaixing) and is the planet Venus, which is why 'white' (*bai*) was used for his personal name and 'great white' (*taibai*) for his courtesy name. Li Bai was superbly good-looking, with a fine clear-cut physique and the sublime appearance of one who has but drifted airily and ephemerally into this mortal world. By the time he was nine he had thoroughly mastered the ancient classics, could produce extempore masterpieces of his own, and was universally praised for his brilliant intellect and dazzling powers of speech. People further referred to him as an immortal of heaven who had been incarnated in mortal flesh, and that was how he came to be known as Li the God in Exile. A poem by Du of the Ministry of Works, the poet Du Fu,* dedicated to him, mentions this name:

> God in Exile, that was the nickname
> some eccentric gave you in years gone by,
> You write, the storm of controversy rears,
> You versify, spirits are moved to cry.
> Thus from those days your fame ever swelled,
> its waves surging further each day,
> Your brilliance drew your monarch's rich favours
> and your name shall endure when all others
>   decay.

Li Bai also called himself Green Lotus Hermit. Drinking being his greatest pleasure in life, he never sought a career in the government. His ambition was to roam freely the whole world over, to see all the famous scenic mountains on earth, and to taste every fine wine in the universe. First he ascended Mount Emei, next he dwelt amid the marshes of Cloud Dream, then he led a life of withdrawal at Bamboo Brook by the Zulai Mountains, where in the company of Kong Nest-Gaffer and another four he passed his hours morning and night in heavy imbibing. They were dubbed the Six Recluse Gentlemen of Bamboo Brook. Someone mentioned that the wine of Wucheng

*Better known in the West as Tu Fu, Li Bai's contemporary and China's second most famous poet.

n Huzhou had a marvellous taste. Ignoring the vast distance between him and Wucheng, Li Bai set off for the place and as soon as he reached its wine shops settled down to unrestrained and merry drinking, for all the world as if he were the only soul around. As he was doing so, a certain Marshal Kashyapa-Bodhisattva passed by, and hearing the sound of Bai's wild singing sent one of his retinue to enquire who it was. Bai on the spot improvised a quatrain of reply:

> I am Green Lotus Hermit, the God in Exile,
> in wine shops thirty springtimes, dodging fame
>   and reputation,
> Why need you come inquiring, Marshall of
>   Huzhou,
> —I'm Golden Grain Buddha's reincarnation!

Marshal Kashyapa-Bodhisattva was astonished. 'Can this be Li the God in Exile from Szechwan?' he wondered. 'I have known of his fame and wished to meet him for a long while.' So he invited him to come and see him and detained him for ten days' drinking, lavishing gifts upon him.

'With such genius as yours, Green Lotus,' he remarked as Li was about to depart, 'it would be as easy as picking mustard and cress for you to acquire the green and purple seals of high-ranking government office. Why don't you make a trip to Changan and take the imperial examinations?'

'Nowadays the government at court is complete chaos,' said Li Bai, 'ruled by no impartial principles whatsoever. How high one comes in the examination placings is decided by secret fawning and underhand dealings and whether one passes the examinations at all depends on whether one has slipped the necessary bribes. If you resort to neither device, then no matter whether you have the noble spirit of a Confucius or a Mencius or whether you have the genius of those political theoreticians of the Han dynasty, Chao Cuo and Dong Zhongshu, you have no means of achieving eminence. The reason why I dally in poetry and wine is simply to avoid being insulted by blind examiners!'

'Things may be as you say,' said the Marshal, 'but everyone knows of you, and as soon as you reached Changan someone would be bound to recommend you to some high post, anyway.'

Li Bai followed his advice and duly took a trip to Changan. One day when he was on a sightseeing tour of the Purple Extremity Palace he encountered the Hanlin Academician and poet Hê Zhizhang. Upon learning each other's names, they both expressed their admiration for one another. Then Zhizhang invited Bai into a wine house, removed his own golden sable hat, emblem of his lofty rank, and pawned it for wine. The two drank together till night, when, reluctant to part, Zhizhang had Li Bai come and bed down in his home, the two of them swearing eternal brotherhood. The following day, Li Bai moved his luggage into Hanlin Academician Hê's residence, and they spent the days discussing poetry and drinking wine, host and guest getting on splendidly together. Time slipped by unnoticed, and suddenly the examination period loomed up.

'This spring,' said Academician Hê, 'it's the official in charge of the Southern Secretariat who is serving as Chief Examiner. He is none other than the Grand Preceptor, Yang Guozhong, the elder brother of the Emperor's favourite lady, Lady Yang. The Examination Superintendent is to be the Grand Captain, Eunuch Chamberlain Gao. Both of them are avaricious men, thirsty for bribes, but you, my dear and noble younger brother, lack the gold and silver with which to purchase their kind attentions. So for all your sky-scraping erudition, you would still never get as far as the audience with our Sacred Emperor. I am somewhat acquainted with the two of them, so I shall write a memorandum to them, entrusting you in advance to their goodwill, and possibly, out of some slight regard for myself, they may be better disposed towards you.'

Li Bai, being of great erudition, was a proud-spirited man. However, since such an opportunity had presented itself and since, moreover, the Hanlin Academician was showing him such kindness, he felt he could scarcely counter his wishes. Academician Hê wrote his notes and sent them to Grand Preceptor Yang and Chamberlain Gao. As they tore them open and read them, the two men both smiled sardonically. 'So,' they at once concluded, 'Academician Hê has pocketed gold and silver from Li Bai and yet has the impudence to write is a letter empty of all enclosures, trying to seek our goodwill gratis and for nothing! When the day comes we must make a special point of remembering that if papers appear with Li Bai's name upon them we must, with no beating about the bush, immediately fail him.'

On the third day of the third month a vast assembly of scholars participated in the examinations in the Southern Secretariat, master-minds from all over the world coming and submitting papers. With his superabundance of genius, Li Bai completed his papers with one unfaltering sweep of his writing brush and was the first to hand them in. Seeing the name Li Bai on the papers, Yang Guozhong did not even bother to look at what he had written, but daubed slapdash strokes across them to cross them out.

'Such a student,' he remarked, 'is only fit to rub my ink for me.'

Chamberlain Gao added, 'He would be inadequate even for rubbing ink. He is only fitted for putting on my socks and pulling off my boots.'

They bellowed an order for Li Bai to be shoved and hustled off the precincts. Yes, yes indeed:

> No matter if one's writings please the world
> —As long as they make a hit with examiners.

His papers unjustly failed by the examiners, Li Bai exploded with bitter resentment, and on returning to the Academician's residence he swore an oath: 'If some day I fulfil my worldly ambitions, I shall without fail oblige Yang Guozhong to grind my ink for me and Chamberlain Gao to pull off my boots for me. Or else I shall never rest contented.'

'Don't be so upset,' urged Academician Hê. 'For the while just settle down in my humble home, and in three years' time when the examinations come round again the examiners will be other men and you are bound to pass.'

He and Li Bai spent all their days drinking wine and composing poetry together, and the days and months passed by until without their having been conscious of it another year had fled.

Suddenly one day a foreign ambassador arrived in the

capital to deliver a state letter. The court sent a messenger with an urgent order to Academician Hê to receive the ambassador, escort him to official lodgings and see him accommodated there. The following day the Epistolary Secretary formally received the foreign ambassador's letter of state. Emperor Xuanzong commanded his Hanlin Academicians to open the foreign letter, but the Academicians were unable to understand a single word of it. 'Your Imperial Majesty,' they declared, prostrating themselves on the golden throne-steps, 'this letter is written in nothing but the footprints of birds and animals, and we in our ignorance cannot understand a word of it.'

Hearing this confession, the Emperor passed the letter on to the Southern Secretariat Chief Examiner, Yang Guozhong, for him to read it.. When Yang tried to do so, it was as if his eyes were suddenly afflicted with blindness and he too was unable to make head or tail of it. The Emperor commanded all his civil and military courtiers in turn to make an attempt, but not one of them could interpret it, and he still remained in the dark as to whether it bore tidings of imminent disaster or good omen.

'What benefit do I derive from having so many civil and military officials,' he roared in fury at his courtiers, his 'dragon countenance' pervaded with utter rage, 'when I am yet left with not a single gentleman of sufficient erudition to share my burdens with me! If we cannot read the letter, with what possible reply are we to acquit this embassy? We shall instead become the disgraceful laughing stock of the foreign nations, who will seek to abuse and insult our southerly court and without doubt resort to military action and invade our frontiers. What on earth can be done? I hereby decree that if within a limit of three days no one is able to read this letter, your salaries shall all cease. If within six days there is still no one who can read it, you shall all cease to function in your offices. If within nine days there is still no one who can manage to read it, you shall all be punished, and I shall select other, worthy and virtuous men to assist me in maintaining the state altars of earth and grain.'

As this imperial decree was issued, all the officials fell into a gloomy silence, not one of them daring to address the Emperor any more, and this further stoked his wrath. When the court dispersed, Academician Hê went home and related what had happened to Li Bai.

'What a pity that this Mr Li did not pass the examinations and acquire a government post last year,' said Li Bai with a slight wry smile. 'What a pity I am unable to lighten the Emperor's administrative burdens.'

'I imagine you must mean, noble younger brother,' said Academician Hê, astounded, 'that with your vast learning and education you are able to decipher the foreign letter. I must recommend you to the Emperor.'

The following day Academician Hê entered court and quite out of turn memorialised the throne. 'I beg to inform Your Majesty,' he said, 'that I have in my home a scholar by the name of Li Bai, who possesses considerable learning and ability. He is just the one to decipher the foreign letter for us.'

Approving the memorial, the Emperor at once despatched a messenger with a rescript to the Academician's residence, to summon Li Bai.

'I am only a lowly commoner from distant backwaters,' Li Bai replied through the imperial messenger, 'a useless ignoramus. There are so many office-bearers in court nowadays who are scholars replete with learning, so why on earth ask for the services of such a yokel from the outback jungle as myself? I do not dare accept the rescript for fear of offering insult to the eminent gentlemen of the court.' The phrase 'for fear of offering insult to the eminent gentlemen at court' was a veiled dig at Yang and Gao.

When the messenger reported back, the Emperor turned to Hê Zhizhang. 'What is Li Bai's meaning in refusing to accept my rescript?' he asked.

'To my knowledge,' replied Zhizhang, 'Li Bai is unrivalled in the whole world for his literary culture and is astonishingly erudite. But last year at the examinations his papers were marked unfairly by the examiner and he was ignominiously hustled from the precincts. Today he would feel it too mortifying to enter court in his ordinary attire, as someone with no post to his name. I beg Your Majesty to accord him some favours, and this time to send an important minister to deliver the message. I am sure that he will then accept your command.'

'I shall do as you suggest, my lord,' said Xuanzong. 'I hereby bestow upon Li Bai the title of doctor and graduate and order that he is to present himself in audience before me clad in purple robe, golden belt and gauze-silk hat and bearing a writing tablet of ivory. May I now trouble you yourself, my lord, to go in person to welcome him into our presence. You must not refuse me this service, my lord!'

Hê Zhizhang took the edict home with him, asked Li Bai to unfold it and read it, and told him how earnest was the Emperor's desire to enlist the aid of his brilliant abilities. Li Bai donned the robes which the Emperor had presented to him, gazed in the direction of the palace and bowed his thanks, then mounted a horse and rode with Academician Hê to court. The Emperor was specially waiting on his throne in readiness for Li Bai. Reaching the golden steps to the throne, Li Bai made his obeisances, kowtowed thrice to express his gratitude for the imperial favours and stood bowed before the Emperor.

As soon as he set eye on Li Bai, Xuanzong seemed like some pauper alighting upon a jewel, someone in the dark discovering a lamp, a starving person chancing upon food, someone in a drought catching sight of a rain-cloud. Opening his 'golden mouth' and 'setting in motion his jade voice', he spoke: 'We have here now a letter submitted to us by a foreign country, which no one is able to understand. I summoned you to me in order that you might "share my troubles" and assist me.'

Li Bai bowed and addressed the throne. 'I am but meagerly lettered,' he said. 'The Grand Preceptor there failed my examination papers, and Grand Captain Gao had me pushed and dragged out of the examination hall. Since you have this foreign letter, why do you not command the Chief Examiner to answer it, instead of leaving the foreign ambassador to tarry needlessly here for so long! I am a failed scholar, an ejected scholar. Unable to satisfy the Examiners, how could I hope to please Your Imperial Majesty?'

'I have personally indicated my appreciation of you,' said the Emperor. 'Do not refuse me this, my lord!' Then he ordered his attendants to respectfully bear the letter to Li Bai for him to peruse it.

Li read it through once, then gave a faint sardonic smile, and facing the imperial throne translated it into Chinese, the

64

language of the Tang, declaiming in one uninterrupted flow. The foreign letter went as follows:

The Great Kaydu of the Land of Bohai sends this epistle to the Emperor in the court of the Tang:

Since you occupied Korea, you have come pressing close to my country and your border troops have time and time again violated our frontiers, which must I am sure be by your own intention. I have now lost all patience and am sending an official to negotiate with you that you may cede one hundred and sixty walled cities of Korea to my country. I for my part have fine objects to send you as gifts: dodder from the Great White Mountain, laminaria seaweed from the Southern Sea, drums from Railing City, deer from Fuyu, pigs from Moji, horses from Shuaibin, silk from Wozhou, bream from the River Meituo, plums from Nine Cities, and pears from Leyou. Of all these Your Majesty may have a share. If you still refuse, we shall marshal our forces and attack you. Then we shall see who will be victor and who will be vanquished!

Hearing Li Bai thus read right through the foreign letter, all the courtiers could not help but be utterly astounded, and all turned towards him, praising him for his remarkable attainments. The Emperor, now acquainted with the contents of the foreign letter, manifested an expression of displeasure upon his 'dragon countenance'. After brooding for some considerable while, he turned to question the two phalanxes of civil and military officials.

'Now that we are faced with the foreigners' threat to launch a military campaign and seize Korea by force, what policy may we adopt to oppose them?' he asked.

The two phalanxes of civil and military officials were like clay models and wooden carvings, not one of them daring to reply. Then Hê Zhizhang addressed the throne.

'When Emperor Taizong (627–49) undertook his three campaigns against Korea, an incalculable number of men lost their lives, yet he was unable to secure victory and the attempts exhausted his treasuries. When by a turn of Providence Gai Suwen died, his son Nansheng struggled for power with his brothers, doing so under our instigation. Emperor Gaozong (650–83) sent his seasoned generals Li Ji and Xue Rengui to Korea at the head of a hundred thousand bold and stalwart troops, but there were a hundred battles large and small before the enemy was conclusively extirpated. In these present times, after enjoying such long days of peace, we lack the generals and we lack the soldiers, and if military strife is allowed to raise its head once more we can scarcely guarantee ourselves victory. If we become involved in those disasters attendant upon military action, when if ever shall we extricate ourselves from them? May Your Majesty give your most careful consideration to these matters.'

'If such is the situation,' said the Son of Heaven, 'how shall we reply to them?'

'Put that question to Li Bai, Your Majesty,' suggested Zhizhang, 'and I vouch for it that he will respond with excellent answers.'

So the Emperor called for Li Bai and asked his advice.

'I beg to inform Your Majesty,' said Bai, 'that the matter is not one which should burden your holy self with any anxieties. Summon the foreign ambassador to court tomorrow, and in his presence I shall reply to the foreign letter, writing in the same script and wording the letter in such a manner as to shame the foreigners and oblige the Kaydu to submit to you with hands clasped in sign of abject capitulation.'

'Who is the Kaydu?' asked the Son of Heaven.

'It is the custom in Bohai,' Li Bai deferentially explained, 'to call their kings Kaydu, just as the Uighurs call theirs Khan, the Tibetans call theirs Zanpu, the Six Zhao call theirs Zhao, and the Heling people call theirs Ximowei, all in accordance with their own customs.'

The Emperor was overjoyed to perceive that he responded with such endless resources of erudition, and there and then appointed him Hanlin Academician. Then he held a banquet in the Palace Hall of Golden Chariot Bells, with every variety of music, dulcimers and zithers sounding forth in ample tones, and palace ladies and princesses proffering the wine and gorgeous maidens passing the cups round. 'My Lord Li,' the Emperor in person proclaimed, 'you may now drink freely and to your heart's content. Let there be no standing on ceremony!'

Li Bai tippled for all he was worth, until suddenly he became heavy with wine and his limbs buckled under him. The Emperor then ordered eunuchs to assist him to the adjacent apartments of the hall and to put him to bed there.

The following day, at the drums of the fifth watch, the Emperor entered the palace hall to open the levée.

> The Whip of Silence rings forth its
> warning thrice,
> Ministers and generals form two orderly ranks.

Li Bai was still in the grip of his hangover when the eunuchs hurried him into court. After the officials had concluded their regular court formalities, the Son of Heaven called Li Bai to approach him, and noticed that his face still bore the marks of drinking, his eyes having a fuddled, blurry look about them. He ordered his attendants to arrange for the imperial kitchens to make a triple helping of sour fish sobering soup. Very shortly the attendants carried in a bowl of the fish soup on a golden tray. Perceiving from the way it was steaming that the soup was too hot, the Emperor with his own hand took ivory chopsticks and stirred the liquid for a long while before handing it to Li Bai. Bai knelt and drank it and at once felt brisk and alert. All this while, the assembled officials were watching with astonishment and delight as the Emperor conferred such favours on Li Bai, astonished that he should thus break with customary etiquette and delighted that he was so well able to appreciate worthy men. Only Yang Guozhong and Chamberlain Gao looked on with misery, gloomy expressions on their faces.

By imperial command the foreign ambassador was summoned into court. When the ambassador had completed his kowtows before the Emperor, Li Bai, clad in purple robe and silk-gauze hat, airily, loftily, with the bearing of some immortal deity ascending to the clouds, stood beneath the left-hand pillar, holding the foreign letter, which he proceeded to read out in clear ringing tones, with not the slightest flaw in the pronunciation of even a single word. The foreign ambassador was utterly dumbfounded.

'Your little country,' Li Bai then informed him, 'has shown

itself remiss in courtesy, but His Sacred Majesty in his magnanimity that is as vast as very heaven has chosen to ignore the lapse. I am by imperial rescript ordered to favour you with a reply. You are to listen to it in attentive silence!'

Quivering and trembling the foreign ambassador knelt down at the foot of the steps. The Emperor ordered a Seven Treasures bench to be placed beside the imperial throne and had his attendants also fetch a white jade inkstone from the land of Yutian, together with an ivory-handled hare-bristled writing brush, some Single Grass Dragon perfume ink and some multi-coloured golden-patterned writing paper, all to be arranged ready in their proper positions on the bench. He bestowed upon Li Bai the honour of sitting on a brocade footstool before the imperial divan to draft the edict of reply.

Li Bai first submitted a request to the Emperor. 'My boots are not clean. They got dirty at the banquet. I hope Your Imperial Majesty will vouchsafe me your indulgence and permit me to remove my boots and tie up my socks before ascending the throne dais.'

The Emperor granted this petition. 'Pull Academician Li's boots off for him,' he ordered a little eunuch.

'May I make a proposal?' Li Bai now asked. 'I beg Your Majesty to pardon my crazy frivolity in advance, or I shall not dare to mention what I have in mind.'

'I give you licence,' said the Emperor. 'You may speak out of place and we shall still not deem you to have committed any offence.'

'When I entered for the examinations in the Spring Examination Halls,' explained Li Bai, 'I was failed by Grand Preceptor Yang and driven away by Chamberlain Gao. Today, as I see the two of them heading the ranks of your ministers, it inhibits the buoyancy of my mood. I beg you with your jewelled voice to instruct Yang Guozhong to bear my inkstone and rub my ink for me, and Chamberlain Gao to pull off my boots and tie up my socks for me, for only then will my spirit attain that grandeur and boldness, which, as I raise my writing brush to draft the edict of reply and to utter words on your celestial behalf, may enable me not to disgrace my monarch's command.'

Since he was requiring a critical service of him, the Emperor was most anxious not to thwart his wishes, so had no choice but to issue the order: 'Yang Guozhong is to bear the inkstone and Chamberlain Gao is to pull off the boots of Li Bai.'

'On that occasion in the examination halls,' both men darkly pondered to themselves, 'we treated him with scorn and insults, declaring that such a student was only fit to rub ink and pull off our boots for us. And now he is able, utilising this moment of imperial favour, to throw the words back in our faces and avenge himself for that ill turn.' With no way out of their plight, since they did not dare contravene their sovereign's command, they were the very picture of pent-up fury. There is a common saying:

> Make no enemies, it does no good,
> for your enemies will never rest,
> Abusing others, you abuse yourself,
> please others and fill your own pleasure chest.

By now brimming with satisfaction, Li Bai ascended in his stockinged feet to the quilted carpet and sat down on the brocade footstool. Yang Guozhong ground the ink nice and thick, then stood in attendance upon him, bearing the ink-stone in his two hands. Strictly speaking, in view of the difference in their ranks, one might wonder how it was that Academician Li was able to be sitting while the Grand Preceptor, in effect the prime minister, was actually standing and waiting upon him. But since Li Bai was to speak on the Emperor's behalf, the Emperor was able to favour him with exceptional courtesies, while Grand Preceptor Yang, having received the imperial command to rub ink, was not granted the right to sit and could only stand there in attendance.

With his left hand Li Bai whisked his beard to one side. With his right he raised his writing brush of Middle Mountain hare-bristle, and, sweeping ceaselessly across the decorative paper, in a very short while had completed the draft of his 'Letter to Daunt the Barbarians', all written in neat and tidy strokes with not the smallest error or erasion. He now submitted it to the Emperor, laying it upon the 'dragon desk'. The Son of Heaven looked at it in utter astonishment. It appeared to be in exactly the same writing as the foreign letter which had been sent to him, and he could not read a single word of it. He had it passed round for the officials to look at, and all and sundry were thunderstruck. The Emperor commanded Li Bai to translate it aloud to him. Bai positioned himself in front of the imperial throne and declaimed in clear, resounding tones:

The Kaiyuan Emperor of the Mighty Tang sends his rescript to the Kaydu of Bohai:

It has always been a basic truth that eggs should not try to combat stones, and that snakes should not fight with dragons. Our dynasty, founded in response to the will of Providence, extends its pacifying rule across the whole world and possesses valiant generals and doughty soldiers, tough armour and keen weapons. Khan Jili broke a treaty of alliance with us and was reduced to captivity, whereas the Tibetan King Nongzan cast a golden goose as a gift and took an oath of allegiance to us. The land of Xinluo has submitted memorials to us in the form of eulogies woven in silken brocade. India has sent birds that can speak, Persia has contributed snakes that catch rats, and Byzantium has presented dogs that drag* horses. White horses have come from Heling, and pearls that shine in the night have been sent as tribute by Champa. The Guligans once presented famous horses and Nipoluo once submitted gifts of wondrous vinegar pickles. All of them, in awe of our prestige and cherishing virtue, bought tranquillity and sought peace. Korea rejected the mandate of heaven and heaven punished her again and again, even so that her royal house, which had survived through nine hundred generations, was in the space of one morning utterly extirpated. For what other reason can this have been but that it was a divine castigation of sins, the all-seeing justice of the supreme order! You, moreover, are but a small nation across the sea, a vassal state of Korea, and compared to China no more than a mere province, utterly inadequately provided with soldiers, horses, fodder and grain. Should your feeble praying mantis wrath display its tantrums and your thin-necked swan arrogance fail to humble itself, the celestial forces will in one fell swoop pounce upon you, your blood will flow for a

*I.e. track? bait? hunt? leave trailing? The precise meaning is not known.

thousand miles, and while you personally will share Jili's captive fate, your country will likewise follow the path of Korea. The Sage, who is now upon our throne in his ocean-vast magnanimity and indulgence, pardons your reckless obstreperousness. You would be well advised to repent hastily of your disaster-courting folly and to devote your energies more industriously to the affairs of government, rather than invite punishment and slaughter and ask to be made the laughing stock of all other nations. Think, think, and think again!

Such is our edict.

The Emperor was enraptured as he heard this, and now ordered Li Bai to communicate it directly to the foreign ambassador and then to enclose it in a sealed packet. Li Bai again called upon the services of Grand Captain Gao, this time to put his boots on for him, and then descended to the lower part of the hall and summoned the foreign ambassador to listen to the edict. As he read it once more, he did so in booming, bell-like tones, and the foreign ambassador, not daring to utter a sound all the while, with face now ashen grey, could only kowtow again and again, make sweeping obeisances, and take his leave of the court. Hanlin Academician Hê saw him off through the gate of the capital.

'Who was that man who read the edict just now?' asked the foreign ambassador in a whisper.

'His name is Li Bai,' replied the Academician, 'and he holds the post of Hanlin Academician.'

'Is that such a high-ranking post that he is entitled to have the Grand Preceptor bear his inkstone and the Grand Captain pull off his boots for him?' exclaimed the ambassador.

'It is true that the Grand Preceptor is a supreme minister and that the Grand Captain is a personal favourite of the Emperor, but they are merely the most eminent of mortals. But Academician Li is an immortal deity who has descended from heaven to adorn and sustain the Celestial Court on earth. So how could any person rank on a par with him?'

With a quick nod of his head, the foreign ambassador said goodbye and returned to his own country, where he gave his king an account of what had occurred. On reading the epistle

71

from China, the king was filled with alarm and held a conference with his compatriots. 'If the Celestial Court has immortal gods to assist it,' they concluded, 'how can we hope to oppose them with any success!' The king wrote a document of submission, declaring his willingness to send tribute and pay homage at the Chinese court every year. But all this occurred later.

Our story has diverged. Meanwhile, in the palace, the Son of Heaven, overwhelmingly impressed by Li Bai, wished to promote him further.

'I have no desire to hold any post,' submitted Li Bai. 'All I want is to be able to live a free and easy life, according to the precedent set by the jester-minister Dongfang Shuo during the Han dynasty.'

'Since you will not accept a post, my lord,' said the Son of Heaven, 'you may choose whatever gold, white jade orbs or rare and wondrous jewels and treasures I have in my possession.'

'Nor do I wish to receive any gold or jewels,' said Li Bai. 'I would like, if I may, to accompany you on your tours and trips of recreation and daily to drink three thousand cups of the finest wine! That will suffice me!'

Aware as he was that Li Bai was an unworldly eccentric, the Emperor had not the heart to coerce him into anything against his will. From then on he frequently held imperial banquets for him and had him lodge in the Hall of Golden Chariot Bells, consulting him about matters of government and bestowing daily ever more bounteous favours upon him.

One day Li Bai was riding on horseback along Changan Street when he suddenly heard the noise of gongs and drums resounding in unison, and caught sight of a bunch of swordsmen and halberdiers approaching in procession, clustered round a prison cart. Bai halted the outriders, questioned them, and learned that they came from Bingzhou and were escorting a general who had neglected to take a military initiative to the Eastern Market to be executed. In the cart Li Bai saw the prisoner, a fine, handsome man of heroic mien and mighty aspect. Courteously, Li Bai inquired his name.

'My surname is Guo and my personal name is Ziyi,' replied the man, in a voice that resembled some tremendous, rich-toned bell.

Able to tell from the remarkable looks of the man that he was one day infallibly destined to become a great pillar of the state, Li Bai shouted to the swordsmen and halberdiers to halt their progress: 'Wait while I go in person to petition the Emperor on the matter.'

All were aware that he was the Academician Li, the God in Exile, for whom the Son of Heaven had with his own hand stirred soup, and none of them dared disobey.

There and then Li Bai turned his horse about and galloped straight off to deliver a supplication at the palace portals, requesting an audience with the Emperor. Having successfully begged a pardon for the prisoner, he personally made his way to the Eastern Market to proclaim the pardon, open the prison cart and release Ziyi, thus granting him the chance to remedy his past offence by future meritorious deeds in the service of the nation. Ziyi bowed his thanks to Li Bai for his great bounty in having redeemed him from the jaws of death, and vowed that one day he would gratefully 'bear rings in his beak and knot grass' in return, and unfailingly remember to repay him. But let us put this matter on one side and mention it no more for the while.

In those days there was a considerable vogue in the palace for growing peonies, which were sent as tribute from Yangzhou. Nowadays we call them *mudanhua*, but in Tang times they were called *mushaoyao*. Four kinds of tuber were grown in the palace, which produced four different colours, crimson, deep purple, pink, and pure white. Emperor Xuanzong had some of them transplanted in front of the Heavy Scent Pavilion, and made a trip there with his favourite lady, the Exalted Lady Yang, to admire and enjoy them, commanding the entertainers of the imperial Pear Orchard Conservatoire to play music for the occasion.

'We are in the presence of my dear lady and we are admiring these wondrous flowers,' he said. 'How, for such fresh blossoms, can we be content to play old songs?' So he at once ordered the Director of the Pear Orchard Conservatoire, Li Guinian, to go and summon Li Bai into the palace.

'Academician Li has gone to the wine shops in Changan Market,' a eunuch piped up.

Guinian accordingly did not bother to search all the streets and other market-places but headed straight for the Changan market, where from an upper storey of a large wine emporium he heard someone singing:

> Three cups and you fathom the laws of life,
> a gallon, and Nature and you are as one,
> Take but the zest that lies in the cup,
> ignore the beck of sober men.

'If that's not Academician Li singing,' said Li Guinian, 'I'll eat my hat!' And he bounded up the stairs with great strides.

Sure enough, there he saw Li Bai seated in sole occupation of a tiny nook, with a single sprig of double-petalled blossoms of Jade-green peach stuck in the vase on his table. He was sitting and drinking with only the flower for company and, although by now thoroughly oiled and befuddled, holding in his hand a gigantic goblet to which he resolutely clung. Guinian went up to him.

'His Holy Majesty is at the Heavy Scent Pavilion and summons you to him, Academician,' he said. 'Come quickly.'

At the mention of an imperial command the other tipplers present at once took alarm and stood up to observe what would happen. Li Bai took absolutely no notice whatsoever, just opened his bleary eyes and recited at Guinian a line of poetry by Tao Yuanming:

> I am drunk, I seek sweet sleep, I bid you go.

Immediately he had recited this line he closed his eyes, on the point of sleep.

But Li Guinian had his wits about him. He beckoned down from the window of the wine house and seven or eight men whom he had brought with him all came upstairs together and, without allowing any room for argument, carried Academician Li, his arms and legs flailing, outside and plonked him on a Jade flower piebald steed. Then, with all of them supporting him on either side and Guinian at the rear whipping the horse forward, they raced non-stop to the Five Phoenixes Tower. Another eunuch sent by the Emperor came to hurry them on

74

and conveyed imperial permission for them to enter the palace
on horseback, so Guinian, instead of helping Li Bai to dis-
mount, gave the eunuchs a hand in supporting him and
headed straight for the rear portion of the palace, past the
Joyful Celebration Pond and up to the Heavy Scent Pavilion.

The Emperor saw at once that although Li Bai was still
astride the horse his eyes were both tightly shut and he had
not sobered up yet. He ordered his eunuchs to spread out a
purple woollen carpet to the side of the Pavilion and to help
Li Bai to alight so that he might lie down and sleep for a while.
He himself went to see how Bai was, and perceiving a trickle
of saliva running from Bai's mouth he personally wiped it
away with his 'dragon' sleeve.

'I have heard,' was Lady Yang's suggestion, 'that pouring
cold water on a person's face can sober him up.' So the Emperor
instructed eunuchs to scoop water from the Joyful Celebration
Pond and his palace ladies to take mouthfuls and spurt it
onto Li.

Startled from his dreams, Bai awoke to see the Emperor
standing there. Horrified, he prostrated himself. 'I deserve ten
thousand deaths,' he said. 'But I am the very god of drinkers
and I pray for the bounty of your forgiveness, Your Majesty.'

The Son of Heaven helped him up with his own august
hands, and explained the situation. 'Today I am enjoying
these splendid flowers with my lady,' he said. 'It is imperative
that I have some new lyrics for the occasion. That is why I
summoned you, my lord, so that you might compose three
stanzas in the pure peace key.'

Li Guinian fetched some golden-flower-patterned writing
paper and handed it to Bai. Bai, drunk as he was, in one unbroken flow of writing at once composed three verses. The
first went:

> Dress evoking clouds, face evoking a bloom,
> fragrant dew-flower zephyr-wafted there by
>   the balustrade,
> Such as you may meet, if not mid heaven's
>   jewelled hills,
> in paradise beneath the moon up there in the
>   Terrace of Jade.

The second was as follows:

> A sprig of Gorgeous Red, her perfume frozen
>   in dew,
> why tear one's heart, to Mount Wu's cloud-rain
>   love aspire?
> What rival had she in the palace of Han?
> poor Flying Swallow flaunting make-up and
>   novel attire!

And the third went:

> Wondrous flowers, state-toppling beauty,
>   together rejoice,
> fair looks that earn their monarch's whiling
>   glance and smiling,
> Both gifted to dispel spring-breeze-borne
>   boundless bitter yearning
> as north of the Bower of Heavy Scent they
>   adorn the wooden railing.

As he read these lyrics, the Emperor was ceaseless in his praise of them. 'Such genius,' he averred, 'beyond all doubt surpasses that of all the many other academicians in the Hanlin Academy put together.'

He at once commanded Guinian to set them to music and sing them, while the performers of the Pear Orchard Conservatoire all joined in with their string and woodwind instruments and the Son of Heaven himself provided an accompaniment on the jade horizontal flute. Upon the conclusion of the singing, Lady Yang drew back her embroidered coif and expressed her gratitude to the Emperor with repeated curtsies.

'Do not thank me,' said the Emperor. 'You may thank the Academician!'

Lady Yang took up a glass Seven Treasures goblet, personally poured out some Western Liang grape wine, and ordered a palace lady to serve it to Academician Li. The Emperor announced that Li Bai was now granted the privilege of a complete tour of the inner palace gardens and commanded unuch attendants to follow him bearing choice wines for him to drink to his merry fill whenever he so desired. Thenceforth he was for ever summoning Li Bai when intimate parties were being held in the inner palace, and even Lady Yang became fond of him and held him in high regard.

Now Chamberlain Gao bitterly resented having had to pull Li Bai's boots off, but could find no way of venting his indignation. One day Lady Yang was leaning against a balustrade, singing over to herself once more the three songs which Li Bai had composed in the pure and peaceful key and sighing with ecstasy at their poetry. First ascertaining that there was no one else in the vicinity, Chamberlain Gao seized this opportunity to have a word with her.

'Most Exalted Lady,' he said, 'your humble slave imagined that when you first heard those songs of Li Bai's you would have been cut to the quick and have borne him the bitterest of grudges. How is it that you care to retain the memory of them with such loving attention?'

'What was there to be resentful of?' asked Lady Yang.

The Chamberlain explained: 'That line "Poor Flying Swallow flaunting make-up and novel attire". Flying Swallow's surname was Zhao and she was an empress of the Western Han emperor Chengdi. As you know, in modern paintings you see a warrior knight holding a golden dish in his hands, and a woman in the dish dancing around with whirling sleeves. Well, the woman is Zhao Flying Swallow. She had exquisite, supple limbs and walked in a delicate, gracious manner, like a sprig of blossom trembling as it is held in the hand, and Chengdi lavished unparalleled love upon her. But what happened? Flying Swallow had a secret love affair with Yan Chifeng, whom she kept hidden in the double partition walls. Emperor Chengdi came into the palace, heard someone cough behind the arras, sought out Chifeng, and killed him. He was of a mind to dismiss Flying Swallow, but her younger sister, Joined Virtue, did all she could to try and save her and he was persuaded to desist. All the same, for the rest of her life she never entered the main palace precincts. Now here is Li Bai comparing you, Most Exalted Lady, to Flying Swallow. It is slanderous. Should you not give it your most careful consideration?'

Now as it happened, Lady Yang had by that time adopted the Turkic man An Roxan as her foster son, and he was allowed free access to the palace and was secretly making love to her. Everyone in the palace was aware of this, only Emperor Xuanzong being kept in the dark about it. Hence, in raising the matter of Flying Swallow, Chamberlain Gao had touched upon a most sensitive spot. Thereafter, inwardly harbouring bitter resentment, Lady Yang was for ever criticising Li Bai in the Emperor's presence for his frivolity, drunken bouts and lack of due deference to his sovereign. Perceiving that Lady Yang was unhappy about Li Bai, the Emperor no longer invited him to the inner palace parties, nor did he allow him to lodge in the palace at all. Li Bai gathered that he was the victim of Chamberlain Gao's machinations and that the Emperor desired to keep him at arm's length, and frequently tried to take his leave, but the Emperor would not allow him to go. So he drank even more recklessly and dissipatedly, and he and his boon companions and fellow-drinkers, Hê Zhizhang, Li Shizhi, Jin Prince of Ruyang, Cui Zongzhi, Su Jin, Zhang Xu and Jiao Sui, became known as the Eight Tipsy Saints.

In his heart, though, the Emperor was truly fond of Li Bai, and it was solely because he was not readily acceptable in the palace that he had somewhat removed him from his intimate circle. In view of Li Bai's frequent supplications to be allowed to return home and his disinclination to linger on at court, the Emperor discussed the matter with him.

'My lord,' he said, 'it is your lofty aspiration to betake yourself to distant parts. I permit you to return there for a while, but shall before long summon you again. Yet you have, my lord, performed magnificent services for me. How could I allow you to return to your mountains empty-handed? Whatever you may need, my lord, I shall provide for you.'

'There is nothing I need,' replied Li Bai. 'As long as I have money "at the head of my staff" to purchase enough to drink myself daily drunk, that will be adequate for me.'

So the Emperor conferred upon him a golden tally, which bore the following words, written in the imperial hand:

I hereby grant Li Bai the title and right of being Academician Without a Care in the World, Free-and-Easy Untrammelled

Scholar, with the privilege of being able to drink wine when he encounters any wine shop and to draw money when he comes to any treasury or money house. Prefectural governments are to give him a thousand strings of copper cash and counties five hundred strings. If anyone, be he an official of the civil or of the military administration, soldier or commoner, fails to show him respect, they will be contravening the imperial decree.

In addition the Emperor gave him a present of one thousand ounces of yellow gold, a brocade robe and jade belt, a superb 'dragon' horse with a golden saddle, and twenty retainers as his entourage. Bai kowtowed his thanks for these bounties. The Emperor further bestowed upon him two golden flowers and three cups of imperial wine, and the privilege of riding from the court in front of the Emperor's own carriage.

All the ministers and officials were granted leave for the occasion and took wine along with them to see Bai off, so that from the Street of Changan right up to the ten-mile halt outside the city there was an unbroken line of bottles. Only Grand Preceptor Yang and Grand Captain Gao, still nursing their grudges, did not go to see him off. Among those who did, only Academician Hê and his six other boon companions kept with him past the hundred-mile mark, and they detained him there in carousing and revelry for three days before parting. In the complete collection of Li Bai's works there is a 'Poem on returning to the mountains and taking leave of my true friends of Golden Gate', Golden Gate and also the term Golden Horse used in the poem both referring to Changan. In the poem he says:

Reverent I accepted my Emperor's citation,
and flame-fast rose to join the fair
  supernal throng,
Till I quit the Golden Horse and depart the
  court this morn,
a flea-bane seed-ball wind-blown bowled along,
Idly I sing an ancient lay of time's
  sad passing,
yet a song's too short a space to sing my woe,

79

I write this to thank you, companions of
    my soul,
and in quest of gaffer anglers in my wherry
    off I go.

Attired in brocade robes and gauze-silk hat, Li Bai rode off
down the road, on horseback, and all the way along his route
he was hailed as a prince of splendour. And sure enough,
when he came to a wine shop he was given free wine to drink
and when he came to a money house he was allowed to draw
money from it. In no time he had arrived back in Jinzhou,
where he met up once more with his wife, Madam Xu. The
local authorities there, learning that Academician Li had
returned home, all came to pay their respects and convey their
congratulations, so that not a day passed but that he drank
himself merry. The days came and the months went, and
suddenly six months had somehow slipped by unseen. One day
Bai told Madam Xu that he wanted to go off on a trip, wander-
ing for pleasure and recreation amid the mountains and
streams. He dressed himself in the garb of an ordinary scholar,
hiding on his person the golden tally bestowed upon him by
the Emperor, and with one young page-boy as company and a
sturdy donkey as his mount he set off to roam at the whim of
his mood and fancy. Wherever he wandered prefectural and
county authorities duly supplied him with wine and money
just as stipulated on the tally.

One day his travels brought him to the area of Huayin
county, where he heard say that the magistrate of the county
was avaricious and oppressive in his dealings with the ordinary
populace. Li Bai thought of a scheme to deal with him. He
approached the magistrate's court, then ordering his page-boy
to make himself scarce he mounted his donkey back to front
and in that manner rode up and banged three times in
succession on the court door. The magistrate was at the time
trying a case at the upper end of the courtroom, and observing
Li kept on reiterating, 'Abominable! Abominable! How dare
he make a mockery of an official, of a "mother-and-father of
the people"!' He ordered his constables to arrest Li and bring
him before the court for trial. Li Bai feigned a slight show of
inebriation and although interrogated again and again would

give no reply. The magistrate ordered the gaolers to march him into gaol. 'When he has sobered up,' he told them, 'have him make a confession, and no nonsense either! I shall sentence him tomorrow.'

The gaolers led Li Bai into gaol. As he saw the chief gaoler, he flipped his beard up in a long peal of laughter.

'This man must be round the bend, off his nut,' said the chief gaoler.

'I am neither round the bend nor nutty,' said Li Bai.

'Since you are *compos mentis* then,' said the chief gaoler, 'you might like to stop larking about and make a confession! Who are you? Why did you ride up here on a donkey and insult the magistrate?'

'If you require me to make a confession,' said Li Bai, 'fetch paper and writing brush.'

As the gaolers placed paper and brush on the desk, Li Bai hauled the chief gaoler unceremoniously to one side. 'Stand back one pace,' he said, 'so that I may write.'

'Let's see what this crazy fellow can write,' laughed the chief gaoler.

And this is what Li Bai wrote:

The Confession of a Man from Jinzhou, by Surname Li,
with the Monosyllabic Personal Name Bai

In youth I acquired wide culture, and a wave of my brush made the gods to cry. In Changan I was one of the famous Eight Saints and of Bamboo Brook's Six Recluses one of them was I. Once I drafted a letter foreign savages to tame and to the ends of this wide world it broadcast my fair name. The imperial carriage many a time good company I kept, and the Hall of Golden Chariot Bells was the bedroom where I slept, and the soup I supped was stirred by the Emperor's own hand and by his sleeve the spittle from my lips was swept. Grand Captain Gao to remove my boots down on his knees did sink, and Grand Preceptor Yang Guozhong stood humbly by to grind my ink. Before the halls of the Son of Heaven, even there I might on horseback pass, yet here in little Huayin county they would stop me riding a long-eared ass! Please consult my tally of gold, where more of my little history's told.

When Li Bai had written this, he handed it to the chief gaoler to read.

The chief gaoler was so frightened that he quite lost his wits. 'My Lord Academician,' he said, bowing with head bent low, 'have mercy on me. I am only following the magistrate's instructions. I have no choice in the matter. I pray you in your magnanimity to be lenient towards me and forgive my crime.'

'You are not implicated,' said Li Bai. 'I merely wish you to tell your magistrate that I have come bearing a golden tally and the imperial mandamus and to inquire of him what offence I have committed that he detains me here.'

The chief gaoler bowed his gratitude and at once rushed to present the confession to the magistrate, at the same time informing him of the gold tally and the imperial edict which it bore. This time the magistrate was like a little child hearing thunder for the first time, with no hole where it can scurry for refuge. He had no choice but to accompany the gaoler to the prison to pay his humble respects to Li Bai. 'Your lowly servant, this inferior functionary,' he said, kowtowing and begging for mercy, 'has eyes that cannot even see mighty Mount Tai right before them! For this single lapse, grave though it is, I implore you to have pity upon me.'

All the other officers, at the news of these events, came to salute Li Bai and beseech his indulgence. They invited the Academician to be seated in the place of honour in the court-room, where all the officers rendered him formal ceremonial honours.

Li Bai took out his golden tally and showed them all what was written on it. ' "Wherever the Academician goes, if any-one, be he an official of the civil or of the military administration soldier or commoner, fails to show him respect, they will be contravening the imperial decree."—What a crime you must have committed! What punishment would you consider you deserve?'

When they read the imperial edict, all the officers of one accord bowed their heads and humbly avowed: 'We all deserve ten thousand deaths!'

Li Bai smiled as he saw them all so abjectly entreating his mercy. 'You have received rank and salaries from the State,' he said. 'How is it then that you lower yourselves to act so rapaciously and oppressively towards the ordinary people? Only if you turn over a new leaf can I absolve you from your crime.'

At this, they all clasped their hands and bowed in supplication, each and every one of them promising to mend his ways and never transgress again. Then, there in the courtroom, they set out a great feast and entertained the Academician to three days' tippling before concluding the party and dispersing. From then on the magistrate was a reformed man and a good pastor of his flock. These events were noised abroad in other counties, where it was universally suspected that the imperial court had sent Academician Li on a secret mission to the provinces in order that he might observe the state of society and investigate local administration. All without exception abandoned avarice for integrity, viciousness for virtue. In his travels Li Bai traversed the whole region of the ancient states of Zhao, Wei, Yan, Jin, Qi, Liang, Wu and Chu, the larger part of China, everywhere lingering to savour the pleasures of the mountains and streams and enjoying to the utmost the delights of poetry and wine.

Later, when the rebellion of An Roxan obliged the Emperor Xuanzong to resort to his carriage and depart the capital on a 'tour' to Szechwan, during which Yang Guozhong was executed by the imperial troops and Lady Yang done away with by hanging in a Buddhist monastery en route, Li Bai, in order to avoid the troubles, went into hiding in the Lu Mountains. Lin, Prince of Yong, presently became Imperial Commissioner of the South-East. He secretly cherished the ambition to set himself up as emperor. Acquainted with Bai's great ability, he forced him to come down from the mountains, wanting to employ him in some unauthorised post. Li Bai would not consent, so Prince Lin detained him at his headquarters. Shortly afterwards, the Emperor Suzong acceded to the throne at Holy Warrior and appointed Guo Ziyi Grand Commander of the Imperial Forces, in which capacity Guo reconquered the two national capitals. Someone accused Prince Lin of plotting rebellion and Emperor Suzong immediately sent Ziyi to transfer forces to the region and deal with him. The Prince of Yong's forces were defeated, and Li Bai at last managed to free himself. He escaped to the mouth of the River

Xunyang, but was there taken prisoner by the sergeant guarding the river, held as a rebel, and escorted to Commander Ziyi's headquarters.

As he set eyes on Academician Li, Ziyi at once bellowed to his soldiers to stand back, while he personally untied his bonds, installed him in the seat of honour and kowtowed most reverentially to him. 'Had you, benefactor, not come to my rescue in the old days in the Eastern Market,' he said, 'would I ever have enjoyed my present standing?' He ordered wine to be brought to restore Bai's peace of mind after all the harrowing treatment to which he had been subjected.

That very night he wrote a memorandum to submit to the Emperor, pointing out the injustice that had been done to Li Bai, further recalling the latter's great deed for the nation in writing the 'Letter to Daunt the Barbarians', and recommending him for some important appointment suited to his great abilities. Yes, truly a case of culling the fruits of past kindness. Ah, yes, indeed:

> Two leaves of drifting duckweed go down to
>   the mighty sea,
> In the sea of human life one may always
>   meet again.

By this time Yang Guozhong was dead and Chamberlain Gao had been banished to some remote region. When Emperor Xuanzong was welcomed back from Szechwan, he was retired as Imperial Father, and he too praised Li Bai's remarkable genius to Emperor Suzong. Suzong therefore summoned Bai into his service as Personnel Commissioner of the Left. Bai, regretfully sighing that it was all too easy to sink or lose one's way in the ocean of government service and that he would not be able to live an easy-going carefree life any more if he accepted, declined the honour. Taking his leave of Guo Ziyi, he boarded a boat and sailed to Yueyang on Lake Dongting. From there he carried on past Golden Mound, Nanking, and moored his boat on the banks of the Yangtse at Coloured Rock.

That night the moonlight was as bright as day. Li Bai was drinking merrily on the river when he suddenly heard from far away in the sky the high faint sound of music, which gradually approached the moorings. None of the boatmen heard it, only Li Bai. Suddenly a great storm and mighty waves arose in the middle of the Yangtse, and a leviathan, scores of feet long, reared up from the waters with a thrashing of its fins. Two boy angels, bearing ambassadorial insignia in their hands, came and stood before Li Bai and announced: 'The Lord on High welcomes the Lord of the Planet back to his seat in heaven.' The boatmen all fainted in astonishment and fright, and when a moment later they revived they saw Academician Li seated on the back of the leviathan. The music leading the way, he rose into the sky and disappeared from view.

The following day these events were reported to the magistrate of Dangtu, who set them down in a memorial which he submitted to the throne. The Emperor commanded that a shrine be built to Li the God in Exile on the Hill of Coloured Rock, and sacrifices held there in both spring and autumn.

In the period known as the Great Pacific Raising of the Nation (976–84) of the Sòng dynasty a certain student was crossing the Yangtse at Coloured Rock one moonlit night when he saw a brocade sail approaching from the west, and on the bow of the boat there was a white shield which bore the inscription 'Lord of Poesie'. At the sight of this, the student in a loud clear voice declaimed two lines:

> Who is it sails the Yangtse, calls him
> > Lord of Poesie?
> I bid him now display his wit, who flaunts
> > a claim so bold!

At once from the boat there chimed back two matching lines:

> This tranquil night is not the hour for
> > ranting forth quatrains,
> I fear lest stars on high amazed drop
> > to the river cold.

Astonished, the student was just about to draw his boat alongside and make enquiries, when the other boat moored at the foot of Coloured Rock. There the man from the boat, clad

85

in purple robe and gauze-silk hat and floating airily as som immortal deity, headed straight for the shrine of Li the God i Exile. The student followed and looked for him in the shrine but there was no trace of anyone inside. Now he realised tha the matcher of his couplet had been none other than Li Ba himself. To the present day, whenever anyone talks of th 'God of Wine' or the 'Lord of Poesie', he always acclaims L Bai first and foremost as worthy of these titles.

> In drafting the 'Letter to Daunt the Barbarians'
> his genius was seen and heard,
> The Son of Heaven served him soup
> which the Emperor's hands had stirred.
> He rode a leviathan to heaven
> and ever since he went away,
> Where the Yangtse flows at Coloured Rock
> sadness lingers to this day.

A Joke Over Fifteen Strings of Cash
Brings Uncanny Disaster

Brilliant insight and nimble wit
are it is true by heaven ordained,
But folly stems often not from Nature,
cannot be trusted, is only feigned.
Indifference is often hatred's cause,
jests sometimes the root of bitter wars.
A heart may be more treacherous
than the Yellow River's ninefold writhing,
More than ten layers of iron armour
a face may inspire one's loathing.
Wine and sex have often ruined
whole families and nations,
But the ancient classics never brought
a good man tribulations!

All this poem sets out to express is the difficulty of being a
human being, because of the narrow treachery of the ways of
the world, the unfathomable and unpredictable nature of the
human heart, the remoteness of the great moral law that under-
lies creation, and the myriad profusions of human emotions
and desires. People bustle and scrabble around in their hordes
in quest of wordly profit and gain, jumbling idiots, tumbling
clowns, culling only calamity, disrupting everything, suffering
endless vicissitudes to preserve their own skins and to get the
best for their own nest. The ancients had all this in mind when
they said: 'There's a time for a frown, and a time for a smile.
'twixt frown and smile, keep cautious all the while.'

This story concerns a gentleman who ended up by getting himself killed, ruining his family, and putting paid to a few other lives into the bargain, all because of a moment's laughter and play after a spot of wine. But let us first cite the following tale as a curtain-raiser.

In the Original Prosperity period (1078–85) of our present dynasty there was a young literatus by the name of We Pengju, courtesy name Chongxiao. When he was only seventeen years old, he took a wife, a girl sparkling as a jewel and as pretty as a flower. Less than a month later, the spring lists were promulgated and the imperial civil service examinations were thrown open to candidates. Master Wei took leave of his wife, packed his bags, and set off for the capital to take the exams. Just as he was about to depart, his wife spoke urgently to him.

'Whether you get an official post or not,' she said, 'hurry, hurry quickly back to me. Don't abandon your loving wife.'

'With my ability I am securely bound for fame and success,' answered Wei. 'No need for you to worry, my dear good lady.'

He took his leave, embarked upon his journey, and arrived in the capital, where he duly achieved fame at the first attempt, being listed ninth in the top list of examination successes. He was awarded a post in the capital and took up his duties amid considerable pomp and splendour and impressive ceremony. Naturally he lost no time in writing a letter home and sending someone to fetch his family to the capital. In the letter he began with the usual good wishes and the story of his appointment, but he then went on to write: 'All this time here in the capital I have had no one to look after me, so I have now taken a concubine. I am so much looking forward to your arrival in the capital, dear wife, so that we may all enjoy my new splendour together.'

One of his household took the letter and made straight for his home, presented himself before the young lady, offered her his warm congratulations, then took out the letter and handed it to her. She tore it open, and, as she was reading through it, suddenly turned to the servant in pain and anger.

'So your master is capable of such ingratitude and faithlessness!' she said. 'No sooner does he obtain a government position than he gets himself another wife!'

柳湖謝氏

'Come on now,' said the servant, 'I've been there with him in the capital, and I can assure you nothing of the sort has happened. The master must be playing a joke on you. As you'll find out when you get to the capital. So don't you fret, lady.'

'Oh, if that's true,' she said, 'then I won't worry any more.'

As, however, the boat and crew were not yet available, while she was busying herself making arrangements and packing for the journey she found someone who was going to the capital and through him sent a letter of greeting to her husband. On arrival at the capital, the letter-bearer hunted out the residence of the Doctor Wei who had met with success in the recent imperial examinations, delivered the letter, was entertained with wine and food, and then went back to his own business. But enough of him.

When Master Wei received the letter, he tore it open and read it. It contained not a word of conventional introduction, preliminary pleasantry or idle chatter. All it said was: 'Since you have taken a concubine for yourself in the capital, I have taken a second husband for myself here at home. Sooner or later we shall come to the capital together to join you.' Realising that his wife was having a joke, he took no notice at all.

Before he had time to stow the letter away, someone announced that a fellow student of his was outside, come to pay him a visit. In lodgings in the capital, ceremony is not as closely observed as at home, and, moreover, the young man was a close friend and fellow student of Wei's and knew that Wei had no other relatives in the house, so he marched straight into the room and sat down. They chatted a bit, then Master Wei got up and went out to the toilet. The young visitor casually turned over the pages of writing on the table, and his eye lighted on the letter. Finding it highly amusing, he deliberately recited it in a loud voice. Too late to prevent this, Master Wei blushed bright red all over his face. 'Just a lot of nonsense,' he said, 'I pulled her leg, so she wrote this as a joke on me.' 'You can't make jokes about things like that,' guffawed the fellow student, then, taking his leave, made off.

Now that fellow student was a youth who delighted in gossip. In no time news of the episode had spread throughout the metropolis. A clique of people who were jealous that such a young man as Master Wei had done so well in the examinations seized upon the matter, which should have been treated as mere piece of insignificant tittle-tattle, and submitted a repo to the Emperor claiming that Wei was too young, lack proper restraint and decorum, and was altogether unsuitab to occupy such a lofty, important position. He was demote to a job in the provinces.

It was too late now for Master Wei to repent of what he ha done. Subsequently he never got any further in the civ service, and a career that had seemed as splendid as a strip brocade silk stretching before him had been allowed to sli through his hands just like that. Thus did a couple of wor said in jest strew a fine career to the winds.

Now let us talk of another gentleman, a fine strapping si foot fellow, who, likewise by a moment's joking, after som wine, managed to bring about his own death, and to involv two other people who also quite unjustly forfeited their lives How did all this come about? There is a poem which somewhat to the point here:

> Miserable the path through life,
> all treacherous meanders,
> Passers-by with sneering mouths
> casually spill their slanders.
> The white cloud harbours no intention
> ever to set sail,
> Yet it too is scudded forth
> by the cruel caprice of the gale.

Now in the reign of Emperor Gaozong (1127–62) the capital was established at Hangchow, which then became known as the 'Provisional Residence'. In its splendour, prosperity and thriving, bustling magnificence it was every bit the equal of the previous capital, Bianliang. On the left side of Arrow Bridge in the city there lived a literatus by the name of Liu Junjian. His forbears had been people of means, possessors of a solid fortune, but by his time fate had proved unkind and nothing went right for him. He started by studying, then later, seeing that it was getting him nowhere, he changed course and took up commerce as his vocation. It was just like turning monk late in life. He was even less cut out for the business of buying and selling, and his capital simply flowed away from him. Gradually he moved from big houses to smaller houses, and finally he rented a small house with two or three rooms. Liu Junjian and his wife, née Wang, had always got on very well together in their younger years, but later, because she had borne him no son and heir, he had taken a second wife, a young lady from a family of the name Chen. She was the daughter of Chen the cake-seller, and everyone in her family called her Second Sister. That had all happened earlier on, when he was not yet so hard-up. The little family of three closely related people lived alone with no outsiders at all in the household. Liu Junjian was a very pleasant and affable character and very popular in the neighbourhood. 'It's just that luck isn't with you at the moment, sir,' all the neighbours would tell him. 'That's the only reason you're finding things such a tight squeeze. Just you wait a bit and things are bound to brighten up for you sooner or later. It was all very well for them to talk like that, but it brought him not the slightest good. He stuck at home, brooding on his miseries and unable to devise any way out of them.

One day he was sitting at home, doing sweet nothing, when old Wang, a man from his in-laws' household, aged nearly seventy, appeared.

'It's the old squire's birthday today,' said Wang. 'He sent me round to fetch you and your good lady and take you back to his place.'

'There!' exclaimed Liu. 'I get so fed-up here day in day out buried in my own problems that I even forget my own father-in-law's birthday!'

Then he and his first wife set about packing some clothes to take with them, and made up a bundle of luggage and handed it to old Wang for him to carry. 'You stay and look after the house,' they told Second Sister. 'If it goes on till late today and we can't make it back before night, we'll certainly be home again tomorrow.'

So saying, they set off, and some six miles outside the city they reached the home of Liu Junjian's father-in-law, Squire Wang, where they all exchanged the usual greetings and polite conversation. There were a lot of guests at the party that day, so there was no real chance for him and his father-in-law to settle down to any very thoroughgoing discussions on the matter of Junjian's desperate financial circumstances. When the guests had all left, the couple stayed behind and slept in the guest-room.

First thing next morning, his father-in-law came to talk things over with Junjian.

'Son-in-law,' he said, 'you can't carry on like this "sitting back and eating the mountain hollow, standing still and eating the earth away from under your very feet, with your throat as deep as the ocean, but your time flashing by as quick as a shuttle"! You will have to devise yourself some more solid means of existence. True, my daughter married you for better or for worse, but all the same she counted on having plenty of clothes and enough food for the rest of her life. Things are just not good enough!'

'My dear and respected father-in-law,' said Junjian with a sigh, 'doesn't the saying go, "It is more difficult to open your mouth and ask people for help than to climb a mountain and catch a tiger"? The way things are in society nowadays, who gives a damn about my situation? Apart from yourself, that is. I just have to put up with the hardship and poverty. Going and asking other people for assistance is a sheer waste of effort.'

'Yes, yes,' said his father-in-law, 'no one can blame you for saying so. But I am not going to let things carry on like this. I can't bear it. I'm going to give you a little capital as a present. You do the best you can with it. Open up a grocer's shop and earn yourself a bit of profit to keep you going. How about that?'

'Thank you, thank you, father-in-law,' said Junjian, 'I'm very grateful. Yes, of course, it would be wonderful.'

While they were eating lunch, the old squire brought out some money, to the tune of fifteen strings of copper coins, and handed it to Liu Junjian. 'Take this for the time being,' he said. 'Just a bit of cash to help you do up a shop window. When you're nearly ready to open shop, I'll step in with another ten strings of coins to help you out. I should leave your wife here with us for a few days, and when you've fixed a date for opening shop I'll escort her back home to you, and join you in a little celebration. How does that strike you?'

Unable to thank him enough, Junjian humped the sack of money onto his shoulder and immediately made for home. By the time he got back to the town it was already getting late and dark, but as his road led past the house of an acquaintance who was likewise planning to set up in the retail business he thought it would be an excellent idea to pop in and have a chat with him. He knocked on the door, an answer came from inside, and out came the friend, greeting him with a bow.

'Very kind of you to call, good brother,' he said. 'Is there something I can do for you?'

Liu told him all about his new plans.

'Well, I've little enough to do and am here at home most of the time,' said the other, 'so if you ever need me, I can come and give you a hand.'

'That would be fine,' said Junjian.

They talked a while about the tricks of the trade, after which the man invited Junjian to stay for a bite, and they downed a few cups of wine. Junjian was not much of a drinker, and feeling himself growing boggle-eyed and blurred, he forced himself up and took his leave. 'Sorry to have troubled you tonight,' he said, 'and if you don't find it too much bother, I'd be very glad if you could drop round to my house tomorrow for a more detailed discussion of business plans.'

The man saw him to the end of the street, said goodbye, and went back indoors, where we shall leave him.

Ah, if only I your story-teller had been born in Junjian's time and been old enough and big enough, I should have grabbed him round the waist to hold him back and snatched at his arm to drag him away, so that he might be spared the dreadful disaster that overtook him. But no, Junjian was to die more miserably than Li Cunxiao, hero of the *History of the Five Dynasties*, who was torn apart by oxen, more wretchedly than Peng Yue in the *History of the Han*, who was slaughtered with all his clan.

Humping his sack of money, Junjian steered his steps towards home, and managing at last to reach his house, knocked on the door. It was already after lamp-lighting time. His secondary wife, Second Sister, being alone in the house and having nothing whatsoever to do, had waited till dusk and then locked the door and dozed off under the lamp. So it was quite understandable that she didn't hear him when he knocked at the door. He hammered for ages and ages before she at last heard him, and with an answering call of 'Coming' got up and opened the door.

Junjian went inside, and Second Sister took the money from him and put it on the table. 'My dear man,' she said, 'where on earth did you obtain such a sum of money? What is it for?'

Now for one thing Junjian was rather fuddled with drink and for another he was rather piqued that his secondary wife had been so long in opening the door, so he thought he would put the wind up her, just for a joke. 'Well . . . I don't really like to tell you,' he said. 'You might be frightened and take it amiss. But I'll have to tell you sooner or later, anyhow. Just that I was in such a pickle, absolutely at my wits' end what with all our money troubles, that I was forced to pawn you to a travelling merchant. I couldn't bear to lose you for good, so I only pawned you, for fifteen strings of copper coins, and if things look up for me financially I'll buy you back—I'll have to allow the fellow a bit of interest of course. But if things keep on going against me as they have been, we shall just have to make the best of a bad job and take it as it comes!'

At first the girl was disinclined to believe her own ears, but the sight of the fifteen strings of copper coins on the table was very convincing. 'We've never had a cross word between us,' she thought, 'and I always get on well with his first wife. How can he be so vicious and cruel all of a sudden?' Still undecided as to whether he was being serious or not, she tried to test him.

'If that's the case,' she said, 'then I'll have to send word to my mum and dad.'

'Oh no, no,' said Junjian. 'If you let on to your mum and dad, they are bound to put a stop to the whole affair. What we'd better do is this: you go and move in with the man tomorrow, and then I'll tactfully find a way of getting someone to break the news to your mother and father afterwards. I'm sure they won't hold it against me.'

'Where have you been drinking tonight, my good husband?' asked Second Sister.

'With the man I pawned you to,' replied Junjian. 'We signed the contract and he treated me to a spot of wine before I came back.'

94

'Why hasn't your first wife come back with you?' asked Second Sister.

'She couldn't bear to say goodbye to you, so she won't be coming home till after you have gone tomorrow,' answered Junjian. 'I couldn't help it. I had no choice, the bargain was clinched in a flash, and I can't go back on it.'

As Junjian said all this, he could hardly suppress a quiet laugh to himself. Without taking off his clothes, he lay down on the bed and dropped off to sleep.

The young lady, however, was far from able to dismiss the matter from her mind. 'What sort of a man can he have sold me to?' she wondered. 'I must go and tell mum and dad about it first. Even if someone turns up here demanding me tomorrow, if they have to go and look for me in my parents' home, something is bound to be fixed up.' Second Sister hummed and haed to herself for a while, then piled the fifteen strings of copper coins behind Junjian's feet, and banking on the fact that he was drunk quietly packed some clothes to take with her, stealthily opened the door and went out, just pulling the door to behind her.

First she went round to the house of a neighbour called Zhu Old Third, with whom she was on good terms, and asked if she could sleep the night there. 'For no good reason at all my husband went and sold me today,' she explained. 'I must first go and tell my parents. Would you mind having a word with him tomorrow? Tell him that since he has found a customer for me, they can both come round to my mum and dad's house and sort things out there. Then we can work out some better arrangement.'

'You're quite right, quite right,' said the neighbour. 'Just you do that, and I'll give your husband the full story tomorrow.'

After a night there, the young lady said goodbye and left. Yes, indeed:

> When the turtle tugs free from the golden hook
> it wags its tail and shakes its head
> never to return again.

Well, let us leave what happened to her on one side for the

while. Meanwhile, Liu Junjian slept on until about eleven o'clock at night before coming round. He noticed that the lamp on the table had still not gone out and that the young lady was not by his side, and, concluding that she was still clearing up the dishes and other things in the kitchen, he called to her to bring him some tea and a bite to eat. Receiving no reply to his call, he was on the point of struggling out of bed, but, still not sober, he slumped off to sleep again.

Quite unbeknown to him, a certain young no-good who had been gambling and lost his money that day and was now in a tight fix came out that night to try and do a bit of pilfering. He chanced to come upon Liu Junjian's door, which Second Sister had only pulled to behind her on departing and which was thus not locked. He gave it a tentative push, and it promptly flew wide open, so he crept stealthily in and got well into the house without anyone being any the wiser. Coming right up to the bed, he was able to take a good look all around by the light of the lamp, which was still burning. There was nothing worth taking. He groped around the top of the bed, and noticed that there was a man sleeping in the middle of it, with a pile of green copper coins under his feet. So he tried to steal a few strings of the coins, but Junjian suddenly awoke and sat up.

'You rogue!' he shouted. 'I borrowed that bit of money from my father-in-law to start some trade and earn my livelihood. And you come trying to steal it from me! What on earth would I do if you did!'

The man did not reply, but lunged out with a punch at his face. Junjian dodged to one side, jumped up, and joined battle with him.

Perceiving that Junjian was very nimble on his feet and handy with his fists, the man took to his heels and tried to run out of the house. But Junjian was not going to let him get away. He pursued him into the kitchen and was on the point of raising the alarm by bellowing to the neighbours to get up and help him catch a thief. In a panic and seeing no way out, the man caught sight of a gleaming wood-chopper right next to his hand. Crises breed solutions. He whipped up the axe, brought it down on Junjian's forehead, and sent him sprawling to the ground. Another blow hacked him flat. It was clear that

Liu Junjian was done for. Ah, the tragedy of it. May his soul accept our humble offerings.

' "First, don't do it; second, don't stop once you've started",' said the man. 'It was you who chased after me. I never came here intending to do you in.' He turned and went back into the room, picked up the fifteen strings of cash, tore off a strip of blanket, carefully wrapped the money in it, fastened it briskly and securely, went out, pulled the door to, and made off.

The following morning when they got up, some of the neighbours noticed that Junjian's door had not been opened, and that there was no sound of any voices from the house. 'Master Liu,' they shouted, 'Wake up, wake up! Morning's here.' There was no reply. They tried to push their way in and discovered that the door was not locked, and, rushing in without further ado, saw Junjian lying on the floor, hacked to death. His first wife had gone to her parents a couple of days ago, but where was his second wife? Of course, the alarm was raised.

'The young lady came to my house last night at dusk to ask for a night's lodging,' said Zhu Old Third, the neighbour in whose house Second Sister had passed the night. 'She said that Master Liu had for no apparent reason taken it into his head to sell her, and that she was going straight to her parents' house before he could do so, and I was to tell Master Liu that since he had found a customer for her, they were both to go over to her parents' house to sort things out. What we must do now is send someone over there to fetch her back so that we can get to the bottom of that side of things. At the same time we ought to send someone to break the news to his first wife and bring her here. Then we can take further steps.'

All agreed to these proposals.

First of all, someone was sent to break the terrible news to everyone at Squire Wang's. The old squire and his daughter wept bitterly. 'He left here yesterday quite safe and sound,' the squire told the messenger. 'I had given him fifteen strings of copper coins to use as capital. And yet now you tell us he has been murdered?'

'I must tell you, squire, and you, madam,' said the man, 'that by the time Mr Liu reached home yesterday it was already dark and he was half drunk. None of us knew of the existence of the money or what time he had returned. But this morning, seeing his door not yet open, we all pushed our way in and saw him lying there on the floor, murdered. No trace of any money, not a single penny, and no sign whatsoever of his second wife. We raised the alarm, and his neighbour on the left, Zhu Old Third, came out. He told us that yesterday evening, when it was dark, Second Sister had come and asked to spend the night at his house. She told him that for no apparent reason Mr Liu had suddenly pawned her to some other man, and that she wanted to have a word with her mother and father. She stayed the night and left early this morning. We all discussed it together and decided that we should come and break the news to you, squire, and at the same time send after Second Sister. If they don't manage to catch up with her on the road, they will go straight to her parents' place and fetch her back, come what may, so that we can question her and get things straight. You, squire, and you, madam, must go and take legal measures to try and obtain justice for Mr Liu's murder.'

Losing no time, the squire and his daughter packed for the journey, had the messenger fed and given wine, and then in great haste hurried into the city.

Meanwhile, Second Sister, having left the neighbour's house at the crack of dawn, had managed to reach the road, but before she had gone a couple of miles her feet were aching so much that she could not move a step further, and she sat down by the side of the road. Then who should come into sight but a young fellow wearing a cap with a Buddhist emblem on it and a straight-seamed, long, capacious smock, carrying on his back a bundle filled with copper coins, and marching along in silken shoes and spotless socks. He came straight on towards her, and when he reached her he eyed her up and down. She was not exactly a stunning beauty, but she had fine eyebrows, dazzling white teeth, titillating lotus-like cheeks, and come-hither eyes that were like rippling autumn pools. Very seductive indeed. Yes, yes:

> The wild blossom is the most alluring flower
> and village wine is the headiest by far.

Putting down his bundle, the young man came up and bowed a very deep bow. 'Where are you going to, young maid?' he asked, 'travelling about on your own like this?'

She returned his greeting with the conventional polite 'Wish you ten thousand blessings!' 'I want to get to my father and mother's,' she then replied, 'but I couldn't walk any further, so I'm taking a little rest here. And where have you come from, sir?'

'I'm just a villager,' he said, his two hands still clasped in front of his heart in a gesture of respect. 'I've been and sold some silk in the city, and earned a bit of money, so now I'm on my way to Chujiatang, over that way.'

'Oh, my parents live on the left side of Chujiatang, sir,' she said. 'Fancy that! It would be wonderful if you would be so good as to let me go along with you.'

'And why not indeed!' said the young man. 'I'm only too glad to escort you, young lady.'

The two of them then set off along the road together, but they had gone no more than a couple of miles when they noticed that two men were running after them, so fast that their feet scarcely seemed to touch the ground, puffing, panting and pouring with sweat through all their exertions, and their coats flapping wide open. 'Hold on there, young lady!' they kept on shouting. 'We want a word with you.'

Puzzled by the oddness of the men chasing after them, Second Sister and the young man both came to a halt. As their pursuers caught up, one of them grabbed her without waiting to give any explanation, and the other seized hold of him. 'Pretty goings-on! And now where do you think you're going?' they demanded.

Flabbergasted, Second Sister took a closer look at them, and realised that they were two of her neighbours, one of them being her host of the previous night. 'But I told you, sir,' she said, 'I told you last night that my husband had suddenly got it into his head to sell me, and so I was going to tell my parents. What do you mean by chasing after me like this?'

'I don't poke my nose into other people's affairs,' said Zhu Old Third, 'but there happens to have been a murder in your house, and that is a matter of public concern. You've got to come back and help us get things straight.'

99

'My husband sold me. I saw him bring the money into the house. Why are you talking about a murder? I'm not going. I won't.'

'You're a cool customer!' said Zhu Old Third. 'If you really refuse to go, we'll have to rouse the local constables, tell them there's a murderer here and would they mind arresting her for us. Otherwise we'll be implicated as well, and don't imagine you'd be left in cosy peace and quiet in your own locality either!'

Perceiving that somehow things had taken a nasty turn and that talking was not improving matters, the young man turned to Second Sister. 'In that case,' he said, 'you'll just have to go back with them, and I'll just have to be on my way.'

This evoked a chorus of shouts from the neighbours who had pursued them. 'You'd be all right,' they said, 'if you didn't just happen to be in the company of this young lady and hobnobbing along the road with her. You'll have to come, too.'

'This is a turn-up for the books!' he said. 'I met this young lady on the road and fell in with her for the journey. What can you pin on me to make me go back with you?'

'There has been a murder in her house,' said Zhu Old Third. 'If we let you go, it will be a case without a defendant, won't it?'

By this time, the choice was no longer in the hands of Second Sister and the young man. A crowd of onlookers had gradually gathered round.

'Young man,' they all said, 'you'll have to go with them. People who do no evil in the day don't jump with fear at the midnight knock on their door. What harm will it do you if you do go?'

'If you won't come with us,' said the neighbours who had chased them, 'we shall know you're telling lies. But we're not going to let you get away with it, anyway.'

So pulling and tugging this way and that, the four of them all made off in the same direction.

When they reached the door of Liu Junjian's house, there was a real old hullabaloo. The young lady went in. At the sight of Junjian hacked to death on the floor, with no sign of a penny of the fifteen strings of cash on the bed, her mouth dropped open, refusing to shut, and her tongue shot out, stuck there in dumb horror.

'What foul luck!' said the young man, also panic-stricken. 'By pure chance I walk a bit of the road with a young lady, and now I find myself mixed up in this crime!'

The crowd was making a great hubbub and showing no signs of dispersing, when suddenly Squire Wang and his daughter strode on the scene, stumbling along in their haste. At the sight of the corpse, they burst out weeping and wailing. 'How could you do it? How could you kill your own husband!' they accused Second Sister. 'And run away with all that money! Everything is as clear as clear can be. How on earth can you account for what you've done?'

'Yes, he did have fifteen strings of cash,' she replied, 'but when he came home last night, he said he was at the end of his tether and was going to pawn me to some man, the money being what he got for pawning me. He said I was to move into the man's household today. I had no idea what sort of man it might be, so I decided to go off first and try and tell my mother and father. So late last night I piled the fifteen strings of cash under his feet, pulled the door to behind me, and went and slept the night in Zhu Old Third's home. Then this morning I set off to tell my parents. Before I went, I begged Zhu Old Third to tell my husband that since he had a customer for me they should both come round to my parents' home to negotiate it properly. I've no earthly idea why my dear husband has been murdered!'

'She's still trying to bluff it out!' said the first wife. 'I can tell you straight and without a shadow of doubt, that yesterday my father gave him fifteen strings of cash to carry home as capital to help him provide for you and me. What in heaven's name would he be doing tricking you into believing it was money he had got by pawning you? The thing is, you've been here all on your own for a couple of days, so you've hooked yourself a lover. Then thinking that because everything was going from bad to worse financially in our home you didn't feel like sticking it out any longer, the sight of all that money gave you a sudden inspiration. So you killed your husband and made off with the money. Then, as a cunning trick, you went and spent a night at our nighbour's, you and your lover-boy planning all the time to run off and escape together. How are you going to explain away the fact that you were walking along with a man? How do you get by that one?'

'Quite right, quite right,' everyone shouted, 'the lady has hit the nail on the head.'

'And you, young man,' she said, turning to him, 'why did you plot with her to murder her own husband? Secretly arranging with her to have a rendezvous in some quiet out-of-the-way place so that you could run off somewhere else together! Why on earth did you do it?'

'My name is Cui Ning,' he said, trying to explain. 'I am not even remotely acquainted with the young lady. Late yesterday I came into town to sell a bit of silk. Here's the money to prove it. On the road back I fell in with the young lady. I happened to inquire where she was going and learned that she was travelling all alone. She mentioned that she was going the same way as me, so I escorted her to keep her company. I haven't the foggiest idea what may have happened earlier.'

None of the crowd was prepared to accept his explanation. They searched in his bundle and found exactly fifteen strings of copper coins, not a farthing more nor a farthing less. 'Vast is the net of heaven and it lets nothing through its meshes!' they all shouted in chorus. 'You and her murdered him. You pinched his money and stole his wife and made off with her for another neighbourhood. And you were quite willing to drag our local beadles and us neighbours into the nasty position of having a murder case on our hands with no one to pin the crime onto.'

There and then, without more ado, the first wife grabbed hold of Second Sister and old Squire Wang grabbed hold of Cui Ning, and with all the neighbours going along to serve as witnesses they surged as one great noisy rabble into the prefectural court.

On being informed that there was a case of murder, the prefect at once called a special session of the court, and ordered all parties concerned in the crime to make their statements and explain the circumstances from the very beginning. First of all, old Squire Wang stepped forward to make his accusation.

'My lord,' he said, 'I am a villager from your prefecture, nearly sixty years old and possessed of only one daughter. Some years ago she married a man of this city, Liu Junjian, who subsequently, in view of the fact that they had had no children, took himself a second wife, from a family by the name of Chen, she herself being called Second Sister. The three of them always got on very well together, without any squabbling or upsets, but the day before yesterday, as it was my birthday, I sent someone round to fetch my daughter and her husband to my home, where they stayed overnight. The following day, being aware that my son-in-law was really down to his last as far as family upkeep was concerned and just could not afford to maintain himself and the other two, I gave him fifteen strings of cash as capital to open a shop and earn himself a livelihood. Second Sister stayed at home looking after the house, and last night, when my son-in-law arrived back, she for some unknown reason hacked him to death with an axe. I might point out, though, that she had a young lover, called Cui Ning, and the two of them were caught running away together and brought back. I pray that you, my lord, will be moved to pity by the sinister death of my son-in-law. The adulterer, the depraved woman, and the material evidence are all here at hand. I humbly beseech you to favour the case with your great perspicacity and see that justice is done.'

'Come forward, the young woman of the Chen family,' snapped the prefect on the conclusion of this exposition. 'What led you to conspire with an adulterer to murder your own husband, rob him of his money and flee with another? How can you explain such conduct?'

'When I married Liu Junjian,' pleaded Second Sister, 'I was only his concubine, but he treated me very well, and his first wife was very understanding and kind to me, too. So how could I ever think of doing such dreadful things? When my husband came home last night, he was rather drunk, and he came in with fifteen strings of copper coins on his back. I asked him where he had got the money and he told me that because he could not afford to keep us all any longer, he had pawned me to another man for fifteen strings of cash, which was the money he now had with him. He wanted me to go and live with the other man today, without even letting my parents know. In a panic I left home in the night, and ran round to a neighbour's house to ask if I could lodge there for the night. First thing this morning, I started out for my parents' home. But first I asked the neighbour to tell my husband that since he had sold me he and the customer could both come round to my parents' home to complete the transaction properly. I had only got half-way when the neighbour I lodged with last night came running after me, seized me, and took me back. I have no idea at all why my husband should have been murdered.'

'Rubbish,' bellowed the prefect. 'There can be no doubt that the fifteen strings of cash were given to him by his father-in-law, and yet here you are trying to tell me that they were the price he received for pawning you. Quite obviously a statement without the slightest foundation of truth! And what, moreover, would a woman be doing running around outside her home at night-time? Clearly you were planning to make your escape. A woman like you could not have done all that on her own: beyond a shadow of doubt there must have been some paramour of yours collaborating with you in this robbery and murder. Come now, tell us the truth.'

Just as Second Sister was about to try and explain, several of the neighbours trooped up in a body and knelt down before the prefect. 'What you have just said, my lord,' they declared, 'was heaven-inspired clarity itself! As she says, she did spend the night at her neighbour Zhu Old Third's house, and left this morning. When we discovered that her husband had been killed, a couple of us went off after her, caught up with her half-way, and found that she was trying to escape with that young man. For the very devil of her, she just would not agree to come back. So we grabbed hold of her and made her. At the same time we sent someone to fetch the dead man's first wife and his father-in-law. When they arrived they told us that the father-in-law had given him the fifteen strings of cash for business purposes, so that he could earn his living. Now that he was dead, we had no idea where the money had got to. We questioned the young woman again and again, and she said that when she was leaving she had piled up the money on the bed. But we searched the young man and found that he had fifteen strings of cash on him, not a farthing more, nor a farthing less. Of course it was him and her. They worked it out together and did the murder. He was caught red-handed with the loot on him. That's proof enough. How can they still try to wriggle out of it?'

Feeling that every word they uttered was the epitome of

sound logic, the prefect summoned the young man to step forward. 'How can such utterly dastardly goings-on be permitted in His Imperial Majesty's own capital city!' he said. 'What led you to scheme to gain another's wife, steal fifteen strings of copper currency and kill the woman's husband? Where were you and she heading today? Confess the truth.'

'My name is Cui Ning,' said the young man, 'I am from the country. Yesterday I came into town to sell some silk, and earned myself fifteen strings of cash. This morning, by the purest chance, I happened to bump into this young lady as I was going along the road. I had not the slightest idea what her name was or who she was. How was I to know that there had been a murder in her home?'

'Fiddlesticks!' bellowed the prefect in fury. 'I don't believe that anything so completely coincidental could ever happen in this world of ours. Fifteen strings of cash were lost, and you just happen to have earned exactly the same amount from the sale of your silk! Beyond the faintest doubt you are trying to fob me off with wild excuses. Moreover, just as one should never ride another's horse, so by precise analogy one should never love another's wife. If, as you say, you had no previous connection with that woman, what were you doing in her company? With such stubborn, lying, thick-skinned rogues one never extracts a confession without a beating.'

Whereupon Cui Ning and Second Sister were subjected to a beating by the prefect's constables. They fainted again and again and were constantly revived to suffer more beating. Squire Wang, his daughter, and all the neighbours and other supporters were clamouring unswerving accusations of the two, and the prefect himself was most impatient to pronounce his verdict on the case. After such a beating, poor Cui Ning and Second Sister could stand no more punishment, and had no choice but to make a false confession of their guilt, in which they declared that, motivated by sudden greed at the sight of the money Second Sister had indeed murdered her husband, stolen the fifteen strings of cash, and made off with her paramour. All the neighbours added their signatures, each drawing a cross with his finger, and the two young people had heavy cangues locked round their necks and were escorted into the condemned cells.

105

The fifteen strings of cash were handed 'back' to the supposed original owner, the squire, who was obliged to spend it all on the tips and expenses demanded of him by the court officials. And even that money was insufficient to foot the bill. The prefect assembled the evidence in documentary form and submitted it to the imperial court. The Ministry of Punishment forwarded it to the Emperor, and an imperial decree came back. It declared that Cui Ning had committed a crime by wrongfully depriving a man of his wife, plotting to obtain and obtaining another's wealth, and destroying another's life, and should be executed according to the law, and that the woman, née Chen, had committed a crime by conspiring adulterously with a paramour to murder her husband, a major sin and wicked evil, and should be put to death by gradual dismemberment in public as a warning to others. Thereupon the prefect re-read their confessions in court, had them both brought forth from their cells, and in the presence of the court, without further ado, wrote the sentence 'Execution' for one and 'Death by a thousand cuts' for the other. They were then led to the market under escort, and subjected to public execution. Had they had mouths for every part of them, those mouths would never have sufficed to tell all their misery and suffering. Yes, indeed:

> When the dumb man tastes phellodendron
> he can tell no one how bitter it tastes.

Now listen to me, dear readers. If Second Sister and Cui Ning had in fact done the robbery and murder, you can guarantee the two of them would have made their getaway that very same night. Why on earth would she have gone and lodged a night with a neighbour? And why go to her parents' the following morning, asking to get herself caught? With only a bit of careful thought, anyone could easily have spotted the injustice that was being done to them. But instead, their judge had to be a muddle-headed fool, solely concerned with tying up the case and ignoring the fact that when you flog someone you can get anything you like out of them. 'Darkly, imperceptibly, your karma is accumulated. Maybe distantly on your sons and grandsons will retribution fall. Maybe near at hand, upon yourself.' Surely their two wronged souls will not let you go unpunished. And that is why a judge, no matter what else he does, must never on any account judge cases in an arbitrary, random fashion, nor ever apply beating and torture just to pander to his mood of the moment. He must always seek a fair and equitable solution, and justice must be done as well as be seen to be done. As they say, a dead person cannot be brought back to life, he is like something broken that cannot be mended. Ah yes, the whole affair certainly merits one's bitterest sighs and most endless regrets!

Anyway, enough of this idle chatter. Junjian's first wife, on returning home, set up a spirit tablet and went into mourning. After a while, her father, Squire Wang, tried to persuade her to remarry.

'I won't insist on waiting till the prescribed three years is up,' she told him, 'but I must at least first complete the Little Blessing, the one-year period of mourning.'

Her father gave his consent to this, and left her to her own devices.

Time flashed by, and soon, by dint of conscientious effort, she had stuck it out for nearly a whole year. Realising that she would be unable to stand the mourning much longer, her father had his man, old Wang, go and fetch her back to his home. 'Tell her to pack up her things and come home. She has mourned for Mr Liu a whole year, and now she can have done with it and remarry.'

She was in no state to choose otherwise, and after careful consideration she decided that her father's suggestion was only common sense after all. So she packed herself a bundle, which she gave old Wang to carry on his back, and said goodbye to the neighbours, promising to come back and see them in a little while. As they made their way out of the city, it being the onset of autumn, a howling wind and ferocious rainstorm blew up, so they had to leave the road and make towards a wood for shelter. But as they walked they lost their way. Ah, dear me:

> Pigs and sheep fleeing to the butcher's shop,
> along the road of suicide, clippity, clippity clop.

As they entered the wood, they heard a great shout from amid the trees behind them. 'I am the Robber King and Keeper of Peace on this mountain,' came the cry. 'Halt, wayfarers. You must pay me a toll.'

Severely shaken, the lady and old Wang looked round, and saw a man leap out towards them. He wore a scarlet kerchief on his head, an old battledress, a red silk girdle and cummerbund at his waist, and a pair of black leather boots on his feet. And in his hand he held a short sword. Waving the sword, he came up to them.

'You scurvy vermin of a highway robber,' said old Wang, just asking to be done in, 'I know your sort. I'll barter this old life of mine for yours.' He put his head down and charged at the robber, but the man dodged aside, and with the impetus of his charge old Wang crashed to the ground.

'You foul-mouthed ox,' shouted the robber in a fury, and stabbed out at him, once, twice, and the blood flowed all over the ground. Clearly it was all up with old Wang.

Seeing how vicious and savage the robber was and reckoning that she had no hope of coming out of the situation alive, Mrs Liu had a sudden flash of inspiration. An idea came into her head, a stratagem of evasion.

'Oh, I'm so glad you've killed him!' she cried, clapping her hands.

The man froze in his tracks, his eyes wide and round with puzzled wondering. 'What relation was this fellow to you then?' he roared.

'Oh, I've had such a terrible time of it,' said Mrs Liu, feigning an air of great relief. 'I lost my husband, and then I was swindled by a match-maker into marrying this old geezer, who's fit for nothing except stuffing himself with food. But now you've killed him, you dear Robber King, and rid me of a frightful pest!'

The man observed that she seemed very willing, and also that she was not bad-looking. 'What would you say to coming with me, as the Robber King's wife and mistress of his stronghold?' he asked.

Thinking at top speed, the lady concluded that there was nothing else for it. 'I should be glad from the bottom of my heart to serve you, King Robber,' she replied.

The robber's wrath was now transformed into delight. He put away his sword and staff, threw old Wang's corpse into a gully, and led Mrs Liu off to a farmstead, a most remote place. He picked up a few clods of soil and threw them onto the roof of the house, and someone came out and opened the gate. When they reached the main hall of his retreat, he gave instructions for a sheep to be slaughtered and wine to be prepared, and then proceeded to enact the wedding ceremony with Mrs Liu. And you know, the two of them got on quite well together! You see, it was a case of

> Though you know full well he's no fit mate
> in the thick of a crisis you string along.

And strange to say, within a few months of making Mrs Liu his own, the Robber King managed to rob a number of wealthy merchants, so that his domestic economy throve. She for her part was very shrewd, and would ply him with sweet words and sound advice all day long.

'There's a very ancient saying,' she said, 'that "The pitcher is sure to get smashed in the well, and the general is bound to die in battle". Now, you and I have got plenty to keep us for the rest of our lives. If you insist on carrying on with this unnatural, senseless line of business, nothing good will come of it in the long run, mark my words. Don't they say, "Romantic Liang Park is all very pretty, it's not a home to hanker after."? Take my advice and turn over a new leaf. Take up another job. Start up a little retail business. That will be enough to keep us.'

Preached at day and night, the robber duly mended his ways, abandoned his profession, and moved into the city, where he rented a house and opened a general grocery store. On feast days and holidays, when he had the leisure, he would often go to Buddhist temples and monasteries, and pray to Buddha and attend vegetarian fasts, at which he made the usual charitable offerings.

'I may have been a highwayman once,' he confided to Mrs Liu one day when he was sitting idle at home, 'but I'm perfectly aware that all wrongs have their victims waiting for requital, just as all debts have their creditors waiting for repayment. I used to spend my days bullying people into handing over their goods, living off theft. Then I got you. Things have gone mighty smoothly ever since, and now I have changed my job and turned over a new leaf. But sometimes when I get to thinking about the past, I can't help recalling that I killed two people I never ought to have killed, and caused the deaths of two others who never deserved it either. It preys on my mind, and I've often thought I would like to do some acts of religious merit, so as to ensure their souls a safe passage to heaven, though I've never mentioned it to you till now.'

'What do you mean, you killed two people you never ought?' asked Mrs Liu.

'One of them,' came the reply, 'was your husband. That time in the wood, he tried to butt me and I killed him. But he was only an old fellow, and I had no particular reason to want to kill him. And now I've got his wife for my very own. He's dead, but he won't be able to rest contented.'

'If you hadn't done it,' said Mrs Liu, 'I would never have been able to share your life, would I? Anyway, the past is over and done with. Don't bring it up any more!' Then after a pause she asked, 'And what about the other man you killed? Who was that?'

'Ah, as far as that man was concerned,' he replied, 'not only was what I did unforgiveable by all the laws of heaven, but two other people were also implicated. They were completely innocent, but they paid for what I did with their lives. It happened a year ago. I had lost a sum at gambling, and hadn't a penny left on me, so that night I went out thinking to filch a few things. Then suddenly I came to a house where they hadn't bolted the door. I pushed it open and went in. There was no one about. I groped my way through an inner door, and saw a man lying drunk on a bed. And there was a pile of money under his feet. So I tried to take a bit of it. I was just about to make off, when I woke the man up somehow. He sat up and said, "That money was given me by my father-in-law to start a business. If you steal it, me and my family will all starve to death." Then he got up and rushed for the door and was just going to raise the alarm when, seeing what a mess I was in, and as there happened to be a wood-chopper lying by my foot, I got a sudden desperate flash of inspiration, and on the spur of the moment I snatched it up shouting "It's either you or me!" and hacked him down with two blows. Then I went into his room and grabbed all the money, fifteen strings of cash it was. Later I made discreet inquiries, and learned that his concubine and some young man named Cui Ning had been wrongly accused of robbing and murdering him, and that both of them had been executed. Though I've been a robber all my life, those are the only two murders that heaven's justice and the human heart could never reconcile themselves to. It's only right that sooner or later I should hold a requiem for the benefit of their souls.'

'So, my own dear husband was murdered by this wretch, too!' thought Mrs Liu, inwardly wailing at the bitter injustice of it all. 'And not only that, but Second Sister and that young man were also dragged in, and for all their innocence suffered execution. And when I recall my part in it! Oh, I should never never have contrived so eagerly to get those two to pay for it with their lives! The two of them down in the Shades of Afterlife will never be able to forgive me, I know it!'

For the time being, however, Mrs Liu put on a cheerful manner, kept her peace, and said nothing. The next day she managed to slip out, and headed straight for the prefectural court to lay a charge and expose the injustice that had been perpetrated.

By this time there was a new prefect. He had held the office for only a couple of weeks. The day's court session had just opened when his attendants marched in a woman who was complaining of injustices. Reaching the steps of his dais, Mrs Liu burst out into loud weeping. Then, stilling her wails, she poured out the whole history of the Robber King's deeds.

'He killed my husband, Liu Junjian,' she said, 'but the judge refused to investigate with any thoroughness, and conducted the case with muddled indifference, as the whim took him. All he was concerned with was to have the case over and done with, and he handed Second Sister and Cui Ning over to the executioners, even though they hadn't the faintest idea what it was all about. Then this man murdered old Wang, too, and forced me to become his wife and live with him. But there's justice in heaven and now heaven has made everything as clear as daylight. Out of his own mouth he's confessed to every

one of the things he did. I beg you, my lord, to "hold high th
shining mirror of your judicial wisdom" and wipe away a
clean as snow the wrongs that have been done.' As she finishe
speaking, she once more burst into tears.

Greatly moved by her presentation of the facts, the prefec
at once sent men to arrest the Robber King. The villain wa
interrogated under beating and torture, and produced a con
fession which tallied word for word with Mrs Liu's statement
He was immediately condemned to death, and a memoria
on the matter was submitted to the Emperor. When the sixty
day period had expired, an imperial decree was sent back
which ran as follows:

The Robber King Peace-keeper of the Mountain has been
tried and found guilty of robbery, murder, and of implicating
the innocent and permitting their killing through the
processes of the law, thereby bringing about the deaths of
three people who had committed no crime deserving of
death, and is sentenced to be executed to a further degree of
severity than normally stipulated, there to be absolutely no
delay in the carrying out of this sentence. The original judge
of the case pronounced verdict in careless disregard of the
circumstantial evidence of the case, and is relieved of official
rank and reduced to the status of a commoner. Cui Ning
and Second Sister died in the most pitiable and unjust
circumstances. The relevant authorities are to visit their
homes and families, and assess and apportion due com-
passionate relief and succour. Since Mrs Liu, née Wang,
was subjected to coercion and obliged to form a marital
alliance with the aforesaid violent brigand, and further in
view of the fact that she was able by her efforts to rectify
the wrong done to her husband and others, while half of
the criminal's property and wealth is to be confiscated by the
Government, the other half shall be assigned to her, to
provide for her maintenance till the end of her days.

Mrs Liu went to the execution ground to witness the
despatch of the Robber King, and took his head away as a
sacrificial offering to her dead husband and to Second Sister
and Cui Ning. After weeping long and bitterly, she surrendered

ll the half of the robber's wealth that she had been allotted to
Buddhist nunnery as alms, while she herself chanted the
utras and prayed to Buddha all day long, and held sacrificial
equiems for the departed souls, completing the human span
f one hundred years of life before passing away. There is a
oem that applies to this story:

> Good and evil both alike
> may invite their own ruination,
> A word of jest may well suffice
> to brew annihilation.
> Let me breathe a word of advice in your ear:
> in all you say be earnest and sincere,
> for the lips and tongue are often doom's
> foundation.

Two Magistrates Vie to Marry an Orphaned Girl

Your dwelling in this mortal world
must stand in some well-omened spot,
And karma and heaven's hidden works
must aid you in your lot.
But men no longer fathom the will
of the Blue Empyrean above,
And vainly toil with body and soul
and rack their brains and moil and plot.

In recent times in the prefectural borough of Quzhou in
Chekiang province there lived a man named Wang Feng, who
had an elder brother named Wang Chun. Each of the brothers
had a daughter, Wang Chun's being called Jewel Beauty and
Wang Feng's Jewel Truth. Jewel Beauty was engaged to
Pan Hua, son of Millionaire Pan, a wealthy man of the region.
Jewel Truth was engaged to Xiao Ya, son of Assistant Sub-
Prefect Xiao, also from the same region. They had both been
betrothed in early childhood.

When Jewel Beauty was only nine years old, her mother
died and shortly afterwards her father, too, passed away. As
Wang Chun was on the point of death, he entrusted his
daughter to his younger brother. 'I have no heir,' he enjoined
him, 'only this daughter of mine. You can regard her as my
heiress, and when she grows up make sure to marry her off
just as arranged to the Pan family. The dowry clothes and
jewellery that my wife left behind you can make over to her

鄭
元
方

and then there is the farmland which the Pans once gave her
as the betrothal gift. You can hand her that to provide for her
pin-money. Don't forget what I've said now, will you!'

When the funeral and burial were over, Wang Feng took
his niece back to his home, and there she became the companion of his own daughter, Jewel Truth.

Suddenly one New Year's morning, Pan Hua and Xiao Ya
both turned up together, quite unexpectedly and without any
prior arrangement, at Wang Feng's home in order to pay their
New Year respects. Now Pan Hua had a delicate complexion
and rich red lips, like those of a beautiful woman, and everybody called him 'Jade Angel-boy'. Xiao Ya, on the other hand,
had a face covered in pockmarks, sunken eyes, and crooked
peg-like teeth, and was the spitting image of a yaksha.* Thus
one of them was handsome and the other was ugly, and the
more you compared the two of them the more you would feel
that the good-looking one was an exquisite jewel of ever-
increasingly scintillating sparkle and that the hideous-looking
one was an ever more colourless lump of mud. In addition to
this, Pan Hua would wear dazzlingly gorgeous clothes, with a
mind to flaunting his wealth, and constantly changed his
attire. Xiao Ya, by contrast, was a stolid, down-to-earth type,
and attached no importance to what he wore. 'Buddhas are
togged in gold, but mortals are togged in togs', goes the
common saying. But people in this world show much shallower
perception than that, and only judge things by the look of the
skin, not by the look of the bones. All the Wang family, men
and women, young and old alike, without exception, admired
young Master Pan's glossy looks as if he were Pan An, the
fabulously handsome youth of old, putting in an appearance
once more. And secretly they all 'trotted their lips and win-
nowed their mouths', tearing strips off the sky-flying yaksha
fiend for his ugliness. Even Wang Feng himself could not bear
the sight of him, and felt inwardly most disturbed.

Very shortly after Xiao Ya's New Year visit, Assistant Sub-
Prefect Xiao died in office, away in another region. Xiao Ya
rushed to the place of decease and escorted the coffin back
home. Although his family had for generation after generation

*A flying demon in Buddhist mythology.

115

held government posts, they had always been incorruptibl
and so had failed to accumulate any savings to bequeath t
him. After the Assistant Sub-Prefect's death, Xiao Ya's mone
daily diminished, while the fortune of Millionaire Pan, wh
was a get-rich-quick parvenu, went each day from strength t
strength.

Wang Feng suddenly conceived a decidedly unprinciple
notion. 'The Xiaos are very poor,' he thought, 'and m
prospective son-in-law is an ugly fellow, whereas not only ar
the Pans rolling in wealth but their young man is a personabl
chap. Why not discreetly swap Jewel Beauty and Jewel Trut
round? Who would know? And that way I would avoi
marrying my own dear daughter off into the hardships of ;
pauper's home.'

Having hit upon this scheme, just before the weddings
Wang Feng palmed off Jewel Truth as his niece and marrie
her to Pan, handing her all the valuables and farmland and s
forth which his elder brother had left in his will. Jewel Beaut
he instead made out to be his own daughter, and gave her i
wedlock to be the mate of the sky-flying yaksha, providing he
on his own account with some very meagre items for he
trousseau. Entirely at the mercy of her uncle's whims, the mos
Jewel Beauty could do was burn with inner indignation, fo
she did not dare express her anger in words.

Surprisingly, though, things turned out contrary to expectations after the weddings. Pan Hua, banking on his wealth
neglected to study the ancient classics or to pursue any trad
or profession, and instead devoted all his energies to whoring
and gambling. His father, seeing his repeated admonition
ignored, died of chagrin and vexation. Pan Hua became al
the more unscrupulous, and throwing caution to the wind
went around day in day out with rogues and shiftless nobodies
eating and drinking and dallying in idle sport. Within less than
ten years he had completely emptied the family purse of it
millions and was left without an inch of land. His father-in-law
frequently gave him sums of money, but it was like trying to
cool glowing charcoal by sprinkling snow on it, of no earthl
use whatsoever, it all melted away in no time. In the end
reduced to starvation, Pan was preparing behind his father-in-
law's back to induce his wife to seek her board and lodging a

contract-bound bond-slave in someone else's household. Getting wind of this, Wang Feng took his daughter Jewel Truth back into his home to be looked after there for the rest of her life and would not allow his son-in-law to call at the house. Pan Hua drifted off to other parts and I have no idea what became of him.

Xiao Ya, on the other hand, stuck at his books and achieved fame and success in his very first attempt at the imperial examinations. He rose to ministerial rank, while Jewel Beauty was awarded the title of Dame of the Supreme Order. There is a poem which is pertinent to these happenings:

> Present wealth and poverty are not fixed for ever
>   more,
> who knows in days to come if we shall flop or fly?
> Your guile, sir, may tip you topsy-turvy,
> for the gods look on and judge us with
>   all-impartial eye.

Dear reader, you wonder why I have mentioned this story of how Wang Feng married off his daughter? I do so solely because people in this world pay attention only to what is right in front of their noses and spare no thought for times to come. They are only concerned to do down others and profit themselves, quite unaware that man may plot a hundred schemes, but heaven's scheme remains a constant single one. You may in your mind devise some slippery, cunning path for yourself, but heaven may well not follow you along it. The best course still is to make a daily habit of doing good.

Today let us tell a tale exactly the opposite of the Wang Feng one, which is called *Two Magistrates Vie to Marry an Orphaned Girl*. This tale is set in the period of the Five Dynasties (907–60), the five being the Liang, Tang, Jin, Han and Zhou. During that time, when Guo Wei, the Grand Progenitor of the Zhou dynasty, was on the throne, he changed his reign-period title to Extended Submission, but although he held the highest position in the line of orthodox legitimacy of succession he did not manage to achieve command over a unified China. There were in fact several rulers who carved out realms for themselves in various regions all over the country, constituting in all a total of Five States and Three Commanderies. The Five States were—Guo Wei's Zhou, Liu Sheng's Southern Han, Liu Min' Northern Han, Li Pian's Southern Tang, and Meng Zhixiang' Shu; the Three Commanderies—Qian Liu's Wu-Yue, Zho' Xingfeng's Hunan, and Gao Jichang's Jingnan.

Our present concern is only with the state under the rule o the Southern Tang dynasty of the Li clan, and with the regio of Jiangzhou over which that dynasty held sway. And withi that region we are concerned with Dehua county in Jiangzhou The magistrate of Dehua county was a certain Shi Bi, who ha originally come from Linchuan county in Fuzhou and ha later taken up residence in Jiankang. Some time after h passed the age of forty, his wife died. He had no son, only hi seven-year-old daughter, Moon Perfume, who with her maid companion accompanied him when he went to his place o office. He was an honest, conscientious official, who took n more than 'a mouthful of water to drink' from Dehua county In addition he was a most astute and equitable judge, settling litigations with great perspicacity, righting grievances, an speeding the processes of justice. And sure enough it proved true that 'When administration is plain and simple and pena action pure and principled, the people will be contented and crime will cease'. When his duties permitted him some leisure, he would take Moon Perfume on his knee and teach her to read. At other times he would tell the maid-companion to play chess, *cuju*-football and a hundred other kinds of games with her, while he himself looked on and gave instructions. As she was a motherless daughter, he cherished her with the tenderest love.

One day the maid and Moon Perfume were playing a game of *cuju*, kicking a tiny ball in the courtyard, when the maid kicked the ball too hard, so that it struck the ground and rose and rolled away from them, with great bounds and bounces, into a hole in the ground. The hole was two to three feet deep, being intended for laying a vat to hold water. The maid's arms were too short for her to reach far enough to catch hold of the ball, and she was just about to jump down into the pit to pick it up that way when Shi Bi stopped her.

'Just a minute,' he said, then turning to his daughter he asked: 'Have you any idea how we could make the ball come out of its own accord?'

Moon Perfume thought for a moment. 'I know', she said, and
at once told the maid to go and fetch a bucket of water, which
he then tipped into the hole. The ball floated on the surface of
he water. They tipped in another bucketful, the hole filled up
with water, and the ball came out of the hole on top of the water.
t had been Shi Bi's intention to test his daughter's intelligence,
and seeing how unusually clever she had been in using the water
o get the ball out, he was beside himself with delight.

Enough of this idle chatter. The magistrate had been in
office for less than three years, when quite out of the blue 'the
tar-god protecting officials did not come out to shine, and
disaster made an unwelcome visitation'. Suddenly one night
he official granary caught fire, and over a thousand piculs of
government grain were destroyed by the flames before desperate
emergency measures to try and save it could even be applied.
At that time rice was very expensive, one picul costing one
housand five hundred copper coins, and in those days of
disorder and national disunity, grain for military supplies was
at a high premium. Under the legal code of the Southern
Tang, if any official in charge wasted or destroyed so much as
hree hundred piculs he was to be summarily executed. However, since Shi Bi was an honest administrator, and the loss
had not been occasioned by an official's corrupt quest for
private gain but rather by a fire that had arisen through
natural causes, his superior submitted memorials in his defence,
explaining the mitigating circumstances and vouching for his
ntegrity. But the wrath of the Tang monarch was still not
entirely appeased, and he dismissed the magistrate from office
and demanded that he pay compensation. The fine Shi Bi was
required to pay was assessed at a total of over one thousand
five hundred taels. He realised all his family property, but that
did not provide half the amount. Placed under insidious
restraint and pressure by the prefect of his region, Shi Bi was
unable to bear the persecutions, became ill with depression,
and died within a few days. The daughter and maid-companion
whom he left behind had to be consigned for sale to the Tooth
Woman—the Official Broker and Go-between, the price
obtained for them to be paid to the government as part of the
compensation money. These further sufferings endured by
members of that household were

Adding rain night after night
to the curse of a leaky roof,
Encountering head-wind buffets
when the boat was already late.

In the same county there was a commoner by the name of
Jia Chang, who had in the past been the victim of slander
which had led to his being put on trial for a murder he had
never committed and thrown into jail under sentence of death.
Fortunately for him Magistrate Shi had acceded to the magis-
tracy and by his further investigations of the case had discovered
the injustice of the verdict and released him. Jia Chang
remained perpetually grateful to him for having preserved him
and his family, but had found no way of repaying him. Of late
Jia had been away from home on a business trip, and he had
only very recently returned when Magistrate Shi died. He at
once went round to the Shis' to express his condolences,
weeping and lamenting over the corpse. He provided the
funeral, himself contributing all the burial clothes and the
coffin. His whole family went into mourning and he it was who
bought some land for a burial ground.

Jia Chang also learned that the Shis still owed a great deal
of money to the government for the grain. He would have
liked to make up the required amount, but he feared that the
wrong conclusions might be drawn and he himself become
adversely involved, so did not dare make a move that might
only be inviting trouble. Hearing a report that the young lady
and her maid-companion and been sent to the Tooth Woman
to be sold on behalf of the government, he rushed off with
some silver to Li the Tooth Woman's house and asked her
what was the 'body-price' for each of them. Li the Tooth
Woman took out an official chit upon which the prices were
written in vermilion ink and had a look at it. The maid was
fifteen years old and she was assessed at only thirty taels.
Moon Perfume was nine years old, but she was assessed at
fifty taels. Now why the difference?—Although Moon Perfume
was so young, she was a lovely, dainty girl, whereas the maid-
companion was only a female servant accustomed to rough
work. Hence the inequality of the assessment prices. Dispensing
with any niggling meanness and haggling over the prices, Jia

hang produced the purse of silver which he had on him, aid out the full sum of eighty taels in pure silver and handed to the brokeress, adding an extra tip of five taels for her. hen without more ado he led the two girls back home with im. Li the Tooth Woman handed in the money received for ae two of them to the government treasury, the local chief ported to the authorities that all of the magistrate's house-old goods and chattels had been sold, and there was nothing ft for the superior official concerned to do but to transfer the ompensation to another item heading. But that does not oncern our story.

Since her father's death, Moon Perfume had done nothing ut weep and cry ceaselessly. Now, not recognising who Jia Chang was, but knowing that she had been bought and was eing led off to his home by him, she felt sure that she was oing to sink into vile and lowly circumstances. All the way o his house she wept bitterly.

'Miss,' the maid warned her, 'you are going to live in omeone else's household now, so you can't behave as you did vhen you were with your father. If you keep on crying like hat, you'll get a beating and scolding, sure as can be.'

This advice only made Moon Perfume all the more heart-broken.

Contrary to their expectations, however, Jia Chang was the very soul of kindness and nobility. He led them into his house and introduced them to his wife. 'This is the young lady of my benefactor, Lord Shi,' he told her, 'and that is the maid who waits on the young lady. In the past, if it had not been for my benefactor, I would have died in fetters and chains. So now we are to look upon the young lady as we would the man who did so much for me. Tidy up another lady's apartment and let the two of them live there. Serve them with the best tea and the best food and whatever you do never treat them with the slightest disrespect. If in the future any of her relatives come looking for her and I am able to give her back to her own kith and kin, then I shall have repaid a little of my debt of gratitude. If not, when she grows up we'll find a suitable match for her here in this county and marry her off, so that my saviour's tomb will after all have his own flesh and blood to watch over it. The maid is to carry on waiting upon the young lady,

keeping her company and doing a little needlework and so on
but there is no call for her to do any outside errands.'

Moon Perfume had always been quick on the uptake, and as
she heard Jia Chang give these instructions to his wife she
hastened over and curtsied to him with the feminine greeting
'Ten thousand happinesses to you!' 'I was bought,' she said,
'and it would have been quite normal for me to become your
slave and maidservant. Treating me with such favours, kind
sir, you are blessing me with a new lease of life. I beg you to
accept my bows and take me as your foster daughter.' So
saying, she quickly knelt down.

Very flustered by this honour, Jia Chang hurriedly knelt on
the ground also and instructed his wife to raise the young lady
to her feet. 'I am a commoner, one of His Late Excellency's
flock, and this mere "ant's-life" of mine was restored to me
by His Excellency's hands. I wouldn't for a moment even think
to treat this maidservant with any disrespect, let alone you,
young mistress! How could I dare to be so reckless as to take
upon myself honours so much above my station? As long as
you are for the time being obliged to debase yourself by
dwelling in my humble home, I must treat you as my guest.
My wife and I will consider that fortune has smiled upon us if
you no more than find no cause to rebuke us for any shortcomings of due deference towards you, young mistress.'

Moon Perfume made repeated bows to convey her gratitude.
Jia Chang further directed the members of his household,
male and female alike, that they were all to address her as
'Mistress Shi'. She for her part called Jia Chang and his wife
'Mr Jia' and 'Mrs Jia'. But enough of that.

Jia Chang's wife was in fact not basically a very noble or
intelligent woman. At first, in view of Moon Perfume's pretti-
ness and brightness, and since she herself had neither son nor
daughter, she conceived the desire to adopt her as her own
daughter and was secretly filled with delight, but when she
heard that she was to treat her as a respected guest her
immediate reaction was one of utter impatience. She could not,
however, ignore the kindness Magistrate Shi had done them,
so she had no choice but to follow her husband's directives and,
in spite of herself, make a show of respect. Later, when Jia
Chang was trading in other parts, whenever he acquired any

fine silks or satins he would hasten first to send the pick of them to Miss Shi for her to make into clothes for herself. When he returned home, the first thing he would do would be to make solicitous enquiries as to whether Miss Shi was well or not. His wife gradually started to grumble more and more to herself about this state of affairs, and as time wore on she showed her claws.

As long as Jia Chang was at home, she managed to fulfil her obligations as far as their daily meals were concerned and would hypocritically mutter a few polite nothings. But as soon as his back was turned, it was quite another story with the meals. And she would for ever be sending the maid-companion out on odd jobs and errands, allowing her not a moment's leisure, and would every day stipulate a certain amount of needlework for Mistress Shi to complete and hand back to her. If Miss Shi happened to be slow in doing it, she would curse her roundly, using the vilest language. Ah, yes:

> Humans have never a thousand days free of
> trouble,
> As flowers never stay more than a hundred days
> red.

Finding the abusive treatment unbearable, the maid confided in her young mistress, and wanted to tell Mr Jia about it when he came home. Moon Perfume, however, adamantly refused to allow this. 'That day when he spent his own money to buy us,' she explained, 'I never for a moment dared hope he might accord us privileged treatment. I know Mrs Jia isn't entirely fair towards us, but that's no fault of his. If you complain to him about her, you will make it seem as if all Mr Jia's kindnesses have meant nothing. You and I are unlucky in life, and the best thing we can do is be patient and make the best of things.'

Suddenly one day Mr Jia returned home from his travels and happened to bump into the maid, who was at that moment fetching some water. He noticed that her face was much more weatherbeaten and haggard than it used to be. 'Young hand-maid,' he said, 'I told you only to wait upon the young lady. Who told you to fetch water? Put the water-bucket down now,

and tell someone else to carry it.' The maid put the bucke
down and overcome by miserable thoughts let fall a few tea
drops. As Mr Jia tried to ask her what it was all about, sh
wiped her tears away with her hand and rushed indoors. H
felt very mystified and suspicious. 'There's nothing the matte
with Mistress Shi and her maid, is there?' he asked his wife o
seeing her. 'No,' was her reply. He had only just returne
home and had many things to attend to, so he put the matte
on one side.

A few days later, some business cropped up with someon
nearby. On his return home, not seeing his wife in her part o
the house, he went himself to the kitchen to look for her for
chat, and ran straight into the maid-companion, who wa
coming up from the kitchen. She had no tray, but was holdin
a big bowl of rice in her left hand, and an empty bowl in he
right hand, with a plate of pickled cabbage leaves on top of it
Mr Jia then took it into his head to dodge out of sight and watcl
what happened next, and saw the maid walk into Mistres
Shi's room. It was beyond his comprehension who was to ea
the food, since it included not the slightest trace of meat o
other substantial food. So instead of going on into the kitchen
he now tiptoed up to the room and peeped through the cracl
in the door. There he saw Mistress Shi using the plateful o
pickled cabbage to help the rice down. Absolutely furious, h
stalked off and embarked upon a quarrel with his wife.

'Oh yes,' said his wife,' we have plenty of meat and stuff
and it's not that I begrudge her it. But if that wench doesn'
come and carry it herself, do you mean to say you expect m
to carry it into their room?'

'I told you in the first place,' said Mr Jia, 'that the Shis
maid was only to wait upon her mistress in her room and ac
as her companion. We have plenty of people in our kitchen to
run around doing jobs, so why should she have to come out o
the room to fetch and carry! The other day when I saw tha
maid out in the street fetching water with tears in her eyes, I
already suspected she must be suffering ill-treatment in the
house. But because I was busy with other things at the time I
never went into the matter. Now it's come to light just how
unkind and ungrateful you have been! You have even been
treating Mistress Shi with a lack of grace. Here we are with a

house chock-full of meat and good food in store, and yet you have to go and give her plain white rice to eat. What do you mean by it? If you behave like that even when I'm here at home, it's obvious that when I'm away you can't even be giving them enough rice to fill themselves. When I came home this time, I noticed how much more worn and thin they've become.'

'That wench comes from another household,' said his wife. 'What call is there for you to be so fond of her? Are you feeding her up so delicate and chubby so that you can take her as your little concubine?'

'Codswallop!' roared Mr Jia. 'What do you think you're saying! I'm not going to bandy words with the likes of you, a blockhead without the slightest understanding of things. I shall instruct the steward every day to buy a separate lot of meat and food to supply the two of them. No need for you to tot it up in your household accounts, and it'll save you from having the food snatched out of your own mouth! That'll delight you, surely!'

His wife did feel she had been a little in the wrong, so she just muttered a few vague words, hummed and hawed a bit, then said no more. From then on Mr Jia directed the steward to apportion the meat and food in two separate lots, while the kitchen-maids were to make arrangements to deliver the food separately. After that for a while things went very smoothly. Yes, you know:

> If only folks would always feel
> as folks when folks first meet,
> The world and folks would then be spared
> the tyranny of hate.

Preoccupied with the business of looking after and bringing up Mistress Shi, Jia Chang avoided trading elsewhere for over a year. His wife for her part resolved to turn over a new leaf, assigning the past to the oblivion of silence.

When Moon Perfume had been living in Mr Jia's house for five years and was approaching maturity, Jia Chang's intention was discreetly to search out a good match for her and marry her off. Then at last he would be able to set his mind at rest and leave home for his business trips without worry. All this constituted an inner burden for Mr Jia, and it was upon him that the onus lay of having to try and arrange matters clandestinely. He knew that his wife was not very well-intentioned, so there was no point in discussing things with her. If luck proved to be on his side, he would fork out some dowry, marry her off, and have everything nicely tied up. Little did he anticipate how impossible it would be to find a suitable partner for the young lady.

There were intrinsic reasons for the difficulties. Mr Jia felt that it would be an insult to Magistrate Shi to lower his sights to a union with anyone of obscure or lowly social status. On the other hand, anyone with any sort of reputation or standing was not likely to consent to marry a girl who had been fostered in a commoner's home. Such were the obstacles to any marriage. Realising that he was not going to be able to arrange a marriage, and since his wife was now behaving more amenably and permanent rules had been established for the supply of provisions in his household, and since he could no longer bring himself to neglect his livelihood, Mr Jia felt obliged to set off once more to trade in other regions.

A few days before he set off, he drummed it into his wife a dozen or more times that she should treat Mistress Shi and her maid with every kindness and consideration. He also respectfully asked Mistress Shi to come out of her room for a talk and repeatedly comforted her with his assurances, and even gave much sympathetic advice to the maid so as to dispel any anxieties she might entertain. Then he had another word with his wife.

'In inherent moral worth,' he said, 'she's several hundred times your superior. So on no account be rude to her. If you fail to do as I say, when I come home again I shall cease to regard you as my wife and I'll divorce you.'

Then he called for the steward and kitchen-maids and gave them each their complete instructions before finally setting out. Yes, indeed:

> As he parted, he consigned her
> to their hands with fervent prayer,
> For he himself had in days gone by
> been blessed by another's bounteous care.

Now all this time, while her lord and master had been lavishing his attentions upon Mistress Shi and her maid, Jia Chang's wife had been feeling extremely fed-up with the situation, but since she could do nothing else, she had been compelled to fall in with his wishes. Brimming over with suppressed indignation, she now, a few days after her good husband had departed the house, began to wield her powers as matron of the household. Looking for trouble, she seized on the pretext of an insignificant little misdemeanour, tardiness in serving up the tea, to quarrel with a kitchen-maid, by way of a rehearsal.

'You slut!' she swore, and gave her a whole series of slaps on the face, 'I paid for you with money out of my own hand, so how can you be so puffed up with yourself, treating me like that! Think you can bank on some little mistress's authority to neglect your duties for me? When the head of the family was home, I let you have things easy. But now he has gone away, we are going to have to return to my way of doing things! And anyway, apart from myself, who stands in need of your services? If they want food, let them carry it themselves. No need for you lot to scurry round after them and neglect the tasks I set you!'

After this dressing-down, she followed up the excitement by calling for the steward and directing him in future simply to enter the sum for the price of the separate portion of meat and foodstuffs, but not actually to buy it any more. The steward did not dare disobey her. Luckily, Moon Perfume was able to put up with the poor, insipid food, and took no notice whatsoever of these measures.

A little more time went by, then one day Moon Perfume's maid went to fetch her some water to wash her face in, was rather slow in doing so, and discovered that the water had already gone cool. She groaned some words that she should not have uttered and Mrs Jia called her over specially to vent her ill-temper on her.

'This water is not meant for you. Someone else has heated it up nice and hot and then you turn up and use some of it just as it takes your fancy. When you were in the Tooth Woman's home, who used to heat up the hot water for you to wash your faces in then?'

Unable to hold her tongue any longer, the maid gave her a

sharp retort: 'Who needs anyone else to fetch water and heat it up! I've done my share of carrying water in the past, as well you know, and these two hands of mine are quite capable of making a fire! Next time I'll fetch the water myself and heat it up myself, so as not to exhaust the strength of my elder sisters in the kitchen.'

These words reminded the woman of the previous incident when the maid had carried water. 'You little bitch,' she swore at her.

'That time you fetched a few buckets of water you showed all your airs and graces, snivelling to the master about it so that I got into trouble and came in for every kind of angry abuse under the sun. Well, now I'm going to get my own back on you. Since you say you know how to carry water and light fires, I'm giving you the responsibility for doing both of those things. From now on, the fetching of the water to be used each day is to be done by you and all the fire-lighting is to be done by you. And if you go wild with the firewood, I'll give you what for into the bargain. Just you wait till your dear master of the house comes back, then you'll have something to weep and wail and snivel and sob to him about. And if you think he'll send me packing, you've got another surprise in store for you!'

From her room, Moon Perfume heard Mrs Jia pouring out the vials of her wrath upon her maid and hurried onto the scene. She greeted her with a courteous 'Ten thousand blessings on you' and a curtsy, made apologies, freely confessing to many errors, and pleaded with her not to take offence.

'It's really all my fault,' said the maid. 'All I can do is beg you, for my young mistress's sake, not to chastise me.'

The woman only became all the more infuriated. 'What "young mistress"! A "young mistress" wouldn't have come into our household! I'm just an ordinary person and it's quite beyond me to understand what rank and titles you have, *young mistress*, that entitle you to turn up here just like that and try and play the lady with me! Although I may be pretty featherweight as far as good breeding is concerned, I don't let other people throw their weight around with me. Let's get things straight, here and now. Even if you were a young lady, it's no secret that you were bought, and we had to shell out a ot of money for you. And you can't get round the fact that I am the housewife and the mistress of this household. It's not you who's called "Mrs Jia".'

Realising that they were not going to see eye to eye in their conversation, Moon Perfume tearfully withdrew to her room. Mrs Jia directed the people in the kitchen that they were no longer permitted to refer to 'Young Mistress Shi' but were to call her by her personal name, 'Moon Perfume'. She further instructed the maid that she was to devote all her energies to fetching water and tending the fires in the kitchen and was not to enter Moon Perfume's room. If Moon Perfume wanted food to eat, they were to wait until she came and fetched it from the kitchen herself. That night she also told a servant-girl to move the maid-companion's bed-quilt into her, Mrs Jia's, room. Moon Perfume sat up deep into the night, and when her maid still did not appear in her room she just had to shut the door and go off to sleep by herself. A few days later the woman called Moon Perfume out of her room and told a female domestic to lock the door behind her. Deprived of her room, Moon Perfume just had to wander round outside. That night she slept in the same bed as her maid. Whenever she started to go to sleep, Mrs Jia would tell her to bring this and fetch that, putting her into service as her slave. Under low eaves, how dare one refuse to lower one's head! Left with no other choice, Moon Perfume just had to make herself small and submissive. Seeing that Moon Perfume had knuckled under, the woman was inwardly delighted and triumphantly marched off without delay to unlock the young lady's room and move every single thing out of it. Everything her husband had previously sent in the way of fine silks and satins, whether or not they had been made up into dresses, she transferred into her own wicker clothes-basket, and she even confiscated the bed-quilt and did not return it. Within herself Moon Perfume cried out in protest, but she did not dare utter a sound aloud.

Suddenly one day a letter arrived from Mr Jia, with which he also sent a lot of things for Young Mistress Shi. 'Look after her well,' he bade his wife in the letter. 'I shall be back soon.'

The woman appropriated the gifts. 'Hm,' she thought, 'I have lowered that Miss Shi and the other wench, her maid, a good peg or two and no mistaking. When my old man gets back, he'll be bound to have a dust-up with me about it. Huh, am I so scared of him that I can't manage to butter him up with a few words and get on the right side of him again? The old lecher, keeping those two filly whores like that! No telling how it will end up! Just before he went off he told me that if I didn't stick to what he said he would divorce me. That shows he's got some depraved scheme on his mind. That Moon Perfume has got a pretty face and she's already a grown woman. Supposing he takes it into his head to hang onto her? Quite likely. And when that happens, it'll be too late for me to argue the toss and start having fits of jealousy. If folks won't worry a long way ahead, you can bet they'll run into trouble just round the corner. The first rule is never start something you shouldn't and the second rule is never pack it in once you've started. So what I must do is sell those two, straight-away. When the old lecher gets back, I'll just have to face the music for one session. We'll have it out in one almighty row, and that will be that. Anyway, what's to stop him buying them back again? A good plan. A good plan.'

Yes, you see:

> With narrow understandings there is no
>   magnanimity,
> With warped hearts come treacherous
>   intrigues.

There and then the woman issued orders to her steward: 'Call Zhang the Tooth Woman round here for me. I have something to say to her.'

In a very short time the steward led in Zhang the Tooth Woman. Mrs Jia introduced Moon Perfume and the latter's maid to her, but then sent them out of the way.

'Six years ago,' she confided to Zhang the Tooth Woman, 'I bought those two wenches. But now the elder one is too old, and the younger one is too delicate and spoiled to do any work, so I want to sell both of them. Find me a customer for them as soon as you can.'

Now originally, the first time they had been sold, it had been Li the Tooth Woman who had transacted the business. She had died in the meanwhile, and Mother Zhang had been

lected from among both official and private go-betweens to be
the Official Broker.

'As it happens,' she said, 'I have the very customer for the
younger one. But I'm not sure if you will agree.'

'Now why should I refuse?' asked Mrs Jia.

'Well,' said Mother Zhang, 'It's the magistrate of this
county. He has a double-barrelled surname, Zhongli, his
personal name being Yi, and he comes from Shouchun. He has
a daughter—his very own, mark you, not adopted—a young
lady by now, who is engaged to the eldest young gentleman of
Magistrate Gao, Governor of De'an County. The magistrate
here, Mr Zhongli, has sent off the wedding gifts, and any day
now they will be coming to collect the bride. Our magistrate
has everything all prepared for the trousseau, but the one thing
he lacks is a maid to accompany the bride to her new home.
Yesterday His Worship summoned me before him and entrusted me with the task of finding one, but I just haven't
managed to find one anywhere. This young lady you have in
your house is precisely the person we're after. But as it's for
people in another part of the country, I wonder if you may not
be unwilling to part with her.'

'The very thing,' thought Mrs Jia. 'Just what I wanted to
find, a customer who lives a long way away. And here he is,
turned up just right! What's more, if it's a magistrate who
takes her, I bet my husband won't dare utter the tiniest squeak
of protest when he gets back!'

'Going as a bride's maid into a magistrate's home will be
ten times better for her than being stuck here with me in my
house, so why should I be reluctant to let her go?' she said.
'As long as I don't lose anything on the price we originally
paid for her, that'll be fine.'

'How much was the original price?' asked Mother Zhang.

'She was nine years old or so,' said Mrs Jia, 'and we bought
her for fifty taels. But now, what with the money we've spent
on her food and upkeep, that'll mean an extra sum on top of it.'

'We can't include the food she has eaten in the bill,' said
Mother Zhang, 'but I myself will stand guarantor for your
fifty taels.'

'And what about that old serving maid?' said Mrs Jia. 'It
would be nice if you could find someone for her, too. The two

131

of them came here together, so if I've got rid of the one I can'
very well keep the other any longer. And there again, she'
over twenty years old, so she'll be wanting a husband too, s
what's the point of hanging onto her!'

'How much are you asking for that one?' asked Mothe
Zhang.

'Well, I got her in the first place for thirty taels of silver.'

'Hm,' mused the Tooth Woman, 'she's coarse goods. No
worth that much. If you'll reduce it by half, I myself, as i
happens, have a nephew, my sister's lad, living with me. He'
thirty now. I promised him some while ago that I would fin
him a wife, but you know how it is, we're not all that well off
so we've kept on waiting and waiting. But him and her woul
make a perfect couple.'

'Well, seeing as how it's your own nephew,' said Mrs Jia
'I'll reduce the price five taels, just for you.'

'Ah,' said Mother Zhang, 'in consideration of the match
making gifts the young woman would normally have to giv
me, couldn't you lower it ten taels for me?'

'Oh well, all right. It's of no great matter,' said Mrs Jia.
'Just you go ahead with all the arrangements on your side.'

'Right, I'll be off this minute to report to His Worship the
Magistrate,' said Mother Zhang. 'If we reach an understanding, I'll hand you the money with one hand and hold out
the other for the goods.'

'Will you get back here by this evening?' asked Mrs Jia.

'No,' said Mother Zhang, 'I'll have to talk things over with
my nephew this evening as well, so I won't be able to make it.
I'll come back with the news tomorrow. The odds are that I'll
pull off both deals.' So saying, she took her leave.

Turning now to the magistrate, Zhongli Yi . . . He had been
holding the post for one year and three months. The magistrate
before him, a Mr Ma, had been the one who had filled the
vacancy left by Magistrate Shi. After Mr Ma had left, promoted to another post, Zhongli Yi had taken over the magis-
tracy in his place. Magistrate Zhongli and Magistrate Gao of
De'an came originally from the same village. Magistrate Gao
had two sons, the eldest aged seventeen called Gao Deng, and

he younger aged fifteen called Gao Sheng. It was Gao Deng who was to become Mr Zhongli's son-in-law. Mr Zhongli had n fact no sons of his own, only the daughter, whose intimate courtesy name was Spray of Cheer, who was just sixteen years old and for whose marriage they had selected the fifteenth day, he day of the full moon, of the tenth lunar month. It was now vithin the last few days of the ninth month and the happy day vas drawing very near. Mr Zhongli had set Mother Zhang the ask of finding a marriage maid in urgent haste, so as soon as he had found the solution to her problem over at the Jias', Mother Zhang reported back to him.

'If we can obtain the right person,' said the magistrate, then even fifty taels is by no means unreasonable. Come to the reasury tomorrow and draw the money for the price, and she can come over here tomorrow evening.'

'Just as you command, Your Worship,' said Mother Zhang. That evening when she returned home, she discussed matters with her nephew Second Zhao, telling him that she had found a suitable and reasonable match for him and wanted to see him married off and settled down. Second Zhao spent the whole night in ecstasies and the following morning togged himself up as smartly as he could in readiness for playing the role of bridegroom. First raking together the twenty taels body-money from her own home, Mother Zhang then proceeded to the county court to obtain a chit from His Worship the magistrate. She then went to the treasury and exchanged it for fifty taels of silver, and on arrival at the Jias' house handed over both sums to Mrs Jia, setting forth each item of the agreements one by one in great clarity. Mrs Jia pocketed both sums for herself. Very shortly two constables despatched from the county court turned up, with two chair-bearers bearing a little sedan-chair, and halted before the Jias' gate.

Now up to this moment Mrs Jia had mentioned nothing of all this to Moon Perfume and Moon Perfume knew nothing right up until the moment had come and she was sent out to get into the sedan-chair. She had no idea where they were taking her and she and her maid-companion shouted and screamed for all they were worth, wailing and crying at the tops of their voices. Not bothering to quibble over niceties, Mrs Jia with Mother Zhang's assistance pushed and shoved

her out through the main gate. Only then did she receive some
explanation, from Mother Zhang.

'Don't you cry any more, young lady,' she said. 'Your
mistress has sold you to the local county magistrate and you're
going to be the marriage maid of His Worship's own young
lady daughter. Oh, you're going to be ever so posh and well
off now, I can tell you! Anyway, you can't mess magistrates
about, especially when things have gone so far, so it's no good
your crying.'

So there was nothing left for Moon Perfume to do but dry
her tears, climb into the sedan-chair and allow herself to be
carried off.

On arrival, the chair was borne into the rear apartments. As
she met Mr Zhongli, Moon Perfume greeted him merely by
clasping her hands and saying 'Ten thousand blessings!'

'That's His Worship himself,' said Mother Zhang by her
side. 'You must greet him much more ceremoniously than
that!'

So Moon Perfume had no choice but to kowtow. As she
stood up again, she found tears were flowing all over her face.
Mother Zhang told her to wipe her eyes and led her into the
private residence, where she was introduced to the magistrate's lady wife and Miss Spray of Cheer. They inquired her
intimate personal name and she told them that it was Moon
Perfume.

'That's very nice, "moon" and "perfume" together,' said
the lady. 'There's no need to change it. She can start waiting
upon my daughter straight away.'

Mr Zhongli tipped Mother Zhang very liberally.

> Poor dainty fragrant maiden from exalted halls
> forced to serve a while as a boudoir skivvy.

By the time Mother Zhang left the magistrate's residence it
was already late in the afternoon, five o'clock or after. When
she arrived back at the Jias', she saw the maid-companion
there, eating her heart out for her mistress and weeping
bitterly down in the kitchen.

'I'm now going to marry you off to Mother Zhang's nephew,'
Mrs Jia announced to the girl. 'You'll be a happy couple, the

wo of you together, so you are much better off than Moon
Perfume. Don't be miserable any more!'

Mother Zhang also tried to comfort her.

Second Zhao had washed himself clean in the local baths
and dressed up in a smart shiny hat and a brand-new suit, and
bearing his wedding lantern himself he turned up to collect
the bride. Without any dithering or dallying, Mother Zhang
told the maid to say goodbye to Mrs Jia. As the maid had big,
natural, unbound feet, Mother Zhang was then able to take
her arm and walk her on foot back to her home, where Second
Zhao and the girl became man and wife.

But let's not ramble off on long-winded sidetracks. Turning
again to Moon Perfume, the day after she entered the residence
of His Worship Mr Zhongli, Madam Zhongli instructed the
newly arrived maid to sweep out the central apartments.
Moon Perfume obediently took the broom in her hand and
set off to perform the task. Zhongli Yi had finished his toilette
and prepared the business for the morning court session and
was striding out of the rear apartments when he noticed the
new maid standing in a stupefied daze with a broom in her
hand in the middle of the courtyard. Mystified, Mr Zhongli
quietly moved nearer and saw that there was a hole in the
earth of the courtyard, and that Moon Perfume was facing that
hole and shedding floods of tears into it. Unable to fathom this
mystery, Mr Zhongli stepped right into the central apartments,
called Moon Perfume over to him, and asked her what it was
all about. She just sobbed all the more pitifully and kept on
mumbling that she did not dare tell him. He had to question
her again and again before she would at last cease her tears
and answer him.

'When I was a little child,' she explained, 'my father used to
teach me to play the game of *cuju*-football here and I once let
the ball drop by mistake into this hole. My father asked me,
"Can you think of any plan to make the ball come out of the
hole of its own accord, without your needing to pick it out?"
I said I could and at once sent my maid-companion to fetch
some water and pour it into the hole. When the hole was full,
the ball floated out of the hole by itself. My father said I was a
clever girl and he was terribly pleased. That is years and years
ago now, but I still remember it, and seeing this place again

made me feel sad and somehow I just felt miserable an
sobbed. I beg you to have mercy and forgive me. Don't punis
or scold me, will you.'

'Who was your father? What was his name?' asked M
Zhongli in astonishment. 'What brought you here when yo
were a little child? You must tell me all the details.'

'My father was called Shi Bi,' said Moon Perfume. 'He wa
the magistrate here six years ago, but a fire that broke out c
its own accord burnt the granary and the imperial governmen
dismissed my father and commanded him to pay compensation
He fell ill with the misery of it and died. Then the authoritie
sold me and my maid into the household of Mr Jia who live
in this county. Mr Jia had once been unjustly imprisoned an
my father had saved his life, so in gratitude he treated me ver
well indeed and has looked after me all this time till now. Bu
he went somewhere else on a trading mission, and his wife
who couldn't bear me in the house, sold me again. That's ho
I came here. That's the whole truth. It is. I have told no lie
and kept nothing back.'

> Now, as a bosom's sorrow at last is spilled,
> surely even a man of iron or stone must weep.

When Mr Zhongli had heard all she had to say, he wa
indeed filled with fellow sympathy and sorrow, and grieved in
compassion for one of his brother officials: 'As Shi Bi was, I
myself am a magistrate. Sheer misfortune made him victim o
a disaster of Nature and his own dear daughter has been
reduced to a lowly condition indeed. If I hadn't heard of the
matter, that would have been the end of it. But heaven ha
brought his daughter into my house, and if I fail to afford her
succour in her need, where then is decency between colleagues
What sort of a fellow would Mr Shi now dwelling down at the
Nine Fountains of Afterlife then deem me!'

He at once asked his wife if she would come and have a
private word with him, and recounted all the details of Moon
Perfume's history to her.

'Since that's the case,' said his wife, 'as she is the daughter o
a magistrate, she must certainly not be treated as a maidservant! But just now our daughter's wedding date is drawing

136

very near, so what alternative arrangements are you going to make, my lord?'

'From now on,' said Mr Zhongli, 'Moon Perfume is not to do any menial jobs, and she and our daughter can address each other as sister. I know how to arrange matters. Don't worry.'

Immediately he wrote a letter and sent someone with it over to his prospective in-laws. On tearing open the letter and reading it, Magistrate Gao discovered that it was a request for the date of the wedding to be postponed a while. The letter said:

Although it is a father's and mother's natural heartfelt desire to see their children married, it is a noble gesture to sacrifice one's own ends in order to compass the welfare of others. Of late, bearing in mind that my little daughter is to leave her boudoir and be wed, I in preparation acquired a marriage maid for her, a certain Moon Perfume. Perceiving that this maid was of such dignified grace and such serene and meticulous deportment, I was astonished, and upon making careful enquiries discovered that she was the daughter of Magistrate Shi, the previous but one tenant of my present office. Mr Shi was a civil servant of impeccable principles, but as a result of a granary fire lost his post and indeed his own life. In addition, his daughter was sold by the Official Broker and later, by another sale, came into my own mean home. The daughter of a man who was the incumbent of the same post that I myself now hold is to me as my very own daughter. The young lady is already over fourteen, having thus attained the age when the hair is pinned and a girl is marriageable. Not only do I find myself unable to demean her to the role of marriage maid for which she was intended, but I cannot, moreover, even permit my own daughter to wed before she herself is married. I shall now in all haste select a husband for the young lady and use my daughter's meagre dowry for her wedding instead. The marriage with your noble scion must be slightly postponed and another propitious date selected.

With my sincere and humble best wishes, in the abject hope that you will understand and forgive me. I, Zhongli Yi, kowtow to you.

After reading this letter, Magistrate Gao thought to himsel
'Ah, so that's how things stand, eh! Well, here indeed is a cas
deserving of chivalrous magnanimity, and I can scarcely allo
Mr Zhongli to monopolise all the lustre of it!'

Immediately he wrote a reply:

Although the date for the splendid 'union of phoenixes' ha
indeed been appointed, how could I fail to share you
aspirations in this matter? Like you I lament for an
sympathise with the plight of one who pursued our ow
calling. Since you, venerable in-law, have adopted our lat
colleague's daughter as your own daughter, shall I, worthles
though I am, not wish to attune my heart to your desires
Perusing your epistle again and again, one is filled wit
melancholy and compassion. As the young lady is the issu
of an upright official and by no means disgraces the porta
pillars of her lineage, would you, dear in-law, consent t
bestow her upon my son and heir as his bride and wed he
to him on the date formerly stipulated for the wedding
chosing another, lofty match for your own dear daughter, s
that everything may be concluded to the advantage an
satisfaction of all and sundry? Long ago, in the time o
Confucius, Qu Boyu felt ashamed that a gentleman of virtu
should stand alone, and now I should like to participate ii
your exalted liberality. I, Gao Yuan, kowtow to you.

A messenger delivered the letter to Mr Zhongli.

'So,' he thought, as he read it, 'In-law Gao wishes to wec
his son and heir to the young orphan lady. Although one
cannot, to be sure, deny that it would be a high-minded move,
my daughter and his son have been engaged for a long, long
time, so how on earth can we change course now? I still think
it would be best if we waited until I have, at leisure, married
off Miss Shi, and then prepared another wedding trousseau for
the fulfilment of my own daughter's marriage.'

So without delay Mr Zhongli wrote another letter and sent
someone to deliver it to In-law Gao's. Mr Gao opened it and
read the following words:

Although to seek for one's son the hand of a helpless young

lady deprived of a family to support her is indeed a sublime sentiment, to alter a marriage which has already been determined upon would, all the same, be to pervert the principles of true morality. My little daughter and your noble scion have for long been destined for one another, the omens having prophesied their union as one to be a 'pairing of splendid phoenixes', and it is intended beyond all doubt that they shall sing together in perfect wedded harmony. Were your noble offspring to cast aside one betrothed wife for another, we should be violating ancient precepts of right and proper conduct, while to have my daughter abandon one promised husband and seek for another would almost inevitably incite the condemnation of others. I beg you, sir, to think this matter over and over again with the utmost care, and for myself feel that we must adhere to our previous settlement.

In dread and consternation, I, Yi, send you this, with my best regards.

Mr Gao read right through this letter, then heaved a sigh. 'On the spur of the moment,' he thought, 'I made my suggestion without a sufficiently thoroughgoing meditation on the matter. Now, reading Mr Zhongli's words, I feel utterly ashamed of myself. But I can now see a way of providing complete satisfaction on both sides, a way which will enable Mr Zhongli to fulfil his handsome aspirations and at the same time permit me to share the pleasures of good repute, so that for ten thousand generations to come our actions will be related as a tale of noble deeds.' Losing no time, he wrote a letter back:

Although, in suggesting that we change one daughter for another, I intended the proposal in the deepest and most well-meaning of friendly spirits, your citation of precepts of morality to oppose the casting aside of one prospective wife in favour of another was indeed most appropriate and correct. My second son, Gao Sheng, is just sixteen years of age and has not yet been bound with the bonds of betrothal. If your dear daughter were to come to my eldest son, and Miss Shi were to be allotted to my younger son, we should then have two fine husbands with two fine wives, making two magnificent couples, and our two families would be securely linked in ties of noble affection for generations to come. There is no need for you to go to the trouble of providing complete wedding trousseaux and dowries: let us instead concentrate our attentions upon the delight which the unions on the happy day will afford us. I abjectly venture to pray that you will condescend to agree and there will be no need to divine anew for an auspicious date.

I, Yuan, in great trepidation, convey to you my repeated respects.

'Such an arrangement,' exclaimed Mr Zhongli in great delight, when he received this letter, 'is the very way to settle things ideally for all concerned. As a gentleman of honour Mr Gao in no whit falls short of the sublime souls of antiquity I must concede superiority to him, and do so with all reverence!'

He informed his wife immediately of what had happened. They split the one dowry into two portions, supplementing them somewhat with additional clothes and jewellery, and treating the two girls absolutely alike, with no distinctions between them in the generosity of their provision for each. Two days before the fifteenth of the tenth month, Mr Gao made ready two gaily decorated, dainty sedan-chairs, and to the accompaniment of the rattle of drums and the piping of shawms and piccolos they went to collect the two brides and escort them in welcoming procession back to their new home. After having first of all sent off the dowries and wedding trousseaux, Mr Zhongli summoned forth his two daughters Spray of Cheer and Moon Perfume and called upon his wife to instruct them in the principles of womanhood. Then the two girls said their goodbyes and set off. Moon Perfume was so grateful for the kind favours she had received at the hands of Mr and Madam Zhongli that she could hardly bear to leave them, and mounted the sedan wailing and weeping.

Of course, we scarcely need mention all that happened as the brides were sped along their wedding route. They reached the county of their destination on exactly the appointed day of good omen, and the two couples, the prettiest picture you ever saw, went through the wedding ceremonies and 'joined

vedding cups'. Mr Gao and his wife were overwhelmed with
oy. Yes, as they say:

A century of blessings is from this day assured,
By nuptial bonds, that heaven tied, secured.

Further to our story, one night, three days after Mr Zhongli
had married off the two girls, he dreamt that he saw a literatus
wearing an official's hat and bearing an official's ivory writing
tablet, who stood before him and said to him:

I am Moon Perfume's father, Shi Bi. In my mortal life I
was the magistrate of this county, but when fire broke out in
the granary I had no means of fulfilling the demands for
compensation and became so miserable that I died of
melancholy. The Emperor on High upon investigation
discovered how incorruptible and honest I had been in the
conduct of my office, took pity on me as innocent of any
crime, and by his imperial edict conferred upon me the title
of City God of the capital of this very county. Moon Perfume,
my daughter, has been the object of your noble bounties, my
lord, and you have raised her from the mire and achieved a
splendid marriage for her. Such acts beyond any doubt
constitute virtue for virtue's sake, and I have already in a
memorial informed the Emperor on High concerning your
conduct. In your fate it was originally decreed that you
should have no son and heir, but because of your charitable
deeds the Emperor on High has bestowed a son upon you
and will magnify the glory of your household. You yourself,
sir, will rise to high office and enjoy a long and peaceful life.
Mr Gao of the neighbouring county, sharing your kind
feelings, chose to take my orphaned daughter as the wife of
his son, which conduct the Emperor on High delightedly
commends, and for which the Emperor on High grants the
two sons of Mr Gao the future blessings of lofty office and
rich remuneration as a reward for their father's virtue.
You, sir, are to convey the order to mortal men that they
are to spread good deeds throughout the world and that on
no account must they oppress the weak or do violence to the
solitary, nor in order to profit themselves do harm to others.

141

The Way of Heaven illumines everywhere with its brightne:
and leaves no smallest stone unturned in the thoroughne:
of its investigations.

So saying, he bowed twice. Mr Zhongli returned his bow
but as he straightened up suddenly trampled on the front fla
of his gown, tripped over and fell sprawling. Abruptly awak
ened, he realised that it had been a dream. He at once told h:
wife about it, and she too could not stop sighing in astonish
ment. As soon as dawn broke the following day, he took
sedan-chair to the City God Temple, where he burned incense
performed various rites and contributed a hundred taels of hi
own salary with instructions to the Taoist priest to renovat
the temple buildings and to inscribe these events upon a ston
memorial tablet so that knowledge of them might be sprea(
abroad for the edification of the general public. He also wrot
a detailed letter reporting his dream to Mr Gao, and Mr Ga(
handed the letter to his two sons to read too. One and all wer
utterly amazed. Madam Zhongli, who was over forty, suddenl
became pregnant and gave birth to a son, for whom they chos
the name Tianzi, 'Heaven-bestowed'. Later, Zhongli Yi gav
his allegiance to the Sòng dynasty and rose to the lofty rank o
Grand Academician of the Longtu Chamber, living to ove:
ninety. His son Tianzi became Top Graduate in the imperia
examinations of the Great Sòng Dynasty. Gao Deng and Ga(
Sheng both pursued government careers under the Sòng
regime and rose to high ministerial posts. But that all happened
later.

Going back to Jia Chang, who was away in other parts a1
the time of these events, he returned shortly after and so
discovered that Mistress Moon Perfume and her maid had
disappeared. On inquiry he was apprised of the reasons why,
and had several enormous rows with his wife. Later he learned
that His Worship the magistrate Zhongli had made Moon
Perfume his daughter and married her off, along with his own
daughter, into the Gao family. Now deprived of other outlet
for his goodwill, Jia Chang went with twenty taels of silver to
try and buy back the maid and restore her to Mistress Shi as a
gift. Second Zhao and his wife were a fond and loving couple
by now and could not bear to be separated, but they expressed

hemselves willing to go and live in as retainers providing it was as a couple. Mother Zhang could not put any obstacles in their way, so Jia Chang led Second Zhao and wife all the way to De'an county, where he put his proposal to the magistrate, Mr Gao. First ascertaining all the ins and outs of the situation, Mr Gao went indoors and questioned his daughter-in-law, Moon Perfume. Discovering that the two accounts agreed, he took Second Zhao and wife into his household, offering liberal recompense of gold and silks to Jia Chang. Jia Chang declined to accept any of them and returned home. Bitterly indignant at the mean-minded things his wife had done, Jia Chang swore that he would stay with her no longer and took a concubine, by whom he had two sons—that too being a reward for good deeds. Someone who lived in later times wrote a poem expressing his admiration of the nobility embodied in these events:

> Others choosing wedding partners
> seek ties with clans of note and estate,
> Who would espouse an orphan maiden
> just to ensure her a fortunate fate?
> But see how heaven never neglects
> men of benevolence,
> How their unblazoned charity receives
> its ample recompense.

Yang Jiao Throws Away his Life
in Fulfilment of a Friendship

At the drop of a hat, as fickle as clouds,
as capricious as April showers they play,
No need to count—so many are they,
give worthless whim its niggard sway.
Look at the friendship of Guan and Bao
that endured from pauper days,
Modern men now cast such virtue
like worthless mud away.

In ancient times in the state of Qi there lived Guan Zhong, whose courtesy name was Yiwu, and Bao Shu, whose courtesy name was Xuanzi. The two of them became friends as young boys, in days when they were both very poor and low in the social scale. Later, when Bao Shu became the first of the two to attain high public responsibilities and eminence, serving in the government secretariat of Duke Huan the ruler of Qi, it was his recommendations that earned Guan Zhong the post of Prime Minister, thus providing him with a position more highly ranked than his own. The two men carried out their administrative duties in complete spiritual accord with one another, from beginning to end working together in unmarred unison. Some of the words once uttered by Guan Zhong merit quotation.

In three battles I was thrice put to flight, but Bao Shu never took me for a coward because of it, aware as he was that I

冠萊公

had an elderly mother to look after. Three times I took up a government career and three times I was expelled from my post, but Bao Shu did not conclude that I was worthless, realising instead that the right time had not yet come for me. Once I gave Bao Shu advice that made things worse, but he did not consider me ignorant on account of it, understanding as he did that things cannot always go well for us. Another time, when Bao Shu and I were doing some trading, I took the greater share of the profits, but he did not deem me avaricious, understanding instead that it was poverty that drove me to do so. It was my mother and father who gave me life, but it was Bao Shu who appreciated my qualities and picked me out with his true friendship!

And so it may be understood why whenever people of olden times broached the topic of that true friendship which embodies mutual understanding and appreciation, they would unfailingly single out Guan and Bao.

Our present story is about two friends who met by chance and became friends and sworn brothers. Each of them subsequently threw away his life, and each of them left behind him eternal fame . . .

During the Spring and Autumn period (770–481 B.C.), the King of Chu, King Origin, held scholars in high esteem and regarded the moral laws of the universe as matters of great importance, welcoming noble minds to his court and seeking out the services of honourable knights. An innumerable host of them throughout the world, hearing of his goodly reputation, came to render their allegiance and offer their abilities to him.

On Piled Rock Mountain in the land of the Western Qiang there lived a noble gentleman named Zuo Botao. Orphaned as a child, he had applied himself vigorously to his studies, had developed such genius as can afford great benefits to mankind, and had by his studying perfected his acquaintance with those administrative arts that can ensure a peaceful and contented populace. At that time the states and kingdoms of China were preoccupied with their efforts to annex each other. Few rulers were attempting to govern through benevolent policies or according to high-minded principles of virtue, the majority of them preferring to try to achieve hegemony by brute force. Because of this, Zuo Botao had not embarked upon any career in government service. But eventually hearing that King Origin of Chu was an admirer of virtue and a lover of honour and was seeking everywhere for noble knights, he took up a single sack of books, said goodbye to his fellow villagers, neighbours and friends, and hurried straight off towards the kingdom of Chu.

Ages later, he came to the region of Yong, where it was bitter winter and there blew ceaseless winds and rainstorms. There is a lyric to the tune 'Western River Moon' which is devoted to a description of scenes of winter rain:

> Hissing north wind cuts your cheeks,
> dull-plod drizzle soaks your coat,
> Bully winter brags and crows,
> whipping up ice and brewing the snow,
> Where are the gentle breaths that blow,
> that kinder seasons puff and float?
> The line of the hills is blurred in gloom,
> the rare-peeping sun glints the glimmer of doom.
> The wandering lad on the edge of the sky
> is all aches of longing for hearth and for home,
> The traveller trudging the open road
> shall repent the folly that stirred him to roam.

Braving the rain and pushing on into the teeth of the wind, Zuo Botao travelled on and after another day's journey his clothes were all soaked through. It looked as if dusk was about to fall, so he walked into a village, intending to seek lodging for the night. In the far distance he caught sight of the light of a lamp shining out through a grove of bamboo and hastened towards it. A very low bamboo fence and the thatch hut that it encompassed came into view. He pushed open the bamboo gate and lightly knocked on the wicker door. A man opened the door and came out. Zuo Botao stationed himself under the eaves and hastily greeted him with the customary courtesies.

'I am from the Western Qiang,' he explained. 'My name is Zuo Botao and I am bound for the kingdom of Chu, but meeting unexpectedly with this rain in the course of my journey and failing to find any wayside inn, I would like to ask you if I might lodge in your house for the night, with a view to continuing my travels in the morning. Could you possibly think fit to grant such a request, sir?'

At these words, the other hastily returned his courtesies and invited him into the house. Inside, Botao noticed there was nothing apart from a couch piled high with books. It dawned on him that the man was a scholar and he was about to bow his respects.

'This is no time for standing on ceremony,' the man protested. 'Allow me to make a fire and dry your clothes, and we must have a chat together.'

He at once set light to some bamboo to make a fire, and while Botao was drying his clothes he himself cooked a meal and warmed up some wine which he served to Botao, treating him with great consideration and hospitality. Botao inquired his name.

'I am Yang Jiaoai,' he replied. 'I lost both my parents as a child and live here on my own. I have always had a passion for reading books and studying, and have completely neglected the farming side of my life, so that now when I am blessed by the good fortune of meeting such a noble gentleman come from distant parts, to my deepest regret I lack the wealth and material wherewithal adequately to entertain him. I abjectly crave your forgiveness.'

'That in this miserable rainstorm I have been granted shelter,' replied Botao, 'and that, moreover, I have been provided with food and drink, fills me with undying gratitude.'

When night came on, the two of them lay down feet to feet to sleep but spilling their considerable learning in conversation they talked on and on and kept themselves awake all night. Dawn brought no let-up in the pouring rain and Jiaoai detained Botao in his house, caring for him to the utmost of his resources, and the two of them became united in friendship, swearing brotherhood with one another. Botao being the elder by five years, Jiaoai installed him as his elder brother, himself assuming the role of younger brother. Botao stayed on for three days before the rain at last ceased and the road dried out.

'Noble younger brother,' said Botao, 'you have the capacity

to hold down a ministership and you have such lofty politic.
ideals. It is a great pity that you should have no ambition t
seek enduring fame but are content to pass out your da
amid the woods and streams.'

'It is not that I have no desire to embark upon a governme
career,' said Jiaoai. 'It is just that no opportunity has hithert
presented itself.'

'At this moment,' said Botao, 'the King of Chu is from th
purest of motives seeking the services of fine men. Since yo
my noble younger brother, are of such a mind, why not com
along with me?'

'I am only too glad to accede to your command, my eld
brother,' was Jiaoai's reply.

So they gathered together a little money for expenses alon
the road and some other provisions for the journey, abandone
the thatch hut, and headed south together.

They had not travelled two days when the rain came o
again and they were forced to halt at an inn. Then, all thei
money exhausted and left with only a sack of grain betwee
them, which they took turns to hump on their backs, they se
off once more, in spite of the rain. While it was still raining,
gale blew up, which in turn gave way to a massive snow
storm. Can you picture it? Just look at it:

> Wind stokes the chill of the snow,
> snow borrows the wind's grim might;
> Frenzied 'willow-floss' panics profuse,
> 'swan-feather on feather' of whirling white.
> It harries, it raids, its ranks run amok
> from north, south, east, west, on all
>   sides around,
> It canopies earth, overwashes whole heaven,
> bleaching the manifold hues of the ground.
> For the wandering bard on his plum-blossom
>   quest,
> the scene that delights his spirit most,
> But the traveller on his weary road
> almost breaks his heart, almost gives up
>   the ghost.

Once they were past Qiyang, the two men's route lay along road across Mount Liang.

On their way they made inquiries of woodcutters, who all informed them that for a hundred miles ahead there were no human habitations, and that it was all steep mountains and vast wildernesses, abounding with packs of tigers and wolves, and advised them that they had best abandon their journey. Botao consulted Jiaoai. 'It is an old saying,' said Jiaoai, 'that "Life and death are up to fate". Since we have come this far, let us press on ahead. Otherwise we shall only regret it for the rest of our lives.'

They carried on for another day, and that night took shelter in an ancient tomb. Their coats were so thin and threadbare that the cold wind whistled through their bones! The next day the snow was falling yet faster and more heavily, and it seemed over a foot deep in the mountain valley.

'Upon reflection,' said Botao, unable to bear the freezing cold any longer, 'since there is no human habitation a hundred and more miles ahead of us, and as we lack sufficient grain to eke out our food and have only thin coats to protect us, I feel that one of us might manage to reach Chu on his own, but if the two of us both try, even supposing we do not freeze to death, we are bound to starve to death on our way. And what good would it do us to rot away here amongst the wild vegetation? I shall take off the clothes I am wearing so that you may put them on, noble younger brother, and you may take this grain all for yourself and push on along the road as best you can. I really cannot go a step further, I would prefer to die here in this spot. When you meet the King of Chu, he is certain to employ you in some high-ranking post. Then will be quite soon enough for you to return and bury me.'

'What nonsense are you talking!' said Jiaoai. 'We two were not brought into this world by the same parents, yet the spirit of honour surpasses the ties of flesh and blood. You cannot imagine that I could countenance the thought of abandoning you in order to seek glory and advancement on my own?' Refusing to accept the suggestion, he took Botao's arm to give him some support and helped him onwards.

'The snowstorm grows fiercer,' said Botao, after they had

gone less than a couple of miles. 'How can we carry on? Let
find a place to rest by the side of the road.'

They caught sight of an old withered mulberry tree, whi
seemed an ideal place to shelter from the snow, but there w
room for only one person to shelter in its hollow trunk,
Jiaoai helped Botao into it and made him sit down. Bot:
bade him strike stones to obtain a light and burn some twi
to ward off the cold air. By the time Jiaoai returned with son
fuel, he saw Botao stripped stark naked, all his clothes piled
a heap.

'What on earth are you doing, my elder brother?' he aske
in astonishment and dismay.

'I have thought it over,' said Botao, 'and can think of r
other solution. Dear younger brother, don't destroy your ow
chances. Put these clothes on quickly, take this grain with yo
and be on your way. I shall wait here for death.'

Jiaoai held him and wept bitterly. 'We must remain togeth(
in life and in death,' he said. 'We cannot part!'

'If both of us starve to death,' said Botao, 'who will bury ou
white bones?'

'In that case then,' said Jiaoai, 'I shall most gladly take o
my clothes so that you may wear them, and you may take th
grain with you. I would much prefer that I should be the on
to die here.'

'I have often been ill in my life,' said Botao, 'while you on th
other hand are young and sturdy, and stronger than me. No
am I any match for your wealth of erudition. Once you hav
had an audience with the King of Chu, you will ascend t
some lofty and splendid post in his government. Of that ther
can be no doubt. Whereas it makes no odds at all if I die now
Do not tarry here any longer, dear noble younger brother
You must hurry on your way.'

'If I were to leave you here to starve to death in this mulberr
tree while I went on alone to success and glory,' said Jiaoai, '
would be a thoroughly dishonourable person. I shall not do it.

'After leaving Piled Rock Mountain,' said Botao, 'I cam(
to your home, and I felt as soon as we met that it was as if w(
were old friends. Realising that you were a man of no ordinar
mettle, I persuaded you to set out in quest of a career at court
Since now we are thwarted by these snowstorms, it is surely

eaven's will that I should end my life now. It would be a
rime on my part to let you die here, younger brother.'

With these words Botao tried to leap into the stream in front
f them and commit suicide, but Jiaoai clutched onto him,
vrapped his coat round him, and helped him back into the
nulberry tree. Botao pushed the coat off. As Jiaoai made to
pproach him once more in an effort to dissuade him from
uch thoughts, he perceived that a sudden change had taken
)lace in Botao's bearing and expression and that his limbs
vere all shuddering with cold. Unable to speak, Botao waved
iaoai from him, ordering him with a gesture to be on his way.
iaoai wrapped his coat around him once more, but Botao was
ılready chilled to the very core of his being, his limbs stiff and
igid, his breath coming in heaving gasps. He was steadily
ıpproaching his last.

'If I linger here any longer,' thought Jiaoai, 'I shall freeze
.o death myself, too. And if I am dead, who will provide for
ny elder brother's burial?' So he knelt in the snow and made
:epeated obeisances to Botao. 'Your worthless younger brother
.s now about to leave you,' he wept. 'I pray that you will aid
ne with your powers from the Shades beyond. If I achieve
:ank and fame, be they however modest, I shall not fail to
provide you with a handsome burial.'

Botao nodded his head in half reply and a moment later had
ceased breathing. There was nothing left for Jiaoai to do but
take the clothes and grain and depart, lamenting, sobbing and
weeping, and at each step turning his head back in sad longing.
Someone later wrote an elegy on Botao's death in the mulberry
tree:

> Winter brought snow and laid it three feet deep
> as the travellers wended their thousand-mile
>   track,
> A long-drawn trudge in the snow and biting cold
> and the rice was running low in their sack.
> Two needed grain that could nourish but one,
> if both journeyed on, not one would arrive,
> If two were dead, neither would gain,
> the only hope was that one might survive.
> Zuo Botao

truly noble soul!
Died that another
might reach his goal.

Somehow bearing up against the winter cold, half starving
Jiaoai reached the capital of the kingdom of Chu, where h
took some repose in an inn outside the city. The following da
he went into the city and asked someone how he should g
about presenting himself before the ruler of Chu in response t
the call for men of ability. 'A reception lodge has been estab
lished outside the palace gate,' was the reply, 'and the Chie
Minister, Pei Zhong, has been put in charge of receiving an
engaging the gentlemen who are coming from all over th
world.'

Jiaoai at once went to the reception quarters, and just at th
moment he arrived in front of them the Chief Minister chance
to be alighting from his carriage. So Jiaoai approached an
bowed to him. Noticing that although Jiaoai's clothes were i
rags his bearing and air were remarkably impressive, Pe
Zhong hastened to return his courteous greeting.

'From whence have you come, noble knight?' he inquired

'My name is Yang Jiaoai,' replied Jiaoai, 'and I am a
Yongzhou man. I heard that your exalted nation was inviting
the services of talented men, and have come here specially to
offer my ability and allegiance.'

Pei Zhong ushered him into the reception lodge, and had
him served with wine and food and provided with lodgings.

The following day Pei Zhong came to the reception lodge to
ask after Jiaoai, and sounded him on various problems that
were preoccupying his own mind, by way of testing the extent
and nature of his learning. Never once was Jiaoai stumped for
an answer, proferring advice with great fluency and ease.
Highly delighted with him, Pei Zhong returned to court and
memorialised the King about him. The King at once sent for
Jiaoai and sought his theories on the best course to take in
order to enrich the nation and strengthen it militarily. Jiaoai
submitted ten policies, all of which were vitally relevant to the
crucial matters facing the kingdom. King Origin, overwhelmed with pleasure, arranged a royal feast for his entertainment, appointed him Middle Minister, and bestowed upon

im one hundred ounces of gold and one hundred bolts of
oloured silk. Jiaoai bowed his thanks again and again, yet
vept copiously as he did so.

'What is it that moves you to weep, and with such grief,
Your Excellency?' asked King Origin in astonishment and
concern.

Jiaoai narrated in detail the story of how Botao had sacrificed
his clothes and the grain for his sake, and the tale inspired the
King with great sorrow. All the other ministers were likewise
filled with sadness and bitter regret.

'What would you wish us to do?' asked the King.

'I beg you to grant me some leave,' said Jiaoai, 'so that I may
go and lay Botao to rest. When that has been accomplished, I
shall return to serve Your Majesty.'

The King then awarded the deceased Botao the posthumous
title of Middle Minister, made lavish provision for the
expenses of the burial, and sent a retinue to ride as escort for
Jiaoai.

Taking his leave of King Origin, Jiaoai hastened to the area
of Mount Liang, sought out the withered mulberry tree of
such old sad memories, and sure enough, discovered Botao's
corpse still there, the dead man's face looking exactly as in life.
Repeatedly bowing in reverence to him and weeping, Jiaoai
called his retinue to summon an assembly of the elders of the
surrounding country locality. Then he divined a suitable spot
in the flat land of Reed Embankment, with a large brook to its
fore and a high cliff to its rear and embraced by peaks on all
sides, all of which made for an excellent geomantic site. Next
he bathed Botao's body with liquid perfumes, clad him in
ministerial hat and robes, and placed him in a coffin which was
encased in a further coffin. He then laid him to rest and
raised a tomb-mound above him. All around the tomb he had
walls built and trees planted, and thirty paces from the tomb
a sacrificial hall erected, with a sculptured image of Botao,
ornamental pillars surmounted by an inscription tablet, and,
beside one of the walls, a tile-roofed room where vigil could be
kept. On the completion of all these constructions Jiaoai held
a sacrifice in the sacrificial hall, weeping in most fervent
lamentation. Indeed, of the country elders and his retinue
every one without exception shed tears. Then finally, the

sacrifice over, all dispersed and went their separate way leaving Jiaoai to spend the night in the shrine annex.

That night Jiaoai sat up by bright lamp and candle light sighing ceaselessly in mournful memory of his friend. Suddenl a gust of dank, gloomy wind howled in and made the lamp an candle flames flicker. Looking round, Jiaoai saw someon standing in the shadow of the lamp, now stepping forward now shrinking back, and from him came the faint, muffle sound of weeping.

'Who are you?' shouted Jiaoai angrily. 'What do you mean by bursting in here in the depths of the night?'

The man said nothing. As he stood up and looked, Jiaoa saw that it was Botao. 'My dear elder brother,' he exclaimed in amazement, 'so your soul has not travelled far. There mus be some special reason for your visit to me?'

'I am grateful to you, my dear younger brother,' said Botao, 'that no sooner had you been appointed to a position at court than you petitioned the King on the matter of my burial, that I was granted a lofty posthumous title, and that you have attained to such perfection in your provision o beautiful coffins and burial clothes and shrouds and all the other things for me. But my tomb is located next to the grave of Jing Ke. He was the man who when alive failed in an attempt to assassinate the King of Qin, and was slain. His friend Gao Jianli buried his corpse here. He is a most ferocious spirit, and comes every night bearing his sword and rants and raves against me. "You, who died of nothing better than cold and starvation," he curses at me, "how dare you have your tomb built in a location above mine, thus depriving me of the geomantic advantages. If you do not move elsewhere, I shall dig up your grave and throw your corpse into the wilds!" In such a distressing crisis I have come to you, dear brother, in the hope that you might rebury me elsewhere so as to avoid such a calamity.'

Jiaoai was on the point of questioning him further, when the wind arose once more and Botao suddenly disappeared.

Waking up with a start from his dream there in the sacrificial hall, Jiaoai noted down all that had occurred, and when daylight came summoned the local elders once more and asked them if there was any other tomb in the neighbourhood.

'In the shade of the pines,' they told him, 'there is the tomb of Jing Ke, and to the front of his tomb is a temple.'

'He was the man who was killed in an unsuccessful attempt to assassinate the King of Qin,' said Jiaoai. 'For what reason does his grave come to be situated here?'

'Gao Jianli was a local man,' they answered, 'and when he knew that Jing Ke had been killed and his corpse flung into the wastelands he stole the corpse and buried it here. Jing Ke's ghost was always haunting the place, so local people built a temple here, and sacrifices to seek his blessings are held in it all four seasons of the year.'

Upon hearing this account, Jiaoai now believed the truth of his dream. At the head of his followers he marched straight across to Jing Ke's temple, where he pointed at Jing's icon and roundly abused it. 'You were a common fellow from the land of Yan,' he roared, 'who had the good fortune to be taken in and looked after by the Prince of Yan. He presented you with fabulous beauties and rich treasures, and provided everything for your pleasure, but you evolved no worthwhile policies to requite his magnanimous bounties. Instead you stalked into Qin and embarked upon an action which not only put paid to your own life but further led your nation to its unneedful doom. Yet you come here to intimidate and delude the local people and demand sacrifices! My elder brother, Zuo Botao, is one of the supreme scholars of the age, a knight of gentility, honour and unsullied principles. How dare you try to exert violent pressures upon him! If you persist in such actions, I shall destroy this temple and dig up your tomb, to eradicate you for eternity!'

On completion of this tirade, Jiaoai went back to Botao's tomb, where he addressed a reverent exhortation to him: 'If Jing Ke comes again tonight, you must inform me, dear elder brother.' Then he returned to the sacrificial shrine and that night also waited up by candle light.

Botao duly made an appearance. 'I am grateful for what you did today,' he said, sobbing, 'but Jing Ke has a large number of henchmen, contributed by the natives of this locality. What you could do is make men of straw, dress them in clothes of coloured silk, place weapons in their hands, and burn them in front of my tomb. Once I have them to help me, it will prevent

Jing Ke from plaguing me.' With these words he disappeared

Through that same night Jiaoai directed the making of doll from bundles of straw, clad them in coloured clothing, gav them swords, spears and other weapons to hold, and stood ; few score of them by the tomb and burned them, simul taneously uttering the prayer: 'Even should nothing untoward occur, I pray that you will tell me what comes to pass.' Ther he returned to the sacrificial hall.

Later that night Jiaoai heard the sounds of a storm tha resembled the clamour of battle. Stepping outside to see wha was happening, he saw Botao fleeing towards him. 'The mer you burned were of no avail,' declared Botao, 'and now Jing Ke has Gao Jianli to assist him, and it cannot be long before my corpse will be evicted from its tomb. I can but hope tha you will quickly transfer it to another place of burial in order to avoid such a calamity.'

'How dare that fellow abuse my elder brother!' said Jiaoai. 'I must throw all my own strength into the battle against him.'

'But you are a mortal, younger brother,' said Botao, 'while we are ghosts of the Shades. Whatever his courage, a mortal is cut off from us by his links with the dusty world, so how can he fight with ghosts? Even the straw men can only assist with battle-cries and are helpless to repel such violent spirits.'

'Go now, elder brother,' said Jiaoai. 'I have a means of dealing with them tomorrow.'

The following day, Jiaoai again went into Jing Ke's temple and uttering mighty curses struck at the icon and destroyed it. He was on the point of setting fire to the temple when several of the local elders appeared on the scene. 'This is the incense temple for the whole area,' they told him, imploring him again and again to desist. 'If you desecrate it, we fear you will bring down disaster on us ordinary people.'

In no time, all the local people had assembled there, all having come expressly to beseech Jiaoai to abandon his intention. Unable to override them, Jiaoai could only resign himself to their demands. Then he returned to the sacrificial shrine, where he composed a memorial to convey his gratitude to the King of Chu, which read as follows:

In giving me his share of our grain, Botao enabled me to

156

survive, to meet Your Majesty, from whom I received the generous bounty of exalted rank and thus my life's fulfilment. Please grant that I may, in a life to come, strive with all my heart to repay your grace and favour.

With most earnest exhortations, he consigned this memorial to his retinue, then made his way to Botao's tomb, where he wept unrestrainedly. He then addressed the following words to his followers: 'That my elder brother is menaced by the violent spirit of Jing Ke, and has no refuge, is a situation that cannot endure. I wished to burn yonder temple and dig up the villain's tomb, but feared lest I be tyrannically overriding the desires of the local populace. I prefer rather to die, that I may become a ghost down by the Springs of Afterlife and, exerting my strength in my elder brother's cause, do battle with that vicious spirit. You are to bury my corpse to the right of this tomb, so that we shall be together in death as we were in life, and so that I may repay my brother my debt of gratitude for his having given me his share of our grain. When you return to the King of Chu, beg him by all the means in your power to adopt the policies which I proposed, so that he may for ever preserve his frontiers and his altars of state.'

No sooner had he said these words than he snatched out the sword that hung at his waist and put an end to his life by cutting his throat. His followers rushed to try and save his life, but were too late. Without delay they then provided burial clothing, coffin and shrouds and laid him to rest beside Botao's tomb.

That night towards nine o'clock a fierce storm arose, and lightning and thunder mingled together in the noise of wild battle-cries that could be heard for miles around. When the area was inspected at dawn, it was discovered that the top of Jing Ke's tomb had been cracked open as if by some explosion, his white bones were scattered before his tomb, the pines and cypresses beside the tomb had been uprooted, and a fire which had flared up in his temple had razed it to the ground. The local elders were utterly amazed and disconcerted, and all presented themselves before the tombs of Yang and Zuo, where they burnt incense and paid fervent homage.

Jiaoai's retinue returned to the capital of Chu, where they

acquainted King Origin with all that had passed. Deepl
moved by Jiaoai's lofty sense of duty and loyalty, he despatched
officials to build a temple in front of his tomb, posthumousl
promoted him to the rank of Chief Minister, presented him
with a temple dedication-tablet inscribed with the word
'Shrine of Fidelity and Honour', and erected a memorial ston
to commemorate the events. Till the present day, withou
interruption, incense has continued to be burnt at the templ
for him. From that time on, Jing Ke's spirit ceased to exist
The prayers of the local people at their seasonal sacrifices wer
richly answered. There is an ancient poem:

> Virtue that pervades all heaven and earth
> may dwell in one human heart, such narrow
>   confines,
> By two knights' tombs in serene autumn, linger
> two noble souls yet, when the chaste moon shines.

On Big Tree Slope a Faithful Tiger Acts Best Man

All the world, in witless worries,
schemes itself to ceaseless troubles,
None wise enough to live the life
of floating foam and drifting bubbles.
All plot their little livelihoods
a thousand years ahead,
It should be justice they bequeath
eternity instead.
Westward slopes the evening sun,
who shall halt its downward track?
Eastward flow the vanishing rivers
never glancing back.
Ah, people fail to comprehend
the bent of heaven's will,
They toil their bodies, rack their brains,
at dead of night they worry still.

These lines would urge people to cherish the common weal, to run their affairs according to the principles of natural, universal morality, and not to scheme greedily after selfish profit or plot the harm of others. There is a common saying, 'Plot and wangle as you will, 'Tis you shall cull the crop of ill.' If you do not stick to what is moral and right, then of course heaven will not aid you.

Once upon a time, there was a man whose surname was Wei and personal name De, and who came from Quanzhou in Fukien province. As a child he had gone with his father when the latter had set up a shop for the smelting of tax-silver into ingots, in the prefectural capital of Shaoxing. His old father was the sort who believed in giving others a fair deal and was not out for a profit all the time, for which reason he acquired a large number of customers, and his business was a thorough success. In only a few years he earned himself quite a tidy sum. When Wei De grew up he married the daughter of one Tailor Dan who lived in the neighbourhood. Because she was quite good-looking, local squires would have been only too willing to fork out a good deal of silver to get Miss Dan as their concubine, but Tailor Dan would have none of it. Observing that old Wei and his son had a solid livelihood and were open-handed with their money, and neighbours into the bargain, and seeing that his daughter would be taken on as sole and number one wife, he had plumped for the marriage with young Wei.

But to everyone's surprise, just after the wedding Tailor Dan fell ill and passed away. In less than two years, old Wei had also died of some illness or other. Wei De talked things over with his wife, Madam Dan, and suggested that, since neither of them now had any close relatives anywhere in the neighbourhood, the best thing they could do was escort his father's coffin back to his old home and stay there. At first Madam Dan was unwilling, but she could not override her husband, so she just had to give in and do as he said. He first sold up all the heavy furniture and other items in the shop, realising what he could in the haste of the situation. Then he made ready their luggage, hired a long-distance boat, and selected a favourable date for embarcation. On the chosen day he loaded his father's coffin into the boat, went on board with his wife, and set off.

Now the captain of the boat, whose name was Zhang Shao, was by no means a nice sort, and went in for sly pilfering along the waterways for his living. Because he wanted to keep this trade all to himself and was scared stiff that any crew he had might spill the beans, he had searched around and found a dumb man who could pole a boat and would do as his mate on board. Now, learning that Wei De had been in silver-casting for a good many years, he felt sure he must have his

扇肆女

avel bags full of the stuff. He also noticed that Madam Dan
as very beautiful. Zhang himself had no wife. These two
ings together put him in a vicious frame of mind, and from
e first moment his passengers came on board he conceived
nasty idea.

No convenient way of putting this idea into operation had
et arisen when, one day, because the wind was blowing so
ard as to make progress virtually impossible, they moored the
oat beneath Mount Jianglang. Zhang De now thought of a
rick. On the pretext of having no firewood, he said that he
anted to go up the mountainside to chop some faggots to
ring back for fuel, but, claiming that there were tigers on the
nountain which often came out and tore people to bits, he
nsisted that Wei De go along with him to keep him company.
Vei De failed to detect the ruse, and went off with him.
Deliberately taking a winding route, dodging this way and
hat, Zhang Shao led him deep into the hills. There he looked
ll around to make sure that there was no one else about, and
lecided that the spot was the very place for him to strike. He
ut some brushwood down, and told Wei De to tie it into
undles. Wei De lowered his head, all his attention fixed on
icking up the firewood, and was thus unprepared for Zhang
Shao, who came up from behind and hacked out at him with
is axe, hitting him square on his left shoulder and sending
im sprawling to the ground. Then Zhang struck out again,
nd brought the axe down on his head. Blood gushed, and
Wei De was done for.

'A neat job! A neat job!' Zhang Shao kept on saying. 'This
day next year I'll get my wife to observe the anniversary of her
husband's sad decease.' With these words, he stuck the axe in
his belt, ignored the firewood, and, unencumbered by any
burden, flew at top speed back down to the boat.

Seeing him return alone, Madam Dan asked him where her
husband was.

'What a tragedy!' said Zhang. 'We met a tiger, and your
poor husband got carried off and eaten by it. I was lucky
enough to manage to run away fast and escape from the
tiger's jaws. I didn't even dare gather up the firewood we'd
chopped.'

At this news, Madam Dan beat her breast, and wept brokenly.

'It must have been fixed in his horoscope when he was born that he was going to be killed by a tiger,' said Zhang Shao in an attempt to calm her down. 'It's no good crying.'

As she wept, though, Madam Dan was thinking: 'I've heard that tigers come out in the hills at nightfall, but I don't believe they show themselves and kill people in broad daylight. What's more, the two of them set out together, side by side, so why should a tiger specially have to go and pick on my husband to eat? And this man hasn't suffered a scratch! It's very strange indeed!' Then she spoke aloud to Zhang. 'Although it may have happened as you say,' she said, 'I haven't seen it with my own eyes. Even if he really has been eaten by a tiger, there must be a few of his bones still left. Can I trouble you to lead me to the spot, so that I may pick them up and bring them back here, as a gesture in memory of our love for one another?'

'I'm scared of tigers. I daren't go,' said Zhang Shao. She then began to weep and wail most plaintively.

'If I don't take her for a walk,' thought Zhang to himself, 'she'll never give up hope.' 'Madam,' he said, 'I'll take you to have a look. Don't cry.'

Madam Dan followed him out of the boat, and set off along the mountain path with him. Previously, when cutting the firewood, the two men had taken the fork to the east, but Zhang Shao, afraid lest she see the corpse, now led her off along the west path. She wept every step she walked. They went on for a long time, seeing no trace of any tiger, while Zhang Shao fobbed her off with all kinds of irrelevant comments, fully expecting her to get tired and yearn to turn back. Little did he realise how determined she was to see her husband's blood and bones, before she would believe that what he had said was the truth. As it dawned on him that she was not willing to retrace her steps, Zhang tried to persuade her with a lie. 'Young lady,' he said, pointing ahead of them, 'you're set on carrying on, but look, look, isn't that a tiger coming towards us now?'

Madam Dan had no sooner raised her head to look and ask 'Where is it?' when they heard from within the forest a weird roaring gust of wind, and all of a sudden out sprang a tiger, white-browed and showing only the whites of its eyes in its fury. It swerved neither to right nor to left, but pounced

162

raight upon Zhang Shao. Too late to duck aside, Zhang only managed to let out a single cry before the tiger closed its teeth ound the scruff of his neck and ran off into the depths of the orest to enjoy him.

Madam Dan had fainted to the ground, and it was a long ime before she came round. Seeing no Zhang Shao, she ealised that he must have been carried off in the jaws of the iger. Now she believed that there really were tigers on the nountain, and that what Zhang had told her about her usband having been eaten by a tiger was true. Overcome with lread, she did not dare continue any further, and, recognising he path along which she had come, wended her way back, veeping every step she walked.

Before she had managed to get away from the mountain, lowever, she saw some half-human-looking creature come lurtling out from the east path making a beeline towards ler. Her only thought was that it must be another tiger, and .rying 'I'm done for!' she fell backwards. Then suddenly she leard words being spoken in her ear. 'My lady,' a voice said, how on earth did you get here?' And two hands helped her to ler feet.

Opening her eyes, she saw that it was her husband Wei De, vith blood streaming all over his face—that was what was naking him so inhuman in appearance. As it happened, Wei)e's time had not come after all, and although he had been vounded by the axe blows he had only swooned away and topped breathing for a while. After Zhang Shao had left him, ie had come to once more, struggled up, torn off his foot-:loths, and bandaged up his head with them as best he could. Then he had made his way down the mountain, intending to eek out Zhang Shao and have a word with him. Purely by hance he had come upon Madam Dan.

Seeing her husband again, Madam Dan at first thought that ie had indeed been wounded by a tiger. But as she heard his iccount of all that had happened, she at last realised what a rile lying trick Zhang Shao had tried to play. She realised, oo, that the tiger that had dragged Zhang off in its jaws had)een sent by the gods to punish and do away with evil.

Husband and wife thanked heaven and earth with infinite gratitude. When they arrived back at the boat, the dumb man made signs with his hand, asking why the captain of the boat had not returned. Wei De and his wife explained everything that had happened from beginning to end, whereupon the dumb man put his palms together in Buddhist salutation, suddenly chanted the words 'Amitabha, Amitabha Bodhisattva!', and, now able to speak, told them of all Zhang Shao's previous evil deeds. When they tried to question him further, however, he became dumb once more. This too was a miracle.

All the way back, Wei De helped the dumb man manage the boat, until they came to his old home. There he sold the boat and built a Buddhist chantry for the dumb man to live in and keep incense burning night and day. Wei De and his wife were Buddhist believers till the end of their days. Someone later discussing this tale composed the following poem:

> He cried tiger, when tiger there was none
> but the tiger in his heart that sprang to light.
> Had his heart been good, any tiger on that
>   mountain
> would have kept itself well out of sight.

Now we have just been saying that a tiger was sent along by the gods to punish and eliminate evil, and such happenings are indeed quite within the bounds of possibility. For it seems that, being king of the animals and a creature of most marvellous insight, the tiger can, for example—as is attested in the records of history—be so influenced by the virtue of a noble-minded, benevolent official as to cross a river voluntarily and cause no more harm in his area. In another instance, a tiger submitted to an eminent Buddhist priest and made himself a protector of the Buddhist dharma. There is plenty of evidence of such things. Now we shall tell the story of a tiger who was the recipient of kindness and gratefully repaid it, bringing together a human couple, a man of honour and his truly chaste wife, and providing the subject-matter for a splendid tale that will never lose its relevance. The sort of tale by which

> By its telling
> chaste women are glorified,

164

> At its words
> the worst of rogues are terrified.

During the Heavenly Treasure period (742–56) of the Great Tang dynasty in a country area under the administration of Zhangpu county in Fuzhou, there lived a man whose surname was Qin and personal name Zili. Both his parents were alive, and the family more or less got by. In his childhood, Qin Zili had been engaged to marry Tide Music, daughter of Lin Bujiang from the same county. The betrothal gifts of tea and dates had already been delivered to the bride's family, and they were only waiting till the boy grew up for the marriage to take place. From the age of eleven, Zili refused to study, and once out of the schoolhouse all he cared for was practising spear drill and wielding the quarterstaff. Since he was their only son, his parents decidedly spoiled him, and made no effort to restrict him in any way. By the time he was fifteen he was tall and strong, with ape-like arms, an expert archer and outstanding exponent of the fighting arts.

Well, the common saying tells us that birds of a feather flock together, and of course a band of young layabouts struck up a friendship with him, and they would all go off together, hawking and falconing, racing on horseback and beagling, shooting and hunting, all for the pleasure of it. Once they had shot three tigers in one day. Suddenly an old man in yellow robes appeared, and, leaning on his staff, came up to them.

'You young gentlemen are very courageous,' he praised them. 'Why, even those mighty paragons of tiger-hunting Ka Zhuang and Li Cunxiao could not surpass you in boldness. But you should love life and hate killing, for all creatures share similar feelings. It's always been said that "If men thought not to slaughter tigers, tigers would not wish to kill men". What motive drives you young gentlemen to kill them? This animal is the king of the animals, and should not be killed in frivolous sport. In days gone by, there was Lord Huang who had magic powers and was able to put down tigers with his red sword. But even he was killed by a tiger in the end. If you young gentlemen set too much store by your courage, and make a hobby of unrestrained killing, depend upon it, you will some day violate the taboos of the gods, and slim indeed will be your chances then of avoiding some unforeseen and fatal woe.'

As he heard this sermon, Qin Zili awoke to the error of his ways, and there and then broke an arrow and swore an oath, vowing that he would never kill tigers again.

One day he had gone alone into the mountains to do some hunting and had obtained a little game, when half way back, reaching a spot by the name of Big Tree Slope, he suddenly saw a fawn-striped tiger which had chanced to fall into a cage-trap which the hunter happened not yet to have visited. As it saw Zili approach, the tiger knelt with its forelegs on the ground, bowed its head, drooped its ears, and made a soft whining noise, as if begging for mercy.

'Doom-ridden beast,' said Zili, 'I've already sworn I'm not going to kill any of your kind any more. But you went running into this trap yourself. Not my fault. Nothing to do with me.'

The tiger stared fixedly at him, and kept on whining and whimpering.

'If I take it on myself to set you free now,' said Zili, 'you must never in the future kill any human being. Never!'

The tiger nodded its head as he said that. Zili smashed the trap and let the tiger out, and given a new lease of life it skipped off crazily.

'Some fellow stood to gain by capturing that tiger,' thought Zili, 'and here I am patting myself on the back, telling myself how kind I am to free the tiger. If my trying to do good means that I'm depriving someone else of their earnings, then I'm neither being consistent in my own morals nor showing any concern for others.' So he placed the game he had bagged in the trap, and returned home empty-handed. Yes,

> Where generosity's feasible
> generosity you must show,
> Where chance for charity occurs,
> charity you must bestow.

Now because Qin Zili would not apply himself to a proper trade or career, the family finances were bit by bit dwindling away. Moreover, being fundamentally generous by nature and fond of entertaining guests, he would frequently bring a band of pals home to plague the place, pestering his parents with demands for wine and food. Mr and Mrs Qin were so fond of their son that there was nothing they would not do for him. At first they just about managed, with a struggle, but eventually they could no longer afford such goings-on, and had to have the matter out with him.

'You're grown-up now,' they said, 'and if you don't turn your attention now to making a career for yourself and building up the home instead of running around as you do all the time, I don't know when you ever will! Other people's sons of your age go in for farming or trade or shop-keeping—they manage one way or another to make something of themselves so that they can support their mum and dad. But all you think of is spending. You've got no idea of bringing anything in. So things are steadily heading towards rack and ruin in the household. And then you turn up here with three or four friends wanting wine and food every other minute, completely ignoring the fact that your parents are almost down to their last and just putting on a brave face, creating endless trouble and distress for them. Even if we pawn or sell off clothes and trinkets, that won't keep us going indefinitely. The time will come when we'll have nowhere to turn and nothing we can do, and you'll live to see us starve to death! Well, now we've let you know how things stand, and if in future you bring anyone round here and there's not even a cup of tea for them to drink, don't start getting worked up about it!'

Qin Zili fell silent at this telling off from his parents, and just walked out of the house without a word. For quite a few days, no one came round to disturb the household with carousal. But a month or so later he led ten or so huntsmen home, and asked to borrow a pan to boil some rice in.

'Go on, let him cook some,' said Mr Qin.

But Mrs Qin was adamant. 'It doesn't matter if he wastes our firewood. That's not the point. But we have been trying to get the lad to turn over a new leaf, and he has been so much quieter and better behaved these last few days. I've been so glad about it. But here he is making a nuisance of himself again. It's the thin end of the wedge, and if we give in to him now we'll never be able to turn any of them away in future! The next time, he'll be wanting to treat them to tea and wine.

I'm near the end of my tether! Let's tell them straight, be firm to them and not spoil him, eh?'

Seeing that she was not to be moved, Mr Qin retired. Mrs Qin shut the door to the private rooms and called out from inside: 'My house isn't a mansion. If you're stuck for firewood, go and scrounge it off someone else!'

Hearing this, the crowd had no choice but to take themselves off. Qin Zili had shame and embarrassment written all over his face. 'Since I was a kid,' he thought with a sigh, 'I've always lived off my mum and dad. Never been able to earn a penny myself, and there hasn't been much coming into the family either. Can't blame them. I've heard there's a rebellion in Annam, and that the court is recruiting soldiers all over the country. Our prefect has received documents from the Military Commissioner, and stuck up loads of recruiting notices. A few of my pals have already gone and enlisted. With all my skills, if I throw myself into the thick of the fighting I may well come back "clad in brocade of glory". Sticking around in this poky hole and causing his parents worry and distress is no thing for any man worth his salt to be doing. Ah, but there's one thing: if mum and dad get to know that I'm thinking of joining up, I know they won't allow it. Well, when fame and fortune stare you in the face, emergency measures are called for. I've got an idea.'

Losing no time, Qin Zili fobbed off his parents with an excuse, and went straight into the prefectural capital to join the army. The prefectural governor put him through various tests, and as his mastery of the military arts showed him to be head and shoulders above the majority, he was made a company commander and signed on at the Military Administration Bureau. In a very short while, the required quota of soldiers had been recruited. The commanding officers called the roll, numbered off the men, distributed rations, equipped the troops with clothing, armour and weapons, and selected a propitious date for the start of the expedition. On the chosen date, to the sound of exploding firecrackers, they marched away.

Qin Zili had not even informed his parents, and it was not until the army had been en route for three days that, encountering an official messenger from his county, he wrote a letter home. Mr Qin tore it open and read it. It said:

Dear mum and dad,
Your son Zili is a useless good-for-nothing and a burden to you. Now I have enlisted in the army, been appointed company commander, and am on my way to Annam. If luck is with me, I shall do great deeds and come back home 'clad in brocade of glory', depend upon it. No need for you to have any worries about me, mum and dad!

When he had finished reading, Mr Qin remained dumbfounded for ages, unable to get out a single word.

'Where's our son gone?' asked Mrs Qin. 'What has he got to tell us in his letter? Aren't you going to tell me?'

'If I tell you,' said Mr Qin, 'I'm afraid you'll get in a state! The lad's gone off and enlisted in the army, and he's marching with the troops in an expedition on its way to Annam.'

'Oh, I thought it was something really terrible,' said Mrs Qin with a smile. 'After he's been away for ten or fifteen days, we'll just send for him to come back, and that will be that.'

'You womenfolk are completely out of touch with reality!' said Mr Qin. 'Annam is four thousand miles away from here, and it's difficult enough even getting letters through. And what's more, he's on government service and not free to come and go as he pleases. Now he's gone, and there's more ill than good to be reaped in that merciless fighting. What if he should go and get himself killed on the battlefield? Who shall we have to keep us company and tend to us in our old age then?'

At that, Mrs Qin started weeping to heaven and earth, and by this time Mr Qin himself was weeping helplessly too.

Several days later, Mr Lin, their prospective in-law, got to hear of the letter as well, and came round especially to see what it was all about. Unable to keep it from him, Mr and Mrs Qin just had to tell him the whole truth. They commiserated together for a while, then Mr Lin went back home to tell the rest of his household, who were all very upset. Yes, it was just as the poem says:

> Of joys there is none greater
> than joy of friendship newly started,
> Of sorrows none more wretched
> than sorrow for friends departed.

If others go their separate ways
'tis little grief by us imparted,
If dear and near ones are torn from us,
it leaves us broken-hearted.

Time sped like an arrow, and soon three years had passed. Since Qin Zili's departure, there had been not a scrap of news from him. Mr Lin frequently sent people round to the Qins' to see if they could pick up any word, but every time it was like a golden needle falling into the ocean, or a silver pitcher dropping in a well, there was not the faintest trace or echo back. A few others from the same county had enlisted and gone away, but the same applied to all of them.

At last Mr Lin's worthy wife, Madam Liang, had a word with her husband. 'It's three years since Master Qin went off,' she said. 'He's still not back, and we've no idea whether he's dead or alive. Our daughter is grown-up now, and we're under no fixed obligation to keep her hanging around for ever. You ought to try and arrange a split with those Qins. I know we're all on cosy terms with one another, but their son is their concern, and our daughter is our daughter, and you have to look after your own flesh and blood. Our daughter doesn't even know what her husband-to-be looks like, whether he's got a long face or a round face, never set eyes on him, so surely you can't think to make her a widow for the rest of her life when she's never even been married?'

'What you say is quite right, mother,' said Mr Lin, and hastened round to the Qins'.

'My little daughter is grown-up now,' he said to Mr Qin, 'and there has been no news whatsoever of your young gentle-man. If he should never come back, how would we sort things out then? My old missus has been fretting night and day about it, so I've come round to discuss the matter with you, my prospective in-law.'

Mr Qin already knew what he had in mind. 'Aye,' he said, 'my good-for-nothing son is a regular scoundrel, wasting your dear daughter's fragrant springtide of life. But since we've come so far, and things being as they are, I can only beg you, my in-law, to do your best to persuade your good lady wife to be patient and wait another three years. If he hasn't

eturned after those six years, then you'll be perfectly free to
ved your daughter to someone of more worthy background,
ınd I should have nothing more to say on the matter.'

Feeling that there was sound sense in what Mr Qin said,
Mr Lin could only retreat, murmuring his respectful agreement. He went back and informed Madam Liang. Madam
Liang had always known that her prospective son-in-law was
not learning a proper trade, and had inwardly been none too
happy about it. The fact that three years had passed and he
had still not returned had suited her down to the ground. But
when she heard that she had a further three years to wait, she
was bitterly annoyed. How she wished she could shrink every
ten days into one, that she could get through those three years
in one second's flash, and reach the day when her daughter's
hand could be given to someone more worthwhile.

Indeed, time sped like an arrow, and suddenly another three
years had passed.

'Our agreement with the Qins has expired now,' said Mr Lin.
'I'll go round and see him again. Let's see what he's got to say
now, if anything.'

'It's an old, old saying,' said Madam Liang, 'that once
you've given your promise, you can't fetch it back with a team
of four horses. He made the promise, so he can't blame us
now! There's a road to this house. Let him come round
himself. Why should we go and see him? Let's wait till our
daughter has a partner. That will be quite soon enough to tell
him.'

'What you say is quite right, mother,' said Mr Lin. 'We
ought to let our child know, all the same.'

'That wench Tide Music,' said Madam Liang, 'is rather
stubborn and contrary. If you just tell her that because young
Master Qin has not returned after six years away we want to
marry her to someone else, and she refuses outright, then old
Qin will have the laugh on us. This is what we must do . . .'

'What you say is quite right, mother,' was Mr Lin's response
to her advice.

The following day, as Madam Liang and her daughter, Tide
Music, were sitting together, Mr Lin came into the house.
'Mother,' he said, deliberately creating an atmosphere of
alarm, 'do you know what? No wonder young Master Qin

hasn't been sending letters home. He was killed in battle three years ago. A soldier came back from Annam yesterday, and he saw it with his own eyes.'

At these words, Tide Music's face went the colour of china clay, and with tears brimming in her eyes she hurried off deeply distraught to her own room. Her mother feigned sad sighs, muttering repeatedly, 'Oh, poor fellow.'

Several days later, Mrs Lin, Madam Liang that is, had a word with her daughter. 'You can't bring the dead back to life again,' she said. 'He's dead and gone, but it's a real pity for you, alive and still so young. So I've already told your father to go and find a match-maker to arrange for you to marry someone else. You must enjoy yourself while you're still young, and not let the pleasures of married love slip you by.'

'No, mother, you're mistaken!' said Tide Music. 'Dad engaged me to marry into the Qin family when I was a little girl, and I've been engaged to Master Qin ever since. A woman doesn't drink the nuptial tea of two families. While young Master Qin was alive, I was his woman. Now he's dead, I'm still his woman. You can't change your mind just because someone has died! I absolutely refuse to do it!'

'Don't be so pig-headed, child,' said her mother. 'You're the only child we have, you've no brothers. And if you get married, your mum and dad will at least have half a son to fall back on. Anyhow, there's no real virtue in a woman remaining a chaste widow when she's never even crossed the threshold. And here are your old parents, still in the land of the living. Don't you give a thought to what a bleak and miserable old age we'll be faced with in days to come! No, all you do is hanker after someone dead and gone. What an unloving daughter you are! What a stupid creature!'

After such a scolding, Tide Music didn't dare answer back, so match-makers and go-betweens shuttled to and fro between their house and the families of prospective candidates. Unable to browbeat her parents, she thought of a ruse.

'I would not think of disobeying anything you suggest,' she said. 'But how could I bear it—no sooner than I hear of Master Qin's death, to go marrying someone else? Let me stay here and mourn for him for three years in fulfilment of the love that a wife owes her husband. After that I shall do just what-

:ver you say. Otherwise, I shall certainly not obey your orders
—I would gladly die in preference!'

Mr Lin and Madam Liang, seeing how very determined
heir daughter was to live up to the ideal she had set herself,
and afraid that she might otherwise commit suicide, were
forced to let her have her way. It was a case of

> When one person sets a determined course
> a thousand cannot wrest them from it with all
>   their force.

Now it had seemed obvious to Mr Qin and his wife that
when their son had still not returned home after the six years
were up, the Lins' daughter would marry someone else. But
when they heard that the girl had resolved to stay in mourning
at home for three years, they were overwhelmed with delight.
'If she can hold out and if, as we hope, our son comes back
within those three years, then she will still be our daughter-in-
law!' they told themselves.

Time sped like an arrow, and suddenly yet another three
years had passed. By now Tide Music was really convinced
that her fiancé was dead. For the past three years she had worn
plain white clothing and eaten vegetarian fare, just as if she
had indeed been observing a period of mourning for the dead.
But now the period was up, she had actually lost all appetite
for strong-tasting foods and meat, and refused, furthermore, to
change her plain clothes for gaily coloured ones. And when the
matter of negotiating a marriage was broached to her, she was
ready to commit suicide.

Mr Lin discussed the subject with his wife. 'Our daughter
being so stubborn,' he said, 'it looks as if there's no hope of
bringing off a marriage. What on earth can we do?'

'We must secretly pick someone for her,' said Madam
Liang, 'and go through all the formalities of receiving the
betrothal gifts at my elder brother's home and not tell her
anything of what's going on. On the eve of the wedding, we'll
just tell her that our nephew, my brother's lad, is throwing a
party, and they're sending people to take her there. Trick her
into changing her clothes and mounting the sedan-chair, and
then the musicians and other members of the wedding train

can intercept her half-way and escort her to the groom's home. When things have gone so far, I don't think we need fear she'll refuse to comply.'

'What you say is for the best, mother,' said Mr Lin.

Mr Lin duly arranged matters with his daughter's maternal uncle, Uncle Liang, and promised his daughter's hand to the young gentlemen who was the third son of Service Secretary Li, an official in the administration of that area. Everything, right from the negotiations up to the giving of the betrothal gifts, was done in Uncle Liang's house. When Mr Lin and his wife went to receive the presents, they told their daughter that it was Uncle Liang's eldest son who was getting engaged. Not for a moment did Tide Music entertain any suspicions. As the happy day drew near, Uncle Liang made out that he was finalising his son's wedding and that he would specially collect the whole of his brother-in-law's family and bring them to his home for the reception of the bride, while Madam Liang promised that they would certainly all come. On the day, Uncle Liang sent people round with two sedan-chairs to fetch his sister and his niece. First dressing herself up, Madam Liang then told her daughter to change into some richly coloured clothing and come with her.

Completely unaware of the trick that was being played, Tide Music could scarcely do otherwise than change her clothes and go along with her mother. Young ladies who have never stepped outside their boudoirs have no idea of what roads lead where. When they had been on their way for some while, suddenly in a dip in a hill there appeared lanterns and torches and they heard the noise of music clamouring to the sky, as all the crowd of the bridal cortège which had been waiting there approached and lined up in front of the sedan-chairs, the musicians blowing and banging away at their instruments. Tide Music realised that something drastic was happening to her, but all she could do was weep and wail helplessly inside her sedan-chair. None of the train took the slightest notice of her, being intent solely on hurrying the chair-bearers along at flying speed.

As they reached a certain spot, dark clouds suddenly crowded in from all quarters and there was a tremendous downpour of rain. Everyone took shelter among the trees of he forest, waiting until the rain stopped, and then marched on in procession once more. They had not gone many steps, however, when all at once a wild gust of wind blew up, extinguishing the lanterns and torches, and a fawn-striped tiger with white forehead and ferocious upturned eyes came bounding through the air down towards them. With a great yell, everyone scattered and fled in different directions.

> What became of their lives, 'tis not yet said,
> but already I see their courage dead,
> their wits in bits, their spirits fled.

The wind dropped, and the tiger had gone. All the members of the cortège called out 'Thank heaven', relit the torches and lanterns, re-established order in their ranks, and moved off in procession once more. But presently the chair-bearers shouted out, 'Hey, something's gone wrong here! When we started, both sedans were full. Now one of them's empty!' When lights were shone on the chair in question, it was discovered that it was the bride who had disappeared. The door of the sedan had been smashed to splinters. What could have happened to her? —She must have been dragged off in the jaws of the tiger!

At this news, Madam Liang set up a whining and wailing. What a joyless lot they were, that crowd of bridal escorts with no bride to escort! The band had stopped its piping and drumming, and half the lanterns and torches had gone out. A conference was held. 'What on earth can we do now?' everyone wondered. It would not be easy for the members of the cortège to go searching for the bride in the dark of night, nor was their valour up to the task. And if they all just split up and went their separate ways, they were afraid they might meet another tiger. Best to stick together, and go to the Lins' home and see what could be done when they got there. As you might say, 'Cheery they trod the outward track, Weary they came slinking back.'

Meanwhile, Mr Lin was just tidying things up in his house when he heard a frantic knocking on the door. Rushing to open it, he discovered that the two sedan-chairs had been carted back, and that each and every one of the numerous cortège was hanging his head in utter misery, like a cur without a home

175

to go to. He gave a start of alarm, unable to guess what was behind it all. 'Can my daughter have refused to go through with it, and got up to some tricks in the sedan-chair?' His heart thumping away as if it had several hundred hammers inside it, he impatiently asked what was the meaning of all this. Madam Liang in her sedan burst out crying, sobbing and choking, unable to utter a single word. The others related what had happened in their mid-journey encounter with the tiger.

Mr Lin too beat his breast and wept, overwhelmed with grief and filled with useless regrets: 'If only I had known my child would meet such a vile fate, I would have let her have her way and not marry. It wouldn't have mattered. And now what a miserable end she's come to, and it's all our fault!'

He ordered men to go and notify the families of Service Secretary Li and Uncle Liang, and at the same time assembled a party of farm labourers, made ready some hunting gear, and waited for the dawn, preparing to comb the mountains, catch the tiger, and search for his daughter's remains. All the time he was

> Mournfully, mournfully lamenting,
> longing for his little maid,
> Ceaselessly his fury venting
> in curses on the tiger's head.

Here our story takes another tack for a while. After enlisting in the army and joining the expedition to Annam, Qin Zili fought with all his might and main and did great deeds. As a result the Military Governor, Geshu Han, employed him as Disciplinary Adjutant in his headquarters, unbuckling his own sword to present to him, and placing great trust in him. After three years, the Tibetans invaded China, and Qin Zili went with Geshu Han when forces were redeployed against the invaders. Once they had repulsed and quelled the enemy, the imperial court appointed Geshu Han Grand Commander-in-Chief, and, at the head of generals and captains from his own headquarters and a hundred thousand bold men, he took up the defence of Tong Pass. In view of his two instances of meritorious service, Qin Zili had by this time risen to the rank of major. What next? An Roxan rebelled, and fought his way up to Tong Pass. By chance, Geshu Han was suffering from some illness at that juncture, and, unable to withstand the enemy, he threw open the pass and surrendered. Qin Zili 'was only one palm, so could not clap'. Incapable of doing anything on his own initiative, he abandoned the men under his command, and alone, sword in hand, made his escape. We shall not go into all the bitter trials and hardships of his subsequent journeyings, but, by one of those strange coincidences that occur in human affairs, he arrived home precisely on the evening that Mr Lin was trying to marry off his daughter.

On presenting himself to his parents, Qin Zili prostrated himself on the ground before them in reverence. 'Forgive your son for the criminal lack of love he has shown towards his parents,' he mumbled.

Only upon scrutinising him more closely did Mr and Mrs Qin recognise that he was their son. He had, to be sure, been big and tall when he had left them, but not so virile and powerful as he was now, and he had grown whiskers all round his mouth, as was the custom up on the frontiers, and his face looked completely different. Recalling all the suppressed anguish of the past, his parents found themselves weeping.

'How is it, son, that you have been away these ten years,' said Mr Qin, 'and we have had no word at all from you? Lots of people said that you had died in battle, and your parents have wept their eyes dry of tears with all their crying.'

'Never mind the ten years,' said Mrs Qin, '—if only you'd come back just one day earlier, you could have done something. Then I'm sure your fiancée wouldn't have gone and married someone else.'

'What's that about my fiancée?' asked Qin Zili.

'Three years after you left,' explained Mrs Qin, 'her father wanted to marry her to someone else, but your dad wouldn't agree to it, so he had to hang on for another three years. Then, when your fiancée heard that you had died, she chose of her own accord to mourn for you for three years. Now we're in the tenth year, so you can scarcely blame her for anything. Just this very evening she has left her home to be married to someone else.'

When he heard this, Qin Zili's eyebrows shot erect with

fury, and he ground his teeth with a loud grating noise. 'What low-down scum dares to go after Qin Zili's wife to be!' he shouted. 'I'll make him acquainted with this sword in my hand!' With these words he stormed out, savage and ferocious, sword in hand.

His parents had never been able to control him even as a little boy, so what hope had they now of holding him back? All they could do was let him go and, in a cold sweat, wait in their parlour for news.

> When Green Dragon Warrior and White Tiger
>   join,
> conjunct stars of prodigious portent,
> The matters of men, marital, moral, mortal,
> are given a new, determined bent.

Now ever since he had been a young lad, Qin Zili had known the road to Mr Lin's house, so he now made off along this road to intercept the bridal party. He had been walking for quite a while when he was overtaken by a heavy downpour of rain, which soaked his clothes. He recalled that the spot where he now found himself was called Big Tree Slope, and that on the slope there was an ancient tree about ten arm-spans in circumference, and all hollow inside, which would serve as a shelter from the rain. He went up to the tree, squeezed himself inside it, and found it was very spacious and roomy. Although the rain was pelting down, it was not long before it stopped.

Zili was on the point of jumping out when there came a huge gust of wind. 'I'll wait till this wind is past, and then go,' he decided on reflection. Then he thought, 'That wind has an uncanny smell about it. Very weird indeed!' Sticking his head out to spy out the land, he caught sight of two red lanterns in the distance that kept flashing vaguely into view and then disappearing. Then suddenly there came a monstrous roaring noise, as if heaven was collapsing and earth cracking open, and something came tumbling towards him, so startling him that he shot back inside the tree trunk.

A moment or two later the wind dropped, and a constant moaning and groaning came to his ears. By this time the

louds had parted and the rain had cleared up, and from the
ar sky faint moonlight peeped forth. Zili moved forward to
aave a look in the moonlight, and discovered that the moaning
vas coming from a woman. He helped her to her feet, and
isked her who she was and what had happened. It was a long
ime before she spoke.

'I am Tide Music,' she said, 'the daughter of a Mr and Mrs
Lin.'

Qin Zili remembered that that was his fiancée's name, but
ust to make certain asked, 'Don't you have a husband?'

'My husband was to have been a Qin Zili,' she answered.
I was engaged to him, but I never actually crossed the threshold. He went and joined the army ten years ago, and we've
had no news of him all this time. My mum and dad wanted to
marry me to someone else instead, but I swore I would rather
die than do that. So they got me engaged behind my back to
someone or other, made out my uncle was sending for us to go
to his house, and tricked me into a sedan-chair. It wasn't till
we were half-way there that I realised what was happening to
me. I was just about to commit suicide, when suddenly a wild
wind blew up, and I saw a ferocious fawn-striped tiger come
charging through the crowd. It made straight for my sedan-
chair, carried me off in its jaws, and threw me down on the
ground here. The tiger's gone now. Luckily it didn't do me any
harm . . . But I don't know your name, sir? If you could take
me home, back to my parents', they'll be certain to give you a
big reward.'

'I am none other than Qin Zili,' he told her. 'First I went on
a campaign in Annam, then I took part in an expedition
against the Tibetans, and later I accompanied Commander-in-
Chief Geshu Han when he went to guard Tong Pass, and I
have only just returned home. I heard that your family were
marrying you off to someone else, and that the marriage was
to take place this very evening. That's why I came this way,
sword in hand to punish those destroyers of universal morality!
But fancy meeting you here! It is heaven that sent the tiger to
restore you to me, and to save me wading in with my sword.
What a fantastic stroke of good fortune!'

'In spite of what you say, sir,' said Tide Music, 'I have never
crossed the threshold, and so would not recognise my husband-

to-be's face. I could hardly take your word alone as proof as readily and lightly as that! I still think you had best take me back to my home, and if my father recognises you as his son-in-law, then I shall not betray the fidelity I have maintained so bitterly all these years.'

'That old swine, your father,' said Zili, 'promising his daughter to two families! Why should I bother going and seeing such an arrant faithless blackguard! I'll carry you back to my house now. First you can pay your respects to your father-in-law and mother-in-law. Then I'll send someone to let your family know. That'll put the old swine to shame!'

With these words, ignoring whether she was agreeable or not, he hoisted Tide Music onto his back, and with his left hand behind him holding her golden-lotus feet and the right one grasping his sword, he made his way back, hopping over the muddy soil.

He had not gone many paces when suddenly he heard the sound of a tiger roaring, and far ahead, high on the mountain, saw two lanterns hovering. Peering hard, he picked out a fawn-striped tiger with upturned eyes and white forehead. Those red lanterns were the light from the tiger's eyes. Zili promptly recalled how, ten years previously in that same spot, he had smashed open a trap and set free such a tiger.

'How did it know that I would be returning home today?' he marvelled. 'How did it manage to go into a crowd of people, carry off my wife-to-be in its jaws, and return her to me? It must be a creature with supernatural powers!' He shouted in a loud voice to it, 'Thank you, tiger, for giving me my wife back!'

The tiger let out a huge roar, and bounded out of sight.

People of later times, when discussing how tigers repay debts of gratitude for kindnesses done to them, considered this a most amazing tale, and many wrote poems on it, of which we here quote only the one by the venerable Hu Zeng (of the late Tang dynasty) as the best of them all:

> People once would only tell
> how tigers slaughter men,
> Now we know that tigers
> repay a kindness done.

How many ungrateful fellows
forget kind deeds and break their words,
In friendship and fidelity
lower than beasts and birds.

Mr and Mrs Qin were waiting anxiously at home when they
heard the ring of footsteps. Hastily lighting a lantern, they
went out to see who it was. They saw Qin Zili, carrying
someone on his back. He came into the main hall, put the
person down, and called out, 'Mum and dad, tonight I want
you to meet your daughter-in-law!'

Mr and Mrs Qin saw that the visitor was a beautiful young
lady, and, plying Qin Zili with questions as to what had
happened, learned the astonishing tale of how the tiger had
repaid a kindness and played best man. They both clasped
their hands to their foreheads, and kept on exclaiming, 'What
amazing good fortune!' Then Mrs Qin took her daughter-in-
law's arm, ushered her into the inner rooms, and gave her
some sweet gruel to restore her.

The following morning, Mr Qin sent someone to notify
their in-laws the Lins. Now that morning, while it was still
dark, Mr Lin had led out the farm labourers and searched and
beaten all round the mountain, but seen no sign of life. With a
sigh, he had done the only thing possible and gone home again.
Now that the man sent by Mr Qin suddenly turned up to
announce the glad tidings, saying that last night their son had
come home and that a tiger had restored his daughter to the
family, he was in no mood to believe a word of it! 'I see,' he
said. 'The Qins have learned that our daughter was dragged
off by a tiger, so they've deliberately concocted this cock-and-
bull story to make a mockery of me!'

But Madam Liang was not so sure. 'Anything can happen
in this world of ours!' she said. 'Why, only the other day one
of our mottled chickens ran off and got lost, and our neighbours picked it up and kept it. A day later, a wild cat came
back to our house with that chicken in its mouth. I chased the
cat away and took a look at the chicken, and it was the same
one that had run away from us. Now there's a strange coinci-
dence! Anyway, a tiger's a great big beast gifted with un-
common intelligence. I heard another tale. There was once a

student living in an out-of-the-way village. He heard a noise
outside his door in the night. He took a look out, and a tiger
paw stretched in through the lattice window. And that paw
had a great big spike of bamboo sticking in it. The student
realised what the tiger had come for, and pulled the spike out.
The following evening, the beast brought along a goat, by way
of thanking him. So you see it's obvious that tigers do under
stand human nature. Maybe heaven has taken pity on our
daughter for the way she stayed faithful, and sent that tiger to
give her back to the Qins. You never can tell. Just you go
round to the Qins to find out if their son has returned or not.
Then at least we'll be clear in our own minds.'

'What you say is quite right, mother,' said Mr Lin.

That very day, Mr Lin turned up at the Qins. Mr Qin came
out to welcome him in, assigned him the guest's seat of honour
and related in detail all that had happened the previous night.
Mr Lin's face was covered in shame and embarrassment, and
he apologised endlessly, and begged to be allowed to 'set eyes
on the faces of his noble son-in-law and his little daughter'. At
first Qin Zili refused to acknowledge his father-in-law, but
after some lengthy persuasion by his parents, and also out of
regard for his wife's self-respect, he felt obliged to come out and
meet him, and, fuming with resentment, make a bow to him.
Then he strode off out of the way.

Mr Qin told Mrs Qin to dress their daughter-in-law up in
her best finery, and ushered Mr Lin into the inner apartments,
where father and daughter, contrary to all former expectations,
met once more. It was like a meeting in a dream, and Mr
Lin's delight knew no bounds. He wanted to take his daughter
home with him. Mr and Mrs Qin, however, would not agree
to that. They selected a favourable date, and there in their
home had the young pair perform the rites to heaven and
earth, go through the wedding ceremony and become man and
wife. Service Secretary Li, on learning of Qin Zili's return, of
course raised no objections.

Later, when the two field marshals Guo Ziyi and Li Guangbi
regained the capital Changan from An Roxan and Emperor
Suzong ascended the throne, the Emperor conducted a
thorough review of the qualities and integrity of his military
officers and civil servants. In the days when he had been

Crown Prince, Emperor Suzong had already heard of Qin Zili's doughty deeds in various campaigns, and since his name was now not to be found in the registers of the rebel clique, he commended him for having steered clear of service with the rebels, and restored him to high rank, as Over-all Commandant of his personal imperial guard. In successive campaigns against the rebels An Qingxu and Shi Siming he achieved considerable success. He survived long enough to retire through old age, and he and his wife passed their twilight years together.

Here is a poem, apposite to our tale:

> If you act meanly and harshly,
> all humans will hate and resent you,
> Be but generous and kind,
> even tigers will befriend you.
> I venture to exhort mankind
> to succour others with fair deeds,
> Where others you can spare from pain,
> show mercy to their needs.